MAGGIE DOVE

SUSAN BREEN

Maggie Dove

For information about this title or to order other books and/or electronic media, contact the publisher:

Under the Oak Press
Irvington, NY

Paperback ISBN: 978-1-7373172-0-3

eBook ISBN: 978-1-7373172-1-0

Printed in the United States of America

For Will, always.

Chapter One

Maggie Dove wanted to be a beacon of light. She dreamed of being the sort of person who made others laugh, calmed crying babies, soothed wild dogs, inspired hopefulness. She wanted her life to be about something grand, yet every blessed thing that happened seemed designed to bring out all that was petty, cranky and small in her middle-aged self.

Take her neighbor, Marcus Bender. Maggie knew, intellectually, that he wasn't an incarnation of Satan. He was just an annoying man. He was the sort of man who blew all his leaves onto her lawn each fall. He drove too fast down her quiet street, and once, when she had to jump out of the way of his car, she saw him laugh. He put a soccer net right up against her property so that every time his kids missed a goal, the ball went flying into her rose bushes. All of this, Maggie recognized, was insignificant. Petty. She tried to ignore it. She wanted to ignore it, and she might have succeeded had Bender not gone after her oak tree.

Maggie loved that oak tree. Her father planted it when she was a girl. She'd climbed on it. Her daughter had swung on its branches. She put ghosts on it for

Halloween and lights on it for Christmas. Maggie loved the graceful shrug of its branches; she loved watching its little flowers unfold into leaves. She loved the little pods that floated over her lawn in the fall. Mostly she loved the way the tree linked her to her past and future. She would come and go, her daughter had come and gone, but the tree was as close to eternal as she was likely to see anytime soon.

Bender wanted her to move the tree. That was the sort of man he was. He thought you should move trees. It blocked his view of the Hudson River. He'd gone to considerable expense to remodel his house, which was the old Bell house, home of Maggie's best friend growing up. He'd transformed the quiet little colonial into a ship. An actual ship, with portholes and decks. He had an art studio on the top floor, though he wasn't an artist. He was a lawyer, but he had an artistic bent and wanted to paint studies of the Hudson River, and he didn't want those studies blighted, as he said, by her oak tree. Blighted!

Maggie said no.

He offered her money. He had a lot of money and was willing to pay to get what he wanted. He seemed genuinely surprised to find there was a person in the world who didn't care about what Bender wanted.

"We'll work this out, Maggie," he said, grinning at her in that wolfish way he had. He was a very good-looking man, athletic, muscular, tanned. He wore suits to work and his broad chest bulged against the constrictions of his shirt. Winifred Bell, who had once been Maggie's neighbor, but was now confined to a nursing home because of Parkinson's, was convinced that the source of Maggie's anger was sexual desire, a conclusion Maggie thought so far off the mark, she didn't even argue about it.

She didn't like men like steam rollers. She liked gentle men, and gentle people. She loved her small town on the Hudson River and the people she'd grown up with and she loved that tree. There was no amount of money he could pay her to make it worthwhile to cut it down. She didn't want to fight about it; didn't want to talk about it. She just wanted to live her life and enjoy her tree.

Then, one April morning, Maggie went outside to see if any new leaves were starting to form. She loved those wispy little clusters that blossomed for a short time each spring, but as she neared the tree she was struck by a sharp odor. She saw a strange dark puddle at the base of the tree; bent down to sniff it and her nostrils burned. Poison. Bender was poisoning her tree.

Maggie called the police and they came over, and were sympathetic, but there wasn't much they could do. They had no proof it was Bender. After the police car went away, Maggie went over to Bender's house, certain he'd been watching the whole scene and laughing.

She pounded on his front door. It must be made of steel. Her hand hurt.

She didn't care. She was furious. Who hurts a tree? It was there to bring solace and beauty. Nothing more.

What was wrong with this man? What was wrong with this world?

He opened the door.

"Maggie Dove!" he said, as though she'd just come over for tea. As though she were not standing there with her fist directed like a battering ram in the direction of his chest.

"Stay away from my tree," she hissed.

"I know how important that tree is to you," he said, speaking soothingly, as though talking her down from the roof. "There has to be a way we can work this out. I want to do right by you, Maggie. Maybe if I made a donation to charity. Do you have one already set up? For your daughter?"

She felt herself gripped by a sensation so intense she could only compare it to labor, but without the payoff. Had she a gun she would have been severely tempted to shoot him, but in that moment, all she could do was hurl her words at him. Her last words to Bender were, "Don't you ever set foot on my lawn again. Not you, or your wife, or your children, or I swear to God, I'll kill you."

Stalking back to her house, she paused to pick up a rock. She brought it inside and took a seat by her window. If he dared! If he dared to come near her tree again, she would throw it at him. She wanted to strike him in the head. She wanted to mark him, so forever after he would have a scar. She wanted to shatter that smug visage of his.

She sat there for hours, watching, waiting, hating. She didn't even have dinner. She didn't move. She watched the sun set. The sky darkened and it was night, and then she felt afraid.

Not of Bender, who was, after all, just a thoughtless man who would get what was coming to him one way or the other, but of herself. She felt something had changed inside her. That because of him, because of what she'd said to him, she was less than what she had been. She was letting hatred get the better of her. She looked at the rock that she'd been clutching in her hands all these hours, and she felt sick, and got up, and set it on her desk.

She stared out at the tree for a long time that night, admiring its elegant lines and thinking about all the joy it had brought her. She watched its graceful dance under the moonlight. She thought how many times she'd hugged it, pressed her face against its sturdy, ridged bark. She felt something inside her unclench. She felt peace and closed her eyes for a bit and when she opened them, an hour or so later, she noticed something lying under the tree.

It was too dark to be sure, but it looked like a doll. With an orange dress. She put on her sweater and sneakers and picked up her flashlight and went outside. That was how she discovered Marcus Bender, dead, lying under her tree, manicured fingers stretched toward her house as though pleading for help.

Chapter Two

Bender looked small. The man who had occupied nearly every waking moment of Maggie's life for the last few months, now looked compact and insignificant, like something discarded. She rolled him over, thinking to do CPR, but there was no question of restoring him to life. He was rigid. She didn't know what to do; didn't want to leave him alone on the lawn, but needed to get help. His house loomed in front of her, lit up like a ship on the ocean at night. She yelled for his wife.

"Noelle! Noelle!"

No movement. Nothing, and so Maggie took off her sweater and put it over his face, thinking to protect him. Then she ran into her house and called the police, except that in her nervousness she accidentally transposed the digits. So she wound up with the pizza parlor instead.

"You can't be wanting a pizza so late, Mrs. Dove," Joe said. "What's up?"

"Something terrible's happened, Joe," she whispered, because it didn't seem right to speak loudly. "Something's wrong. Marcus Bender is dead on my lawn."

She could almost feel Joe snap to attention. He volunteered for the ambulance corps and had served two tours in Iraq. "Are you sure he's dead?"

"Yes, I felt for his pulse. And he's rigid, but I moved him. I know you're not supposed to, but I couldn't leave him with his face in the dirt. He's got blood on his lip," she added.

"That's okay. That's okay. I'll get the police. They'll be there in a minute. You stay inside."

But she couldn't stay in her house. Not with Bender lying defenseless on her front lawn, and so she went back outside. She crouched down alongside of him, thinking to keep him company, not sure what else to do. She was surprised to find herself crying. She'd hated him so much and now he lay before her, so vulnerable. He looked frightened, as though whatever killed him came up on him suddenly. But of course it would have. He was a young man, only in his late 30s. Not a man who should be dying. She supposed he'd gone out for a run, though she'd never seen him running before. He had on a bright orange shirt that reflected light. Almost as though he wanted to draw attention to himself.

"What were you up to?" she asked. "Why did you want me to see you?"

Automatically she looked at her tree, poor little oak that looked ghostly in the moonlight.

No, she would not get mad at a corpse. She shut her eyes and said a prayer and waited for the police, who should be there any minute. The police station was only a few blocks away. Where was Noelle? She looked at his blazing house. She looked up at the moon, which hovered above her, all pale white and sickly looking. Like a voyeur. Like a ghost or one of those balloons that followed you around. Her daughter had been terrified of balloons; they never could have them at parties. Juliet thought them secretive. She was such an imaginative child. So full of stories and light.

Maggie's legs hurt from crouching, but she couldn't bring herself to sit down on the lawn. This wasn't a picnic. Neither could she stand. Then it would look like she was going to kick him and she didn't want that to be the first thing the police saw when they pulled up. Where were they?

How unnaturally quiet the village was tonight. Where were the teenagers racing up and down Main Street in their cars? Where were the trucks on Broadway, the muted TV noise from the other houses nearby? Even the trains were silent. Her street was a dead end, so there was never much traffic, but you could usually hear the van Dornes arguing or Mr. Cavanaugh playing his piano. Even the peepers were struck dumb, the little frogs' insistent racket stilled. Something they did when danger approached.

"Is someone there?" Maggie called out, for suddenly she felt the presence of someone else. A presence right out of the edge of her hearing. She tried to concentrate. She smelled honeysuckle, a sickly and indecent aroma. She felt, rather than heard, someone else's heartbeat.

A coyote? she thought. They came here sometimes, but in packs, and they moved around. A dog? But no, she felt a human presence. She remembered a fact she learned when she used to write mysteries, that a person poisoned by belladonna could develop a heartbeat so loud it could be heard from several feet away.

"Who's there?" she called out. "Noelle?"

She felt anger and hatred, but wasn't sure if it was coming from inside her or outside. Maybe what she was feeling was the malevolence she'd felt toward Bender. Maybe all that evil was taking shape outside her, now that Bender was gone. Maybe something inside him had now been transformed into something malevolent. Something destructive. She wanted to run back into her house, but refused to do it. Never give in to fear. Something she told her Sunday School students all the time, something she believed. So she stood up, ready to face what was coming, and heard the distinctive sound of a large creature crashing in her direction.

Chapter Three

Peter Nelson was the worst Sunday School student Maggie'd ever had. The only way to keep him occupied during class was to let him light the devotional candle. Repeatedly. One miserable Sunday he set off the fire alarm, which caused the entire church to be evacuated, right in the middle of the minister's stewardship sermon. But Peter was also one of the first responders when the towers fell on 9/11. He was brave and fearless. He'd been her daughter's first and last love and he was one of the few people who still remembered Juliet's birthday. He was also assistant chief of police for the village of Darby-on-Hudson, and at the moment he was crashing across her lawn.

"You're all right, Dove," he cried out, gathering her up into a hug. "I wasn't sure from the report."

He squeezed her so hard she thought he might be giving her the Heimlich maneuver, but there was love in those arms, and caring. She disentangled herself.

"Are you all right?" he asked her, warm basset hound eyes trained on her. He smelled slightly of cigarettes.

"I'm all right," she said. "But I don't think Marcus Bender's doing so well."

"No," Peter said, crouching down to begin his work with the body. Pretty boy, they used to call him, back when he was her Sunday School student, because his hair was so blonde and curly. Now that he was nearing 40, only patches of it remained. Soon no one would remember why all the girls chased him.

"This is how you found him?" Peter asked, running his hands over the body.

"No, I rolled him over. I'm sorry, but I couldn't leave him with his head in the dirt."

"That's okay, Dove," he said, rocking back on his heels, looking around him, flashlight raised. The town hall bell chimed twelve times. Midnight.

"Did you see him fall? Hear anything?"

"No," she said, voice faltering slightly. The wind blew. Some forsythia petals blew by. "I didn't see when he got here. I didn't even see him running. I didn't know he did run."

"You did good, Dove. Wasn't anything you could have done for him. He's been gone for a while. I'm just sorry you had to be the one who found him."

Peter took out his radio and pressed it. "All right, Joe. Tell the ambulance boys Marcus Bender's dead. He's been dead for a while. Looks like a heart attack. How long you think it will be?"

Something blared from the radio.

"All right," he said. "But let's get moving. See if Dobbs Ferry has another ambulance. I don't want to keep this guy on Dove's lawn any more than we have to."

She could hear Joe Mangione's voice crackling. "No," Peter said. "We don't need to bring Campbell into this yet. Not with a death from natural causes."

"Where is everyone?" Maggie asked.

She knew the Darby-on-Hudson police force was small, but she'd expected more of a response to a sudden death. There couldn't be too many sudden deaths in a town of 6,230 people. She'd have thought the place would be ablaze with police cars and bystanders.

"There's a four-alarm fire up in Tarrytown," Peter explained. "All the trucks are up there. Everything's up there. And our police chief is in the city tonight. He had tickets for the ballet."

Walter Campbell was the bane of Peter's existence. Up until a few months ago, the brand new police chief had been a hedge fund manager in Manhattan. He made his last million and decided to do something meaningful with his life, so he dumped his wife and three children and moved to a perfect little house in the center of Darby-on-Hudson and dislocated Peter, who had been on track to be appointed police chief himself. Peter hated him, all the more so because the man was ruthless and brilliant.

Peter began making more calls, arranging for the ambulance and the coroner and Maggie found her attention drifting over to Bender, unchanging, immutable. She'd never got over the granite-like irreversibility of death. All conflict resolved, all love absorbed, all feeling extinguished. So much of Bender's personality had been in his eyes, she realized, the arrogance, confidence, hostility. With the eyes lifeless, he seemed so insignificant. Here before her lay the man who had occupied so much of her waking time in the last few months, and he seemed so paltry. One might as well find out one had been obsessed by a gerbil. And yet, how profound her hatred for this man had been.

"He looks so innocent," she said.

"He was a son of a bitch, Dove. Pardon my French. And now he's dead."

"Peter!"

"It's the truth. Thou shalt not lie. One of the Ten Commandments."

How he had struggled to learn those commandments, which the minister had insisted each child memorize before being confirmed. Peter wanted to write them on his hand, but Maggie felt it was wrong to cheat in a religious ceremony, and so they worked on it for weeks, she trying to come up with games to help him remember, finally coming up with a complicated Scavenger hunt involving commandments and clues that did eventually work, though he still had a tendency to rock a bit, like he was walking, when he quoted one of them.

Now he stood up and surveyed the lawn, the road, the Bender house.

"Well, it went fast for him," Peter said, "if you're looking for comfort. He must have felt the pain and fallen over. I doubt he even knew what hit him." Maggie heard the siren's cry. The ambulance would be there in a minute.

"You think it was a heart attack?"

"Hannah will give the official pronouncement, but it looks that way to me. Occupational hazard for these guys, working in the city and living in Westchester. Push themselves all the time and then, wham, the stress gets them. Had another case last month. Exercise bicycle. Wife away. Gets home after a weekend with the girls in Cancun and finds him. He was next to the electric heater."

"Peter, please."

"Sorry, Dove."

"He has blood on his lip," she pointed out.

"That's common. Heart attack victims often bite their tongue. Or he might have hit his lip on a rock when he fell. He must have been running, felt pain and turned toward the light in your house."

Maggie looked toward her house, which sat tidy and close in front of her. Two stories covered in white shingles, the shutters blue, the porch decorated with some new pots of impatiens, her foolish little flower pot in the shape of a chicken. The forsythia was starting to erupt into bloom. Neat white lace curtains. They were see-through. Bender must have seen her sitting by the window. She cringed as she thought what her face would have looked like. She had a horrifying image of that mother in Psycho.

"I can't imagine any scenario in which he thought he'd get help from me," she said.

"He might not have had time to think. You have a pain, you stagger. I wonder how old he was."

"Thirty nine," Maggie replied, then blushed as she realized what she'd given away. She knew all there was to know about Bender. Had spent considerable amount of time researching him on the internet, wanting to understand him. It was the same process she used when writing one of her mysteries, spending hours filling out dossiers for her characters, though it was much stranger, she acknowledged, when you did it for your neighbor. The result was she knew Bender was born in Long Island, went to college at Amherst, was active in its alumni society, made donations to the Democratic Party and the Doctors without Borders, had a degree in archeology but worked in a law firm. He posted frequent reviews of books in an online reading community. He liked Updike, hated Rushdie.

Peter looked at her, tired eyes face reflecting nothing but love. "No one liked him, Dove. Don't fret."

I've always wanted to hold myself to a higher standard, Maggie started to say or thought she should say or thought she should do, though it didn't matter because Peter wasn't paying attention anymore. The street had erupted into sound. The ambulance came whirring down the street, followed by the police car. Joe Mangione got out, changed out of his pizza clothes. Followed by the Lindstrom twins in their green ambulance jackets, and a muscular young woman who Maggie hadn't seen in a while. Thalia Greenburg? Back from London?

They got to business immediately. Although they were a volunteer force, they saw a lot of action. The village was near one of the more dangerous curves on the Saw Mill Parkway and Maggie knew they'd seen some terrible things.

Noise bred more noise. Out came the piano teacher, Ellis Cavanaugh, along with his little white dog, Fidelio. Then the lights of the van Dorne house snapped on, though they didn't come out. They tended to keep to themselves. One of the Lindstrom twins headed over to the Bender house, Maggie assumed to try to locate the widow. Where was she, Maggie wondered. Where was his family? Surely they were home, yet no one had answered when she yelled. No one came out when there was a circus on the lawn.

"Hey Mrs. Dove," Joe said. "You okay?"

"I'm okay," she said. "Thanks for calling it in."

"We did install a 911 system a few years ago," he said. "Just for future reference."

"Hopefully I'll never need again."

"So, what, he came for your tree?" Joe said.

"I don't know," Maggie answered, feeling her cheeks warm, remembering how she'd been down at the police station earlier that day, complaining about this man.

"You call Campbell?" he asked Peter. He looked angry, but Maggie knew that was just the way Joe always looked. He was a small man who'd gone to great effort to get an ambulance corps jacket to fit him just right. He was the neatest one there.

"This is no crime scene. I don't need to disturb him at the ballet for a heart attack."

"Disturb him, Nelson."

"Let me get Dove inside. Then I'll call him."

"Don't bring me into this," Maggie said. "If you're supposed to call your boss, do it, Peter."

"Pish posh," he said, pushing her toward her house. "I'll be right back," he called to Joe. "Someone find that wife and see what she knows. See if she wants to come out and say good bye."

He propelled Maggie up her porch and into her living room and then went into the kitchen to make her some tea. She felt more tired than she expected. Only now did Maggie realize she had on sweat pants and sneakers.

Maggie felt embarrassed. She usually dressed more formally, carefully. When you lived in a small town, there was no privacy. She remembered one afternoon, some months ago, running out to the post office without make up. That Sunday, at church, Agnes Jorgenson said she was sorry to hear Maggie'd been ill.

Now the whole town would be buzzing about her. She could only imagine what people would have to say, and worst of all, they'd be right. Even she was appalled at herself. *"What's the first commandment," Jesus was asked.*

"Love thy neighbor as thyself."

She sank into her couch. The whole room looked so prim and proper. She imagined Bender standing beside her, looking at it, the white curtains, the little china tea cups displayed in her hutch, the doilies that her great-grandmother had tatted. She loved that verb. Rarely came up. The picture of her daughter in a silver frame. Juliet dressed as the Princess Anastasia and Maggie's husband dressed as Tsar Nicholas. They'd gone trick or treating in those costumes for years, even as Maggie stayed home, dressed as Rasputin, and made huge batches of hot dogs. Over the course of Halloween night, the whole village would stop by and grab a hot dog and talk and laugh.

"Here's some fortification, Dove," Peter said as he walked in, carrying a tray loaded down with tea and cookies. He set it in front of her, and then sat down on the edge of her coffee table. That boy never sat down on a chair like a normal person.

"Do you need to take a statement?" she asked.

"No. He had a heart attack, that's all. Don't you worry. Even Campbell can't make more of it than it is."

"You'll call him, right. I don't want you to get fired over this."

How he struggled to graduate from the police academy. Every course a challenge, except for guns and weapons, which he loved.

"You won't do anything foolish?" she asked.

He laughed.

"When have I ever been foolish," he said, but now he jumped back to his feet and peered out the window.

"Go," she said. "Do your job. Don't worry. I'm fine."

"You sure?"

"Yes."

"We'll be here a little longer. The widow wants to see him, but first she wants to dress appropriately. Why don't you call Winifred?"

He stood up, started to go to the door, then stopped to look at the very thing she'd been hoping he'd miss.

"Hey Dove. What are you doing with a rock by your window?"

So he had noticed. She should have known; he was so much smarter than he ever liked to let on.

"I was planning on throwing it at Bender," she said, and he laughed.

Why do people always laugh at the truth? she wondered.

Chapter Four

Her house felt smaller after Peter left. Which made sense, Maggie supposed. Love expanded, hate contracted. She could hear Joe on her front lawn, the familiar caw of his voice. He always sounded like he was announcing a baseball game. Mr. Cavanaugh's little dog was snarling. He acted so much bigger than he was, the dog. Not Mr. Cavanaugh. She felt off kilter. She paced around her living room, not certain what to do.

Had she liked Bender, she would have wept. In the days and months after her daughter died, while other people assumed she was rudderless, she was, in fact, perfectly focused, which gave her days a rhythm. She grieved. That was all she had to do; didn't need to eat, write, love, talk. In some ways she was more focused on her daughter after her death than before, because before there had always been the distraction of real life. But Bender was different; she couldn't mourn him. But she couldn't ignore him either. Couldn't turn on the TV, or listen to music. Couldn't eat. Would not do to have the smell of broiled steak floating over her lawn. Even she could not bring herself to be so cold-hearted.

Her heart pounded. She hoped she wasn't having a stroke. A man was dead on her front lawn. A man she'd hated. She remembered then the feeling she'd had of being watched. The creaking twig. Her house was on a quiet street, the neighboring houses all a good distance from each other, excepting Bender, who had encroached. But between the trees and the darkness and the fact of the van Dornes being preoccupied with themselves, the street was very quiet. Maggie shivered as she thought about someone standing there, watching her, judging her. Thinking about how cruelly she had treated that man. He had a wife, who was even now getting dressed before she viewed his body.

What would she wear?

What did she even look like? Maggie wished she could remember. She must have met Noelle Bender. They'd lived in that house for more than two years, after all. Yet she couldn't conjure up any strong memory of her. Bender was so vivid that anyone standing alongside of him would have paled. She thought she remembered white gold hair and puffy lips.

All Maggie really knew of Noelle Bender was that she wasn't much of a gardener, nor much of an environmentalist. The lights in their house were on all the time and they didn't recycle. And Tim Harrison, the garbage man, told her Noelle didn't give a Christmas tip, a fact that Maggie wished she didn't know and tried to put out of her head, without success. Such details one learned when one lived in a small town. That and she knew one of the daughters had lice and it kept coming back, although Noelle told the school nurse otherwise. And now she knew that the widow wanted to dress up to see her husband's body, and that she didn't come out of the house when Maggie yelled at her, though maybe because she was afraid of Maggie.

Peter was right, she thought. She should call her best friend, but getting hold of Winifred was problematic. Her friend lived in an adult community, and they didn't allow phone calls late at night. But there had to be a way to reach her.

Maggie remembered then that one of the nurses had given her a card some time ago. Had told her to feel free to call if she ever had concerns about Winifred's care. They were kind there and recognized the value of friendship and the only question was, what had she done with the card?

Probably put it in her desk, which was at the far end of the living room. Her one attempt at organization; if you put all stray things in one place, you have a shot at finding them later. She pulled open the top drawer. Alone among all the furnishings in the house, the desk was not an antique. She'd made it herself, from a catalogue, before she wrote her first book. Had she been able to carve her own pen, she would have done that too. She wanted the act of creation to be as much under her control as possible. So she had a hand-made Shaker-style desk that wobbled when she leaned on it too hard, but it was her own, and she imagined that the very wobble had influenced her writing. That she had stayed away from longer words because the desk could take only so much pressure; perhaps she would have had a more literary bent with a stronger desk.

Miraculously she found the card, right next to three others for chimney sweeping. She called and got a startled sounding nurse, who eventually remembered who Maggie was, and when she explained to her what had happened, hearing herself the tremor in her voice, the nurse said not to worry. She'd find Winifred and let her use her cell phone. Just wait a moment, the nurse said, and she'll call back. So Maggie sat quietly, waiting for her friend to call, listening to Joe Mangione hollering on her front lawn, visualizing the nurse going through the halls of the home, finding Winifred, who would be in bed this time of night. Propping up the pillows, punching in the number.

The phone rang and Maggie grabbed it.

"Are you all right?" Winifred asked. Her voice was shaky, but Maggie knew a forceful lady was behind it. Sixty-two years old, with a beautiful figure that she was unable to display, much to her aggravation, because she couldn't walk. The Parkinson's was going after her with all it had, though Winifred was giving the disease a heck of a fight.

"You must have been frightened," Winifred said.

"It seemed so unreal I didn't have time to be frightened," Maggie answered. "I must have sat alongside him for fifteen minutes and I didn't think anything about it, but now I keep seeing him in my head."

That dark, curly hair, the lips pulled back in alarm. A moment of sharp pain before crashing onto her front lawn; a stab of fear but nothing more. A quick way to die, the only trace of violence the blood on his lip that must have been from when he fell down. On a rock, perhaps. She thought of his reflector vest. He'd intended to go for a run; was there anything more tragic? A run to improve your life, that ended in death. A run on her lawn. By her tree.

"Do they know who killed him?" Winifred asked.

"Killed him? He had a heart attack."

"Heart attack? Is that what Young Sherlock says?"

She heard Peter outside, talking to his boss. Thank God. *Yes sir. Yes sir.* A whiff of honeysuckle blew in through the window, a smell she'd always detested.

"Peter seemed pretty sure about the heart attack. Didn't even ask Doc Steinberg to come out."

"A man like Bender. I just assumed he'd been murdered. Seemed the type. In fact, if I didn't know you better, I'd think you murdered him."

"Winifred, don't even joke about that."

Winifred laughed, dropped the phone, scrabbled around for it, and then resumed talking.

"Now don't pretend you didn't hate him, Maggie Dove. This is no time to be a hypocrite. One of the first things I said to myself, the day I moved into this place, was that I was done being seemly. I'll speak the truth and nothing less. You should speak it too."

"I am speaking the truth," Maggie said. "I hated him and I wanted him to go away. But not like this."

"Of course, my friend. But he brought it on himself. It's nothing to do with you; it was his time."

Maggie sank down onto her living room couch, the rotating red light from the ambulance chasing itself around her sedate room.

"I can't help but think that I precipitated the arrival of his time. That all the hate and anger I was feeling transposed itself onto him. Like voodoo. Maybe if I'd been kind to him, he'd still be alive."

"If you were kind to him, you'd be a woman without a willow tree."

Winifred had never been a plant person. Maggie'd always been the one who picked her plants, watered them, filling Winifred's home with orchids because it got perfect light. Winifred would have killed them all.

"Not a willow. An oak."

"Well, it's green and it has roots and he wanted to kill it. You can't say that that wasn't so."

Maggie pressed the phone against her mouth, trying not to speak too loud, conscious of the crowd on her front lawn and yet desperate to confide her secret. "I was watching for him, Winifred. That was why I was up. I stayed up, waiting for him. I was so sure he would show up on my lawn."

"You were looking out the window for Bender?"

"Yes."

"Did you see him?"

"No, that's just the thing. I didn't. I watched and waited and I was so furious because, you see, I knew, I knew he was going to come. I felt it, and so I got a rock."

"What? What rock?"

Winifred wheezed with the effort of her speech. Maggie crouched even more tightly into a ball.

"I had a rock and if I'd seen him, I was going to throw it at him."

For a moment the phone was quiet. Then Winifred began to laugh. "I've played softball with you, Maggie. You'd never have hit him."

"That's not the point," Maggie said. "I had murder in my heart."

"Seriously, you were going to throw a rock through a window. What were you thinking was going to happen? Wait, didn't someone do that in one of your mysteries? But no, the murderer dropped a boulder from the roof."

"I couldn't get up on my roof. And I didn't want to kill him. I wanted to hurt him."

Winifred laughed so hard that Maggie heard the nurse come back in and ask if she was all right. She felt like laughing herself, and might have except that there was still a body on her lawn and a man was dead and his wife was a widow and his children fatherless.

"I feel so foolish. What sort of person plans to throw a rock at her neighbor? I feel like an ant, or a worm. This is not at all the sort of person I want to be."

"You're a good person, Maggie. But you're not a saint. No one is. No one should want to be. Better to be human. Tell you the truth, this hatred of yours for Bender has been the most interesting thing about you in years."

"That's a terrible thing to say!"

"I mean it. All this grieving and crying has made you boring. No offense."

"Boring! My daughter died. My husband died. My whole world disappeared. I think I'm entitled to be depressed."

"That was 20 years ago," Winifred said.

"It could be a hundred years ago. You don't recover from something like that."

"You're not the only person in this world who's suffered," Winifred said. "Look at me. Here I am, in a nursing home, can't even move. I've suffered too."

"I appreciate that, Winifred."

"Come right down to it. I've suffered more than you. You've got your own house and car. You can go out at night. Frankly, I might just as well have lost my daughter because she's not talking to me. It's just like she's dead."

"No, I'm sorry but it's not the same thing. You and your daughter had an argument and if you would simply call Amy and apologize for being a horse's ass, she'd forgive you. She's alive. My daughter's dead," Maggie cried out. "There's not a thing in the world I can do to bring her back."

"Well you have happy memories," Winifred continued, unabashed. "You should appreciate what you have."

"What I have! What I have! I have a dead man on my lawn." Maggie swore, and slammed down the phone. How was it possible that her best friend in the world was also the person who drove her most crazy? Except for Marcus. Who also drove her crazy. What was wrong with her?

Her fury seemed to spatter across her genteel living room, pulsating the way the ambulance light had moments ago. Maggie was so angry she couldn't move; she felt as though something large had settled itself against her chest. She staggered to her feet, swaying under emotion, thinking she would go upstairs, go to sleep, but then she heard someone saying her name.

The windows were open. She'd just yelled in front of half her community. She, who had struggled so hard to maintain a brave face all these years, had just let down her guard and yelled about her grief, and worst of all, the widow was on her lawn. Maggie could hear Noelle saying her name.

She remembered then something her mother used to say: *Listeners never hear good of themselves.*

But it was too late.

Chapter Five

"Maggie Dove?" the voice said. A woman's voice. Soft, cultured in the way movie stars from the Fifties sounded. Fake. "That short old lady? The mean one who was always yelling at Bender?

"She's the one who found my husband?" the disembodied voice went on. "I bet she didn't shed any tears over my Bender. No matter what Bender did, she was on him."

I found him because he was on my lawn, Maggie wanted to shout, but she didn't. No matter what her grievances with Bender were, they felt so insubstantial interpreted through this woman's eyes. Maggie might have writer's block, but she was still enough of a writer to be able to go into someone else's head; to see herself as Noelle must.

"That old lady hated my husband. She must have spent half her time looking out the window to see what my Bender was doing."

I'm not that old, Maggie muttered. *Not yet.*

She wanted to go outside and defend herself, but the conversation had gone on too long to interrupt. Then it would look like she'd been sitting in her house eavesdropping, which she had been. Maggie groaned and sank into her couch, prayed they would all just leave. Now. But they didn't. The night wasn't going to end.

"Didn't your husband try to kill her tree?" Peter asked. Loyal Peter. "Thank you for him," Maggie whispered.

"It was just an oak tree," the widow responded. "Not even a healthy one. There was a brown patch in the middle. And my husband offered to move it."

My God they were an annoying family, Maggie thought. The whole lot of them. The husband was a psychopath, the widow deluded. The younger daughter poorly behaved and the older one swiped Snickers bars on Halloween. Maggie hadn't complained, but she saw that girl come running up her front stoop and pour a whole bowl full of candies into her bag. They took her snow shovel too. During the last big storm she'd left it out on her front stoop and when Maggie went outside to shovel some more, it was gone. They'd taken it. "Can I have it back?" she'd asked the young one, who was standing on her driveway, holding it.

"Sure," she said. Sure.

"My husband offered to pay her, to get her a new one, to move that one. She was beyond reason."

"She's very attached to that tree," Peter said. "She has a long-standing relationship with it. Your husband should have respected that."

Maggie sank deeper into her couch. She wondered how much worse this could all get, though she knew the answer to that. Things could always get worse. That was the surprising thing about life. There were no limits. That was what you learned when you grew up. You might be lucky, you might coast through, but you might be cursed too and if you were, if things started to go wrong, there was no limit. She heard the sound of the phone inside her head, Doc Steinberg on the other end, telling her there'd been an accident. Terrible accident. "You're going to have to be strong, Maggie."

She began to feel that metallic taste in her mouth, the taste of panic and grief, the terror of grief. No one told you how frightening grief was, because it was bottomless, it was quicksand, it could swallow you and you could sink and sink.

"Will there be an autopsy?" the widow asked.

"Yes, there's always an autopsy with a sudden death."

"So when will I be able to schedule a funeral?"

Noelle sounded short of breath.

"I'm sure they'll release the body to you quickly," Peter said soothingly. "You'll be able to have the funeral whenever you want."

"He was always worried about having a heart attack," Noelle said. "His father died of a heart attack and his mother died young too. He was sure he wouldn't live to see forty. He always had huge celebrations on his birthdays. That's how we met.

"He was shy," she went on. "But men often are when they meet me for the first time. It's the nature of the business."

What business? Maggie wondered. What did that mean? What did Noelle do for a living?

"Would you happen to know why he was on Mrs. Dove's lawn?" Peter asked.

"What are you suggesting?" Noelle said. "My husband lies dead before us and you're going to start talking about that tree. Are you suggesting a tree is more important than my husband's life? He would have paid her good money to move it and it's only an oak. Nothing special. Those trees are like weeds. She could have bought herself something special, a Japanese maple. Something pretty. She didn't really care about that tree. She just wanted everyone to think of her as a victim. She would have moved it soon enough if one of her friends had asked her to."

Her words seared Maggie, she wondered if they were true. Had she said no just to be unpleasant?

But the widow changed direction yet again, the enormity of the situation hitting her. "This is bullshit," Noelle shouted, her voice an animal trying to break free of its bounds. "He can't be dead. He just had a check-up. With that bitch, Doctor Steinberg. She said he was in great shape for a man his age, but he could stand to lose five pounds. He was so upset about that. He's such a hypochondriac. I told him we should go out to lunch and celebrate, but he didn't want to. He wanted to go out and exercise.

"How could this happen?" she cried. "How could he be alive one minute and dead the next?"

Maggie had cried out something similar when she lost her daughter. That had been the most shocking part of the whole tragedy, the thin line that separated before from after, a line so narrow it seemed like you should be able to stick your hand through it and grab your old life back. But you couldn't.

Her heart ached for Noelle then. Whatever had divided them, they knew what it was like to share grief. Maggie stood up. She had to go outside. She couldn't stay inside, listening anymore. She walked toward her door, but before she could open it Peter asked, "Do you have family we can call? Someone to help you with the children?"

"They're not my children now," she said.

"Why's that?"

"They're his first wife's. He got custody of them, but she'll never want to leave them with someone like me."

She'd got herself under control.

"They'll say I'm not good enough to take them. I'll probably never see them again. What am I talking about, they don't even like me. Never wanted to live with me in the first place. They'll be glad to say good bye to me."

"I'm very sorry," Peter said, and he sounded like he meant it. "Is there no one I can call?"

"No," she whispered. "No one."

Maggie couldn't take it anymore. No one deserved this. No one deserved to be alone with her dead husband and about to lose her kids and be surrounded by hatred and contempt. She had to go outside, Maggie thought, pushing open the front door and walking onto the veranda. Kindness had to trump humiliation. She stepped out onto the front porch just as the widow said, "Did that awful Mrs. Dove watch him die?"

Maggie came stuttering to a stop, struck motionless on the front lawn, now almost empty, in front of a young woman who stared at her aggressively, angrily. She wore a tight black dress; she must have changed into mourning the moment she heard her husband was dead. A suspicious person might think she had it at the ready.

"No," Maggie said. "He'd been long dead by the time I got there."

"I don't know if I believe you."

She was beautiful and proud. Her eyes flashed, her white blonde hair was combed softly around her and she'd put on make-up, unless she normally went to bed with carefully lined eyes and plumped up glossy lips.

"Let's bring him away," Peter said, indicating Bender, who was covered up.

"Get her away from me," Noelle said.

Maggie didn't argue, went back inside. Only a small part of her, the churlish part, thought Bender had got what he wanted. Her lawn. He'd finally kicked her off her own lawn.

Chapter Six

That night Maggie woke up to the sound of the 2:00 freight train. She'd been listening to that train most of her life, counting up the cars though she usually fell back asleep before she got to fifty. She loved the trains, the town hall clock that sounded every hour, the barking of Cavanaugh's dog every morning, the street sweepers on Tuesday and Friday, the garbage men yelling at the commuters who were going crazy trying to get around them, the peepers that erupted every March, the Halloween parade that took place every October, the Arbor Day ceremony every April, the rhythms of her town.

She loved order. She supposed that was why she was so religious, because she sought meaning in everything. She couldn't picture life without a plan. She imagined the universe as her little village writ large. She suspected that was why Bender upset her so much, because he was a convulsion in the natural order of things. Because he represented chaos and she was clutching so tightly to the rules of her world.

Maggie couldn't sleep.

The train passed, but she was restless. She paced around her bedroom. A deep fog had descended, blocking out the lights of the Mario Cuomo new Tappan Zee Bridge, which normally she could see twinkling. All was hidden. She stared down at her lawn, muffled in fog. She felt her heart beating wildly and wondered if she too would collapse, as Bender had done. She wanted to call Winifred and apologize to her, but she'd already disrupted the nursing schedule once. She'd call first thing in the morning.

She turned on the lights and picked up one of her favorite mysteries. Agatha Christie, of course. *A Murder is Announced.* She became a mystery writer because she loved Agatha Christie so much. People thought she wrote mysteries because she liked murder and mayhem, but in fact she loved the rules of mysteries.

Crime and punishment. Cause and effect. Unlike life, mysteries made sense. Someone died and it was for a reason. Someone else figured out the reason and then she sent the bad guy to jail. It all made sense. The few times she'd read mysteries without a solution she'd thrown them away. That was why she'd stopped writing them. Because when her life lost its order, she could no longer write about it.

A girl. Loved. A beautiful girl who sailed through her life, surrounded by a family and village who loved her. A girl on the brink of incredible success, a talented linguist offered a scholarship to a prestigious school, who went to a party to celebrate. A rainy night. But she was a careful driver. Didn't drink. Left the party early to make her curfew. Put on her seat belt, except that, while she was waiting at a traffic light, a van skid on the slick road and crashed into her. Her passenger, Peter Nelson, who was not wearing a seat belt, was thrown through the car and survived with a few bruises. But Juliet was killed instantly.

How could one write mysteries after that? How could one presume to know how people lived or thought or how things could turn out? Sometimes Maggie wondered how she managed to hold onto her faith after all that, except she loved Him so much, she couldn't let go of Him. But she never trusted God in quite the same way again. She lost so much on that terrible night.

How dare Winifred suggest she'd hung on to her grief for too long? How dare she judge? She'd entered uncharted territory on the day her daughter died. No one had the right to judge her anymore. Only, perhaps, Peter, who had suffered too, who had loved Juliet almost as much as she did. Whose life was also destroyed by her death. Who had clung to her memory just as Maggie did. How could Winifred even suggest that an argument with her daughter was the same thing? Poor Amy Bell who had never been able to do anything right as far as her mother was concerned, because she was awkward and unpopular and wasn't the daughter Winifred wanted.

Again, that terrible pounding of Maggie's heart. Anger was swallowing her alive, and as she looked out the window, she could almost imagine Bender out there still.

Why couldn't he have died on his lawn? What possible reason did he have for running on to her own?

That question ate at her. Bender would not have run on her lawn without a reason. She knew him well enough to know that. She grabbed up a flashlight and went outside. All was quiet. Still. She smelled the widow's heavy perfume, and looked toward Bender's house, lit up, as usual. All was as it should be. The widow in bed, the body in the morgue. Peter gone home. Nothing to worry about and yet the peace did worry her.

She prowled around her lawn, seeking, knowing, peering into the forsythia, crouching down by the floribunda, looking under the hydrangeas, one of the most poisonous of plants. She'd used the leaves in one of her mysteries. She searched around some more, looking into the little space by the stairs where balls often rolled.

Something caught her eye. She walked toward it and saw that it was a bottle of drain cleaner, hidden by her house. A white bottle with a distinctive red devil on it. Maggie picked it up and saw that the bottle was empty, but some drops of liquid still clung to the rim. Someone had used it recently.

So it was true, she thought. He really was going to kill her tree. "You son of a gun," she muttered, and with that every light in his house shut off.

Chapter Seven

Friday morning broke rainy and wretched and Maggie, waking early, saw a figure on her lawn. For a moment she thought it was Bender, come back to haunt her, but then the figure moved and she saw it was the piano teacher, Mr. Cavanaugh, and his dog. Frisky little dog that seemed to think of her lawn as his own personal latrine, but Maggie put that thought in a bag and deposited it elsewhere. She could hate one neighbor, but not two. When you hate one person, it's his fault; if you hate two, it's yours.

"Avante, Fidelio," Cavanaugh called out, tugging his dog in the direction of Main Street. He was a little white pouf of a thing. He always looked puzzled. The dog, not Ellis Cavanaugh.

But no, he wasn't done. Cavanaugh, not the dog. He stood in front of her oak tree for a moment. She couldn't make out the expression on his face. He wore a poncho, and glasses covered his eyes, but she assumed, from the stillness of his position, that he was remembering Bender, perhaps wondering, as she was, how it was possible that the events of last night had left so little trace. The lawn looked as it always did. Life went on, the great tragedy of life, and she had just begun to think about that when Mr. Cavanaugh rocked back on his feet and spit at her oak tree. Then he grabbed up his little dog in his arms and strode in the direction of Main Street.

Maggie was stunned. She'd never seen that man lose his temper and Mr. Cavanaugh had been sorely tried. She'd seen him on the verge of tears. At the high school concert, when Jeremy Burns played Chopin at twice its required speed she'd seen him brush his face with a handkerchief. But never angry.

What had Bender done to him? Maggie wondered.

How many people in this village hated him?

She thought of what Winifred said, that he seemed like a candidate for murder and she suspected she was right. So much ill feeling swirled around the man. Anger created ugliness. She knew it had in her. She blushed as she thought of what her face must have looked like when she yelled at Bender. She'd always thought she had gentle features, but then she never looked at herself in the mirror that she didn't assume a smile first. How different would she look if her jaw was twisted in anger, her eyes hardened? She didn't want to be that person, which was part of why she hated Bender so much. Because he turned her into somebody she didn't want to be.

She considered the phone. Foolish to hold onto grievances. She didn't want to be that person. She wanted to be good. She wanted to be kind.

"I knew you'd call," Winifred said. "You don't have the stomach for a real fight."

"Why are you provoking me?" Maggie asked, sitting down by the window, at the very spot where she'd planned to throw a rock last night. Her desk was cluttered with papers. Everything seemed out of place.

"I don't want to fight," Maggie went on. "I want to have a friendly conversation."

"About what?" Winifred asked.

"About the weather," Maggie said. "It's bad." She wanted to tell her about Mr. Cavanaugh, about the bottle of drain cleaner, but suspected it would lead to a discussion of what an idiot Peter was, and she didn't feel up to that.

"Yes," Winifred said. "There does seem to be a lot of humidity. That reminds me. There's a man I want you to meet."

"No."

"I just want to know what you think of him," Winifred said.

"You've chosen this moment to set me up on a date," Maggie said. "I had a man dead on my lawn just last night."

It was like being back in high school, she thought. She was 62 years old and they were arguing over the same exact things. The two of them used to go to A&S to look for bathing suits and Winifred was always after her for not picking something more glamorous. "Don't be a prude, Maggie Dove."

She didn't want to argue and yet she felt it was expected. This was their relationship. Had nothing changed? Was there no way to break through and establish a relationship on a deeper level? To say, you are the friend of my youth and I love you, but I can't keep arguing about the same thing, but before Maggie had a chance to say anything at all, she noticed some commotion over the Bender house.

"What?" Winifred said, with the talent for knowing what Maggie was thinking. For reading her mind.

"You're never going to believe this."

"What?" Winifred asked. "Is it a man? Is it George Clooney?"

"No. George Clooney is not involved, but there's a woman dragging Bender's kids out of the house." The rain pounded down on the beleaguered group, drops hitting the ground and then bouncing back up.

"What type of woman?"

"She's limping."

"That must be Bender's first wife," Winifred said. "She has Parkinson's."

"How on earth do you know that?"

"I have my sources," Winifred said. Maggie could hear her grin. Winifred had always known things before anyone else. Before she married for the first time, before she got pregnant, she'd planned to be a reporter and she probably would have been good at it.

"Come on now, Ariadne," Maggie could hear the woman cry out. "Come on now, Lorelei. Come with mother."

"You're right," Maggie said. "She must be taking them away from Noelle."

"Maybe there was something in the autopsy that worried her," Winifred said.

"They can't have the autopsy done already, can they? He only died a few hours ago."

"I don't know," Winifred said. "You're the mystery writer. But it seems strange."

The woman was savage with movement, so desperate to get to the car that she seemed to be forgetting about the two children, who were getting drenched, and then she collected herself and pushed them into the car and slammed the doors closed. She was driving an old VW, which was not a car Maggie associated with scenes of anger or children, for that matter.

The VW lurched into action, a shot of smoke blew out its exhaust, and then it drove away and the street was empty.

"It is strange," Maggie said.

Her own hatred for the man, Mr. Cavanaugh's anger, and now this act of what seemed to be desperation.

"I bet the wife killed him," Winifred said. "I'm just not sure which wife."

"It's a heart attack, Winifred. That's what Peter said."

"And Young Sherlock's never wrong."

"I wouldn't say that. But he seemed so confident."

Maggie pictured the way Peter had looked last night, the argument over whether or not to call Campbell, the look of concern on Joe's face. Was he wrong to assume so quickly that it was a heart attack? If he'd messed up, Campbell was not the sort of man to offer forgiveness, she felt sure of that. Yet she knew Peter to be a good police officer. He'd won awards, but then he'd never had investigate anything involving Maggie and she knew he had a blind spot where she was concerned. He was so intensely loyal that had he found her standing over with Bender with a knife she suspected he wouldn't even give her a traffic ticket.

How far would he go to protect her?

What had he done?

She had to know what the village was saying, and there was one place she knew for sure she could get that information.

"I have to go," Maggie said.

"Don't get involved," Winifred cautioned.

"Good bye, Winifred."

Maggie anointed herself for battle. She showered, flossed and put on her favorite J.Jill jeans, which had a nice expandable waist, not that she really needed it. She fluffed up her short white hair, put in her pearls, a gift from her husband. He'd not been an extravagant man. More likely to write her a poem than give her jewelry, but he'd splurged on these after their daughter was born. Her gentle professor, who she'd fallen in love with as a senior in college and run off and married, the most scandalous thing she'd ever done. Dear Stuart Dove.

Finally Maggie put on some pink lipstick and some Chanel Number 5, which she wore for the sole reason that she once heard an interview with P.D. James and she wore it. Then she set out to find out how much trouble Peter was in.

Chapter Eight

Iphigenia's hair salon sat in the center of the village, both physically and metaphorically. Almost every woman in town passed through her doors, and because Iphigenia felt very strongly that all women looked best with blonde straight hair, almost every woman in the village looked slightly similar. On village-wide occasions, such as the Fourth of July fireworks or the Spring Fling, there were so many blonde women of all shapes and sizes that Maggie sometimes thought the whole village looked related.

"Tscha," Iphigenia cried out. "Look at you Maggie Dove. Look at your hair. You look like a rag doll. You ruin my reputation. Sit down. I have ten minutes."

"I really just wanted to ask…"

Iphigenia stood before her, a fury of perfume. She wore her own hair blown up like an Egyptian princess, with bangs, an effect she highlighted by shading her eyes with lots of dark pencil. She was gorgeous. "We can do color too. I have time."

"No color," Maggie said, as Iphigenia propelled forward into her salon.

"Why don't we try something new today?" Iphigenia said. "We were talking about changing the shape."

"Dear God,' Maggie cried out. "Nothing new."

"Of course. Of course. I know, Miss Maggie wants to play it safe," Iphigenia said, sweeping Maggie toward the black chair and swiveling it so that Maggie could settle in more easily.

"That's exactly right. Miss Maggie wants safety."

Iphigenia swung Maggie around so that she faced the mirror, and, confronting her image so suddenly, Maggie laughed out loud. Who was this person with the white hair and blue eyes?

"I'm turning into my mother," she said.

"You're beautiful," Iphigenia said, snapping a black plastic cape around Maggie's neck. "Beautiful. You haven't aged a day. Isn't that right, my friend Agnes, who sits over there so quietly?"

Maggie started. She hadn't even noticed Agnes Jorgenson's sullen figure in the corner, all swathed in black.

"Yes," Agnes said. "You're still beautiful. How are you, Margaret?"

They'd gone to high school together, Maggie and Agnes and Winifred and for some reason Agnes felt compelled to call Maggie by her full name, though Maggie wasn't sure why. No one else in the world called her Margaret.

"I heard you found Marcus Bender's body," Agnes said. She was secretary to the traffic court judge and spent a good deal of time listening to people come up with excuses. She'd learned to trust no one. She had large blue eyes and should have been attractive, except she never blinked. She always looked startled.

Iphigenia clucked. "Such a tragedy. Such a bad thing."

"Bad for Bender, certainly," Agnes said. She gazed at Maggie speculatively. Her lips twitched and Maggie had the strongest possible feeling she was laughing at her. For just a moment she thought of Bender collapsing on her lawn. She imagined his haughty face and the drop of blood on his lips. She shivered as she remembered the feeling she'd had that someone else was there. In the night. Watching her.

"I heard he'd just been to the doctor," Agnes said.

"How many times does that happen? You go to the doctor and the next day you're dead. That's why I never go to the doctor," Iphigenia said, laughing loudly. "Not for ten years."

"That's just foolishness," Agnes said. "You don't have mammograms?"

"No. Nothing. Nothing. And look at me. I'm healthy as a horse."

"You should go," Maggie said.

"No. Me? I want to go just like Bender. Alive one minute and then, dead the next."

She snapped her scissors at the thought, though Maggie noticed her hands were shaking. The scissors came a little closer to Maggie's cheek than she suspected Iphigenia intended.

"Did you do CPR?" Agnes asked.

"There was no call for it. He was dead."

"How could you be sure?" she asked. "I've heard stories about people being buried alive. They used to worry about that, didn't they? That's where the expression comes from. Saved by the bell. Because they'd put a bell down in the coffin."

"Agnes!" Maggie interrupted. "The police were there. Trust me, Bender was not alive."

"Was he stiff?"

"Tscha," Iphigenia said. "Look over there. Edgar Blake must have lice again."

The pharmacy was across the street from the hair salon. Sure enough, Edgar Blake's mother was clutching her son with one hand and a bag with the other, the bag distorted by a familiar shape. Edgar was renowned for his lice; his mother said they kept reappearing, but the general consensus was they never went away.

"Such thick hair, the son has," Iphigenia said. "I think maybe I cancel her appointment for tomorrow. Just to be safe. I don't want any creepy crawlie things in my salon." She shivered dramatically.

"He's in your Sunday School class, isn't he?" Agnes asked.

"Yes."

"Better wear a hat this Sunday," Agnes said. "Or maybe tell the reverend to call and ask them not to come to church."

"Dear God," Maggie exploded, "if the worst thing that ever happens to me is I get lice from one of my Sunday School students, I'll consider myself lucky. For all we know, it's a home pregnancy test. Am I going to cut a 6-year-old boy off from salvation because we saw his mother with a bag?"

Agnes laughed at that. "You're a good Sunday School teacher, Maggie, but I don't know that you're that good. Do you seriously think young Edgar's salvation hinges on going to one of your classes?"

Maggie blushed. What was wrong with her lately? She didn't recognize herself.

"Are you going to Bender's funeral?" Agnes asked.

"No," Maggie said, determined not to get pulled into this discussion. On the street one of the young skateboarders shot by, a tall Asian boy with pants that looked like they would slide right off his hips. He jumped to go over the curb and the skateboard seemed to attach itself to his feet, a move so dangerous and graceful that Maggie almost cried out.

"I can understand that," Agnes said. "I wouldn't go to his funeral if I were you. But I wonder if Peter will go."

"Why wouldn't he," Maggie asked, a twinge of anxiety pinging through her.

Agnes peered toward her curiously. "Let's just say that Bender was not a fan of our assistant chief of police. One might even say that Bender was trying to get him fired."

"Why would Bender want Peter fired?"

"I didn't say he was. I said he might be."

"I don't know what that means, Agnes. Are you saying Peter's in trouble?"

She laughed at that. "My dear, Peter's been in trouble since the day he was born."

Maggie started to reply, but before she could go further, Iphigenia shouted, "Ping. Time's up. Color's ready. Time to do some blow drying." She swept Agnes out of her chair before she could speak. Then aimed the blow dryer at her like a gun, humming loudly, fluffing her hair. Agnes sat rigidly throughout, a prisoner awaiting execution.

Iphigenia was a whirl of fluffing and blowing for the next few minutes, and when she was done, Agnes surveyed herself in the mirror, obviously pleased with the result. She took a check out of her pocketbook, prewritten, and handed it to Iphigenia and walked out the door, stopping, for just a moment, in the doorway.

"Don't you worry, Margaret. Peter's not the only one who doesn't mourn Bender's passing," Agnes said. "I could name ten other people in this village who would have been happy to kill him too."

Having said that she exited through the door, sailing onto Main Street like the queenliest of ships, bowing to those who passed.

"Brrr. I don't like her," Iphigenia said.

"Me neither."

"What makes someone like that?" Iphigenia said, eyeing Maggie's hair speculatively, snipping every so often.

"I don't know," Maggie said. "She had a crazy family, I can tell you that. There were eight of those Jorgenson children, each one stranger and meaner than the next. But the father. He was really a piece of work." He'd been thrown out of town after fondling some girl, or so the rumor had it, though Maggie figured she wouldn't pass on that tidbit. She'd like to think she had a little honor left.

"She's not happy. Her roots are unhealthy. I can tell."

Iphigenia then turned her attention back to Maggie's hair, which she cut and fluffed until Maggie thought she looked a little like Julius Caesar.

"Very young," Iphigenia said. "Very beautiful."

It will grow out, Maggie thought.

"Is it true you haven't been to the doctor in ten years?" Maggie asked.

"I wouldn't want to go through chemo. I'd rather die."

"Do you think something's wrong?"

Automatically Iphigenia put her hand to her breast.

"If you're worried, it's better to find out early. It's not a death sentence, you know, but you're better off finding out. You're probably making yourself sick worrying about it."

"No."

"I'll take you. Make an appointment with Doc Steinberg and I'll go with you and then we'll have lunch. Why don't you make it for Monday?"

"We'll see," Iphigenia said, and then she nodded over at the pharmacy and they both looked at Noelle Bender, who was walking out the door of the pharmacy, carrying a white bag. Lice? Maggie wondered. Or something else? What else came in a box? A home pregnancy test? Good grief, Maggie thought. Living in a small town turns us all into spies, but before she could turn her head, Noelle looked straight at her.

Maggie blushed, and turned away.

After she left, her thoughts turned back to Peter. Was it possible he had some sort of beef with Bender? Of course it was possible. Peter argued with everyone. But how bad was it? Probably he hadn't told Maggie about it because he didn't want to upset her. But she knew who he would tell. She knew who would know.

Chapter Nine

Maggie drove over to Winifred's nursing home, and there she found her friend, as she so often did, staring at the pictures of her four husbands. Winifred liked to define herself as a serial marrier. Although she'd hit a bit of a rough patch in the last few years, having developed Parkinson's, that didn't stop her from looking for husband number five. She'd divorced the four previous ones, being of the view that there was no point in staying in a bad situation, so it was something of an irony that Winifred had wound up in the ultimate bad situation, semi-paralyzed and in a nursing home. Yet she took it with more grace than anyone Maggie knew.

She didn't complain, although she had enough justification. Maggie had noticed that often the people with the most to complain about did it the least, possibly because they didn't need the attention. In any event, Winifred looked awful when Maggie walked into her room, dyed brown hair teased too high, right arm swollen, head craned perilously to the side. Blue eyes sparkling. Those eyes had been looking for trouble for more than sixty years.

"Here she is," Winifred said. "I was just telling young Arthur here about your adventures last night." Young Arthur grinned genially, a soft young man with large spongy hands. He was massaging Winifred's arm, trying to build up her muscles. Winifred was determined to beat the disease and had done a lot of research on the internet, trying to find alternative cures, or any cures, and one thing she was passionate about was exercise.

"Not much of an adventure," Maggie said. "More of a nightmare really."

She sank down onto Winifred's new couch. Unlike every other person at The Castle, Winifred had elected not to bring her furniture from home. Instead she'd gone to Bloomingdales and selected a jewel blue couch and an antiqued white bookshelf. She'd had Arthur spend the afternoon moving everything around to get it just right, which had not made The Castle happy because the administrators were of the view that Arthur was there to work for more than one person. But Winifred didn't care and neither did Arthur. The whole thing was quite nice except Maggie felt the couch had been designed for someone about six inches taller than her. She felt like a child with her feet hanging in space.

"A nightmare," Winifred crowed. "Nonsense. You're a mystery writer. You should be eating up death for breakfast. I would think you'd be delighted to have someone die on your front lawn. If that's not a cure for writer's block, I don't know what is."

"I didn't become a mystery writer because I wanted to see a murder," she said, "but rather because I like to write stories."

"I thought you became a writer because it gave you a respectable way to fantasize about men."

Arthur had moved onto Winifred's other arm, trying to press some feeling into her poor abused limbs. Maggie knew Winifred and her moods well enough to know she was looking for an argument. She'd been like that as a girl too. So excited by trouble that she couldn't calm down. Maggie focused on the bookshelves, which Winifred had filled, three rows deep, with copies of Maggie's books that she still, twenty years after the fact, handed out to doctors and nurses.

"Maggie's detective was quite the dreamboat," Winifred explained to Arthur.

At one point Maggie had told her to stop buying books because she didn't want her to bankrupt herself, but Winifred didn't care. She loved Maggie's books; they were the best books ever written and she'd set them on her shelf between *War and Peace* and *Beloved*.

"She's ignoring me," Winifred said.

"I'm not ignoring you," Maggie said. "I don't want to argue with you."

"Inspector Claude Benet. He had big hands," she said to Arthur. "He was the perfect man. He was like James Bond, but faithful. He was even good at house repairs. That man could change a bulb," she said, cackling wildly.

Arthur laughed along genially. Maggie hoped he didn't go home and relate these stories to his family.

"He was handsome, spoke three languages and played the clarinet."

"Flute," Maggie said.

"Same thing."

"Not really."

"Oh yes, my dear. It's all the same."

Maggie wondered if it would be possible to have a conversation with Winifred that did not end in sexual innuendo. Arthur smiled at her. He was a kind young man who performed his job with grace. She knew he had a mother and grandmother and great-grandmother who lived with him. He talked about them fondly, didn't complain, didn't get mad. What was his outlet, Maggie wondered. What was the secret of his grace? Everyone has a secret.

"And he didn't own a gun. He won all his cases through quick thinking."

"And jujitsu," Maggie said. "He was a black belt."

"Not that it mattered. His suspects always confessed."

Maggie was tempted to come to the defense of her dear Inspector Benet, but decided to say no more. One way or another Winifred would get in the last word, and she didn't want this to get ugly. She was Maggie's best friend, but that didn't mean Maggie always liked her.

"Did you base him on someone you knew?" Arthur asked.

"I suppose I based him a little bit on my husband."

Winifred howled. "The marvelous Stuart Dove."

"My husband was some years older than me…" Maggie started to say.

More howling from Winifred. "Some years! Maggie's own father used to call him dad."

Maggie resumed. "But when he was young, he was quite elegant. I didn't know him then, of course, but I liked to imagine what he would have been like, and so part of Inspector Benet came out of that."

She'd found her husband so mysterious. That was part of his charm for her. She didn't know him fully and doubted she ever could. He knew so many curious people. He was a Russian scholar and had spent years traveling around Russia, and so they were always having visitors. Curious people who showed up in the middle of the night and told stories and drank and ate and argued about religion and love. They were all so over-the-top, most of them Ph.D. students, some writers, and some who didn't fit into any category. They all respected her husband and she loved being part of that world. She began studying Russian herself. Inspector Benet, of course, was fluent.

"Stuart Dove could not change a light bulb."

"He was a professor," Maggie explained. "He was very charming, very cultured."

"He was no James Bond."

"I thought he was," Maggie said, and she looked meaningfully at Winifred, who had once been a champion fencer, who had known back then when to parry and when to go in reverse. Though not now.

"Why, on their honeymoon..." Winifred started to say, but Maggie cut her off.

"That's enough," Maggie barked and finally Winifred snapped her jaw shut.

"I'm in trouble now," she stage whispered to Arthur.

"You're too much," he said, laughing. Maggie wondered what it would take to upset Arthur. Now he'd be a good murderer, Maggie thought, involuntarily. Occupational hazard of being a mystery writer. Every time you meet someone, you wonder what would make them kill.

He began gathering up his towels, putting away his ointments, preparing for his next client.

"So long, pretty lady," Arthur said.

"Bye Arthur," Winifred cawed. "Don't be a stranger."

She stared after him after he left. "I should have married a man like Arthur," Winifred said. "Someone calm and good with his hands."

"I thought Fred was like that."

"Ah," Winifred said. "He was boring."

She gathered herself together then, and looked at Maggie. "So, how much trouble am I in?"

"Not so much," Maggie said, because that was the thing about Winifred. Bad as she was, it was awfully hard to resist that spirit that flamed inside her. "Lucky for you, I'm trying to control my anger."

"Saint Maggie."

“I was over at Iphigenia’s before and I ran into Agnes Jorgenson.”

“Oh my God,” Winifred said. “The light that failed.”

Maggie laughed. “She’s just as wretched as ever. More so.”

“I don’t know why she moved back to town. Couldn’t she have stayed somewhere else and made everyone there miserable? Do you remember when she tried out for cheerleading? When she wanted to be on the team? No one wanted to catch her. Remember how she looked in the uniform.”

Maggie shook her head. She did remember quite clearly. Really it wasn’t all that funny, but it was ridiculous. It was almost as though Agnes had gone out of her way to look foolish. Short little skirt that did not flatter her hefty body, hair tied in pig tails, but instead of looking bouncy, it just sagged onto her shoulders. Plus she had no sense of timing at all. Even the gym teacher, sweet Mary Callahan, had to leave the room so as not to laugh.

“Anyway, Agnes implied that Peter had some reason for being angry at Bender. Do you know about that? I didn’t even know he knew Bender. I wouldn’t have thought their paths would cross.”

Winifred shook her head. She tried to cross her arms, but they were too heavy to move. Her right foot began to twitch. “I haven’t seen him in a week or so. He’s been busy with something. I thought he found a woman.”

Maggie looked at her friend's twitching foot. Seemed wrong to use someone's disability against them as a tell, but she had to know.

"Is it that bad?" she asked.

Winifred's eyes glittered the way they always did when there was danger. She loved trouble. Damned fool, Maggie thought. She put her hand on her friend's, to try and stop the spasm.

"Winnie," she said. "What has Peter done?"

Winifred's entire body clenched in rebellion. She would not tell the secret, no matter what sort of torture she endured. Maggie wondered if she was the bravest person she knew or the most impossible. She wondered what on earth Peter could have done. She loved him so much, but he was like Winifred. They were both drawn to trouble. They had a self-destructive side that she found terrifying. She couldn't protect them. She couldn't protect anyone.

Suddenly Winifred cried out.

"There he is!"

"Who?"

"That man I wanted you to meet. Remember?"

"No."

She began calling to him, but her voice was dry and nothing came out. She gestured toward Maggie, suggesting that she go and waylay him, but Maggie wanted no part of it, and soon enough he was gone. She only had a general image of him, a blur of white hair, laughter.

"Frank Bowman," Winifred rasped. "I want you to meet him."

“Are you kidding me?” Maggie said. “Right now, at this moment, when I’ve had a dead man on my lawn and I’m preoccupied with Peter, that’s what you think I need?”

Winifred recovered her voice. “I’ll tell you what you need,” she said.

But Maggie was up and out. “That’s it,” she said. “That’s it.”

Chapter Ten

Maggie Dove roared out of the nursing home. She rammed her foot down on the accelerator of her red Audi TT and had the pleasure of seeing one of the nurses shake her head, scandalized. She happened to be near Rt. 684, which wasn't exactly the direction in which she wanted to go. Was in fact in the complete opposite direction. But had the virtue of being always empty and having a 65-miles-an-hour speed limit.

She raced north for half an hour.

She felt like the car could take flight. She could take flight.

Damn Winifred. Damn that Frank Bowman, whoever he was. Damn Marcus Bender, for dying on her lawn. Damn his wife, just on principle. Damn Peter, who was almost certainly in some sort of terrible trouble. Damn Winifred again for always making her feel guilty and prudish. Damn herself for being such a crank.

Maggie turned on the seat heater and her whole body felt like it was dissolving into butter. She blasted the radio. WQXR. Rachmaninoff. Russians. Spies. Her husband.

The sun now shone so bright it didn't seem possibly it had been pouring only a few hours earlier. She passed three cars: two minivans and a Kia. The one great virtue of being 62-years- old was that you could drive a bright red Audi TT and almost never be pulled over by the police.

In an older person, speed is endearing or a sign of dementia.

She'd bought the TT years ago when she'd been investigating cars for Inspector Benet. What sort of car would such a man drive, she'd asked herself, going from car dealership to dealership until she found the TT, thrilled at its sleek shape, so excited she'd bought one for herself. She still felt excited every time she got into it.

Could she come back in another life or as another person, she would race cars. Maggie's one regret, beyond anything to do with her daughter, was that she hadn't done anything adventurous. Hadn't skied or gone on safaris. Had preferred to stay home and read a book, which was an adventure of a kind.

"Frank Bowman," she muttered.

Finally she got off 684 and head back in the direction of home.

Imagine going on a date and having to make small talk, she thought, as she raced past Sleepy Hollow Cemetery. She loved feeling the road beneath her. Loved the sound of the engine running. For some reason she'd always loved the smell of oil, maybe because her father had been so handy. He'd had a workroom and he loved to putter. He wasn't a well-educated man, but he'd loved history and he'd loved Stuart Dove. "And he did not call him dad," she muttered.

Maggie didn't want to be ridiculous. Bad enough she'd been pitied for so long. She'd been the person people always spoke to gently, asked how are you doing with the frightened hope on their faces that Maggie would not collapse on their watch. That she would just reply, "Fine thanks." Which she always did. She'd not wanted to be a burden.

She'd struggled so hard to reach a point that people could talk to her without flinching. Grief was so isolating. People wanted to say the right thing, but they weren't sure what it was. So better to say nothing at all. She wanted to comfort people, to tell them it was okay to say what they wanted. But she didn't have the energy and found it hard to speak without crying. Then there were the callous ones who were afraid bad luck was contagious. And those who thought you should get over it. But over the years she'd managed to reclaim her person. She was no longer an object of pity, but friendship. She would not now switch into ridiculousness by dating one of Winifred's suitors.

Anyway, if she wanted an attractive man to talk to she could talk to Inspector Benet. She'd given him silver hair and solemn brown eyes. She'd made him perfect. She'd found there something appealing about a man with a thick head of hair. In the years since she'd stopped writing, the part she'd missed the most had been Benet, but she still talked to him when she wanted. Occasionally he answered. Between the fictional characters and the lost people she loved, Maggie could spend a great deal of time talking to the air, and why not? Perhaps that was heaven, conversation with those you loved, real or not. Why would she want to disturb that?

Past the shops in Tarrytown, the Junior League thrift store, a church where she'd gone to a funeral, a synagogue, a park, another park, a place where a traitor had been shot during the Revolutionary War. Past Sunnyside where docents dressed in nineteenth century clothes took you on tours of Washington Irving's home. Further south on Broadway, entering her village, passing by the church that she loved so well. Admiring the way the steeple reached to the sky. An old-fashioned building made of stone and marble, for an old-fashioned woman with an old-fashioned life.

She'd only ever had one fight with her husband, and that had been over whether or not to have a child. Stuart thought he was too old. She'd pressed him. She wanted a child, hoped for a daughter. She knew he'd be a good father, and so he was. In so many ways, more patient and loving than she was. How he'd loved walking with his beautiful little girl up and down the hills of their village, along the aqueduct that ran through the village, and alongside the river, skimming rocks, fishing, sometimes swimming. He'd tried so hard to split Juliet away from Peter. He'd never understood Peter's virtues, only seen his faults. Thankfully, Stuart died a year before Juliet did. Maggie's first thought, when the phone call came from the police, was that she was glad he hadn't lived to see this. Glad to think that Stuart was already in heaven, waiting to welcome his daughter.

She stopped writing about Inspector Benet after Juliet died. She tried to keep going, but every time she started a new book, she found herself killing off Inspector Benet. She couldn't foresee an ending in which Benet lived. Every time that man went out to solve a case he got hit by a bus, or stabbed, or, in its final iteration, he was hit by lightning. Her publisher suggested coming up with a different hero. Maybe she'd done all she could with Inspector Benet, but she didn't want to leave him. She'd wanted him to die.

Her publisher suggested she was depressed and should get some help, but she didn't want help. She wanted to mourn.

She turned down Main Street. The river shimmered in front of her like a dream. Every color was as carefully delineated as a needlepoint: here silver blue; there midnight blue; here sky blue. Everything so clear. She couldn't get over the beauty of this river, its timelessness. It was impossible to own, to understand; it could only be appreciated. She thought of Peter. She would have to go talk to him. She prayed his conflict with Bender wasn't too terrible. Suddenly she felt weak, dizzy, couldn't go any further. She wasn't more than two blocks from home, but she worried she'd crash the car. She pulled into the first spot, surprised to see a crowd in front of her, even more surprised when they all turned to look at her curiously. Then they began to do something very odd. They began to clap.

Chapter Eleven

Maggie assumed the crowd was applauding someone behind her, so she turned her head, expecting to see something remarkable. But all she saw was Sal Martini, slumped against a streetlamp, squinting up at the sun. She turned back to the crowd, wondering if she was hallucinating, but then the crowd parted and there was Hal Carter. He was having his annual furnace drive, she realized, and he was trying to dragoon her.

"It's our local celebrity," Hal cried out. "Come up here, Maggie Dove."

Hal Carter used to be considered the most romantic man in town. Not that he looked the part. He was a plumber and looked like a plumber with his overalls, ruddy face and competent hands. For almost all his adult life he'd lived with his mother, and oh what a difficult woman she'd been. She used to slam the door on Girl Scouts just on principle. Didn't approve of begging. She disapproved of any woman Hal ever went out with. Plus, her nose was always running. She liked to shove Kleenex up her nostrils so when you spoke to her it looked like she had tusks. But no matter how difficult the old lady was, Hal Carter never complained. Ever.

People were always trying to set up Hal on a date because, except for the handicap of his mother, he was a good catch. But no. He didn't have time. His mother needed him. Maggie herself had gone out with him on the one and only date she'd gone on after her husband died, but it had been like going out with her brother.

Then, one day, the old lady died. She passed away in her sleep and not one month later Hal began dating Gretchen Anderson, who was easily the loveliest young woman in town. She worked as a docent at the Sunnyside historical site and dressed up in 19th century clothes. You'd see them strolling around town, him all red and voluble and she so placid in her gown. They were so tender with each other. There was such pleasure in seeing someone get what he deserved. He'd suffered and suffered for years and then, in reward, he won a beautiful prize.

The wedding was the biggest occasion there'd ever been in the village. Winifred cried through the whole thing. The bride wore a nineteenth century wedding dress, all ivory and beads. There were even beads in her hair. The bride's mother, who was also lovely, played the piano as Hal and Gretchen danced a minuet.

In the years since his wedding, Hal had become ambitious. People said it was because he wanted a family. It wasn't cheap living in this village anymore, especially for a plumber, however good he might be and there was a suggestion that Hal was not so good a plumber as his father had been. Maggie noticed that since he suffered less, people had become more critical.

So, to drum up business, Hal had started up a contest to find "the oldest furnace in town." Winner would get a free furnace, but all the runners up would get "consultations." Maggie knew for herself that Hal was persistent as a tick. If you were a runner up, you were doomed to get a lot of consultations until Hal finally harangued you into installing a brand new furnace. She'd expected the contest to fall flat, but surprisingly, a lot of people signed up. Especially the new folk, who were sharp lawyers in the city, and then bemused by the ways of the village when they moved here. She suspected they knew they were falling for a line, and they wanted to; that's why they'd chosen to live in this beautiful town.

"It's our own celebrity," he repeated. "Come up here, Maggie Dove."

"I already have a new furnace, Hal," she said. "You put it in last year."

He guffawed at that, the crowd too. She thought that would be the end of it, but he pressed on.

"Tell us about your new mystery."

"It's about a plumber who gets murdered," she said, which just about pushed Hal over the edge. He was a florid man with a loud galloping laugh, the kind of laugh you heard from blocks away. He'd put in a new furnace at Bender's house too, she remembered. She'd heard the sound of his laughter coming from inside the house.

"This lady wrote the best book I ever read," he said. He held out his hand, inviting her to stand up front with him, but she shook her head no. She felt self-conscious talking about her books in the best of circumstances and she didn't want to be forced into endorsing his services, particularly when, now that she thought about it, her new furnace kept turning off last winter.

"Come on up, Maggie. I need your seal of approval."

"Not right now, Hal." She wished he'd stop. She felt something weird in the intensity with which he was pressing her; remembered then the look he'd got on his face when she'd gone out with him that one time. When she'd not invited him into her house for coffee. But surely she was being silly.

For just a moment her vision of him twisted, of the village twisted. There was hatred here, she thought. Hatred in her heart, hatred perhaps in Hal's heart, and who knew where else. Her expression must have changed because Hal backed off. He turned his attention to a thin young man in a suit.

The crowd's attention drifted away from her and Maggie might have drifted away herself, except that she noticed Joe Mangione standing near the front of the ambulance corps building. Now there was a port in the storm. She made her way over to him.

"Thanks for coming so quickly last night," she said.

"It's my job," Joe replied, his voice sounding of Boston. "Don't forget to call 911 next time."

"Right. Say, have you seen Peter today?"

"Nah, well, it's only 3 o'clock. He'll be up and around soon."

"Three o'clock? Has he gotten that bad?"

"We've all got our demons, Mrs. Dove. Right?"

"Did he get in trouble for not calling Campbell right away?"

Mangione looked up and down the street as though Campbell might be hiding somewhere, which was laughable. The man was easily 6 foot 8. There were statues smaller than Walter Campbell, and statues with more warmth to them, Maggie suspected. He was one cold son of a gun. But he was certainly not the sort of man who lurked.

"Ah, Peter's his own worst enemy." Joe shook his head.

"Was he having trouble with Bender, do you know? Did they have an argument?"

Joe crossed his arms. He was so small and brave, but in this society only his smallness was noticed. He was a passionate Red Sox fan and always aggrieved about them. Even when they won, he couldn't get the memory of their losses out of his head.

"Bender," he said. "Now there was a piece of work."

"Why didn't you like him? "Maggie asked.

"Bend-uh," he said. "Thought he owned this town, thought he owned everything, him and his money. His mother died of a heart attack when he was a boy, so what's he got to do? Has to make sure the village has all the best emergency supplies. He donates money for the 911 system. He arranges for us all to take special certification classes. He wants the village to have New York City caliber regulations."

"You didn't want that?"

Joe crossed his arms. He spit into one of the begonias the gardening club had planted in front of the firehouse. "He wanted to improve the physical capacity of the firefighters. He wanted to make the requirements more stringent."

"What does that mean?"

"He wanted a height requirement. His mother died because none of the firefighters was big enough to lift her. He wanted all fire fighters to be over 5'10."

"But that's not legal?"

"No. He couldn't force the village go along with his demands, but he wouldn't donate his money if they wouldn't comply. He gave them a month to make up their minds. They had until May first."

He rocked back on his feet. She wondered if she'd ever seen him without his ambulance jacket on.

"The guys would never have voted you out."

"No," he said. "I was going to quit. I couldn't ask them to make a sacrifice like that for me. I planned to quit today. But now, it's all over. He's dead."

Yet another person who hated him, Maggie thought. The whole village was full of people who wanted Marcus

Bender dead. She shivered. Why move to a small community and then do everything you could to make people hate you? Surely that was an attitude more suited to the anonymity of the city.

Suddenly the crowd hushed, and Maggie, following the direction of the crowd, saw the widow Bender walking down the street. Noelle wore a black dress, slightly different than the one she'd worn the night before, but equally form fitting. She sashayed as she walked, eating the largest ice cream cone Maggie'd ever seen. She didn't know there was anywhere in the village that sold ice creams that large. Impossible not to stare.

Impossible not to listen too, to the whispers around her.

Funeral's tomorrow.

On the river. Humanist minister. What's a humanist funeral?

Heard they took the kids away.

"I feel like we're in 'The Lottery,'" Maggie whispered.

"What?"

"You know, the Shirley Jackson story where they throw a rock at Mrs. Hutchison," though no sooner had the words escaped her that Maggie remembered her own rock. She was ready to throw a rock at Marcus Bender. Only last night. Because of a tree.

There was all too much darkness surrounding this man. She had to break through to the light somehow. She slipped past the crowd, following Noelle, thinking perhaps there was something she could do to connect with her, but as she turned onto her street, as the gap between them grew smaller and she yelled out her name, Noelle paused for just a moment, then turned her back on her and went into her house. Maggie went to the door and rang the bell, but there was no answer, just as there had been no answer last night, when her husband's corpse was on her lawn.

Maggie noticed, though, when she walked onto her porch, that Noelle had flipped the remains of her ice cream cone onto her lawn. Maggie picked it up, desperately wanting to do the right thing, but flipped it, instead, right back onto Noelle's lawn.

"Take that," she said, and walked back to Main Street to retrieve her car. Then she called Peter to arrange for a meeting, to figure out what was wrong and what she could do.

"We have to talk."

"I'll meet you at the park in an hour," he said.

So she took a shower and washed all Iphigenia's shellac out of her hair, put on a warm sweater and jeans and made some turkey sandwiches and coffee and then head out for the park, hoping the news from Peter would not be too bad.

Chapter Twelve

Of course Peter was late. Maggie could have taken a nap and read a book and he would still have arrived ten minutes after her, but she didn't mind. Maggie loved sitting in the park at nighttime. The Mario Cuomo Bridge soared like a sailboat across the Hudson. Maggie loved to watch it at night; she'd loved the old one too.

She'd thrown rocks into the river as a little girl, skipping them across the flat water. She'd swum in the river, as had her daughter, climbing out onto the jetty and splashing around and, depending on the decade, clambering back in covered with sludge, or in recent years, clean water. (Thank you, Pete Seeger.)

Over this very spot the planes that wreaked destruction on 9/11 had come shrieking, and from this site she could see where the Twin Towers once stood. For months afterwards the members of the village had gathered at this point, staring down at the scarred tip of Manhattan and mourning their own who had died in the attacks. Several trees had been planted here to commemorate it, and Maggie, inspired, had a tree planted in memory of her daughter. A spruce. She rarely went to Juliet's grave, preferring instead to sit alongside this little tree. She felt closer to her daughter in this open, happy place, the lights twinkling, the leaves smelling of Christmas, and as she sat there she caught some movement out of the corner of her eye and saw it was the same Asian boy she'd seen skateboarding earlier that day. He was doing tricks with his skateboard right near the edge of the river, scraping the wheels against rocks she knew would stab him if he fell. Reckless. She wanted to warn him to stop. But she knew he wouldn't; that type of person doesn't stop no matter how you caution them.

Instead, Maggie crept forward, thinking that at the least she could help him if he broke his leg. He didn't acknowledge her, but she felt he was aware of her, so purposely did he not meet her gaze. He exuded strength. The wheels made a pleasing, whirring sound.

He began to jump.

Maggie was not a risk taker herself, but she admired the quality in others.

A tugboat went by; the ground shook with the power of an oncoming train. Suddenly the boy looked up and grimaced and Maggie, startled, heard Peter's voice.

"Come on. You know that's illegal here."

The boy crossed his arms; looked like he might argue.

"You want me to take you to the police station," Peter yelled. "No skateboarding allowed here."

The boy smacked his skateboard to the ground and rolled off, the angry click ricocheting like a bullet as he left the park.

"Are there not enough signs?" Peter asked, as he sat down alongside her. "There's one right there. No skateboarding in the park."

"You were awfully harsh with him."

"Rules are rules."

Maggie was touched to see him wearing the leather jacket she'd given him so many years ago. He ran his fingers through his hair, and it looked like some loose wisps might go flying right off. "Lucky for you I wasn't as strict as you are."

Strange phenomenon she'd noticed with Peter in specific, but other bad boys in general, that they were much less patient as adults than you'd expect them to be. You'd think they'd have more sympathy. But they didn't.

"You spoiled me, Dove," he said, with the grin she remembered. "I took advantage of you."

"Yes you did. But I never minded. Children need to be spoiled a little."

"Not that one," he said, nodding in the direction of the skateboarder. "He'll get in trouble for sure. Goes too fast."

"Can't cause that much harm on a skateboard."

"Tell me that after he plows into you and you wind up in the hospital with a broken hip."

Peter stretched his neck; she heard the crack. Time was such a strange thing. Only yesterday, it seemed, this boy had been coloring in front of her. He loved to sharpen the crayons until they turned into little stubs.

Later, when he was a little older, he put air freshener on his iguanas by mistake, and killed them. How he'd cried. She thought of what Agnes had suggested about his getting into a fight with Bender. Was it possible? Anything was possible. He had a temper.

"Everything all right with Walter Campbell?" she asked. She handed him one of the turkey sandwiches and he crammed half of it into his mouth.

"Everything's fine," he mumbled.

"Don't say that. It makes me nervous."

He laughed at that, put his arm around her. "Walter Campbell has it in his head that I should have closed off your lawn as a crime scene. I should have insisted he come back from the ballet. Now he's all in lather about it. Says I'm insubordinate. And the widow's mad because she says someone murdered her husband."

"Was there something wrong with the body?"

"No, no. The preliminary autopsy was fine, and they released the body to be buried tomorrow. They just have one more test to do. They're doing a liquid chromatography."

"Don't they do that for poisoning?"

"It's a possibility, I guess."

"But how could it be a possibility? I thought he died of a heart attack."

A train went past, a slick metallic sound. Progress, the future. She shuddered.

"Campbell has an instinct about these things," Peter said, chewing the second half of the sandwich more slowly. "He says he can tell something's wrong. Why not? He's a genius, with millions in his bank account. Why shouldn't he spend some of the village's money on these tests?"

She looked at the man, but saw instead the boy, with his eyes that always burned with passion. Who loved her daughter so much. Who was content to sit alongside her and read, even though he was no great reader, just because he knew Juliet needed quiet. Maggie used to love the way he held her, almost tentatively, as though she were so valuable he didn't dare press her too hard.

"I wish you could get along with him," she said.

"A-hole," he said. "Pardon my French."

"He's your boss," Maggie pointed out.

"What's he going to do to me?"

"He could fire you."

"Then I'll get another job."

There was a chill breeze off the river. Little white ripples darted on top of the water, but not so many years ago, during Hurricane Sandy, those little waves had crashed over and flooded the park and caused terrible damage.

"Agnes Jorgenson told me you had a fight with Bender," she said.

"Well, Agnes Jorgenson. She'd know. Wouldn't she?"

"Did you have a fight with him?"

Peter jumped up and stood by the rocks at the side of the river. Too dark to skip rocks now, but he'd loved to do it when he was young. Had quite a talent for it.

Could make a rock skip four times, which had been a source of great frustration to Juliet because she could only make it go two times.

"Did you hear what he did to Mr. Laws?" Peter asked.

"Eugene Laws? From the high school?"

"Yeah. He's got two years to go until he can retire. But Bender heard he was a bad teacher. He heard his success rate with the AP tests wasn't up to par."

"Eugene Laws is a disaster," Maggie said. "Everyone knows it. But what would Bender care? His daughters aren't in high school, are they?" It was one of those facts of village life, that if your kid was on track to go to a good school, you made sure she didn't get into Laws' class.

"Bender didn't care that his daughters weren't in high school yet. They would be someday, and he wanted it to have high standards. Nothing second rate about our school system. He made it a one man mission to get rid of Laws. He raised it at school board meetings and circulated a petition."

"And what happened?"

"Oh, they got rid of him. They've hired somebody new for next year. She has a master's degree from Columbia."

"In fairness to Bender, she's probably an improvement."

"I know, Dove, but that's not the point. There's something passing from this village. Don't you feel it?

These people move in and they don't care about the village. Just themselves and their property values and the schools, so their kids can go to the best colleges and make a lot of money. Everything has to be top-rate, but where's the room for the normal people? Where's the heart?"

"So you had a fight with Bender about Eugene Laws?"

Peter crouched forward, his back in the posture of prayer. Something bad was coming, Maggie thought. She was tempted to run, just as last night when she'd crouched next to Bender's body. She wanted to get the heck out of there; to run back to her tidy little house and into her bedroom and lock the door. But you couldn't. You just couldn't do that. You had to face down your fear.

"Clemmy Atwood was having her eighteenth birthday party," Peter said. "You know Clemmy. She's crazy and her mother was worried that the kids would go off and drink and then there would be an accident. She wanted to make sure they were supervised. She figured they were all going to drink, but if someone was watching out for them, they wouldn't get too drunk and no one would get hurt." Clemmy Atwood, Maggie thought, her second worst Sunday School student.

"You're a police officer and you were at a party where kids were drinking! Are you crazy?"

"I didn't take any money," Peter said. "But I wanted to make sure they were safe. I couldn't take the risk that someone might get hurt, Dove. I didn't want anyone to be in an accident."

She could still see him as he looked that night, as handsome a boy as it was possible to imagine. A little like Robert Redford, with his beautiful hair and his basset hound eyes and the leather jacket he wore then and always had worn. Juliet had been worrying about what was to become of them. They would be separated by hundreds of miles, and an academic culture so foreign to what Peter knew. She loved him and wanted to marry him, but Maggie'd been cautioning her. Wait a little longer. A little longer.

"You know how strict Walter Campbell is. You know he's going to be furious."

"Nothing went wrong. Everyone got home. No one got hurt, but one of the kids told her parents and she told Bender."

"You're the DARE officer, Peter."

"I'm not saying it's right for them to drink, but I can't be a hypocrite. We drank all the time. Kids got sick. I wanted to protect them."

A boat cruised by. People laughed. How messed up things become, Maggie thought.

"Bender told me he made an appointment with Campbell. They were going to meet on Monday. He wanted to get me fired, and I told him what he could do."

"You had an argument with him?"

"I'm an idiot," he said.

"Yes, you are."

He picked up some dirt and rubbed it in his hands. "It was a lucky thing for me that he died."

Yes it was, she thought. Winifred was right to think he was in trouble. He was doomed and he was sure to get in an argument with Campbell and he would likely argue himself right into jail. If Campbell was right, if Marcus really had been murdered, then there was only one person who stood between Peter and jail and that was her. That was an awful lot of responsibility for someone who'd been in a self-contained world of grief for the last twenty years.

But she didn't see that she had a choice.

Chapter Thirteen

Saturday morning was Bender's funeral and even though Maggie didn't plan to go, she didn't feel she should ignore it. Some solemnity seemed called for and so she dressed with care that morning, put on heels and her black Eileen Fisher pants and her black Eileen Fisher blouse and she figured if nothing else, she looked elegant. Then she combed out her hair, put in her pearl earrings, checked the clock and saw it was 7 in the morning.

So it was going to be that kind of day.

Might as well plan out her Sunday School lesson. She gathered up her supplies and cogitated over what to do the following day, when Edgar Blake, he of the lice in his hair, was certain to show up in her classroom. She had no proof, of course, but she was inclined to believe Agnes on this one. If Agnes said the boy had lice, he did. She couldn't toss him out of class and she couldn't embarrass him but she wondered if there would be a way to get him to wear a bathing cap. He was sort of child who would probably like a bathing cap. Her own daughter had worn a bathing cap for years. Maggie never did figure out why.

If she could get Edgar into a cap, maybe then she could persuade him to watch one of the new movies the church had ordered in which various characters from the Bible were portrayed by vegetables. Maggie wasn't sure why it was easier for people to accept Saint Paul as a potato than as a man, but so be it. Then there was Doubting Thomas as a carrot and the Virgin Mary as a plum. That at least made some sense. Jesus was a little apple with a nose and ears and the Sermon on the Mount looked like a vegetarian buffet.

She looked at her watch and saw it was now 7:30.

She made herself some coffee and sat down at her kitchen table. The sun shone in; it was a glorious day. Disaster always struck on glorious days, she believed. Nothing bad ever happened in the rain. Maggie'd often thought how wrong-headed producers were to set their movies in dark and gloomy nights. It was in the glare of a sunny day that horrors usually took place. She wondered how many people would go to Bender's funeral. He had two daughters. Their friends would go. Family. At Juliet's funeral, the whole town turned out. The principal shut down the high school early so that all the kids could come. The local deli catered the reception afterwards, donating hundreds of dollars' worth of food, and they kept bringing her meals for long afterwards. Every day there would be a knock on her door: Joe Mangione, or the lady that ran the cupcake store, or someone from the church, just stopping by to sit for a while.

She kept thinking about what Peter said last night, about how they were testing for poison. That still seemed odd to her. As a mystery writer, she'd spent a lot of time reading about poisonings and one of the things she knew for sure was that they were hard to detect. That many poisoners went unpunished because no one thought to look. Evidence didn't show up on a regular autopsy. She went over to her computer and typed in gas chromatography. It was a "confirmatory test," Wikipedia explained. The first round of tests are presumptive tests, which screen for the possibility of drugs but are less specific, and less expensive. Confirmatory tests are used only if there is "the possible presence of a drug or toxin." Possible presence. What made Campbell think to look, she wondered.

Suddenly Maggie saw a flash of movement out her window and noticed Noelle Bender walking on her lawn. Walking toward her little oak tree.

What was it with that family and boundaries? she wondered. Why didn't they stay where they were supposed to stay? They had a perfectly good lawn all to their own and a fine house, so why did they have to bother with Maggie's? She watched as Noelle minced her way over to her oak tree and stood there, looking at it. Be patient, Maggie thought. Her husband died under that tree. Maybe she just wanted to meditate a moment.

But it was Maggie's tree. Her oak tree. No, she reminded herself. It was God's oak tree. Well God didn't want it moved any more than she did, she thought.

Oh God. Today was the day of this woman's husband's funeral. How could she be cruel to her? It was odd how some people just brought out the worst in you. You could be a perfectly pleasant person and then someone could press your buttons and turn you into a raging lunatic.

Maggie noticed that Noelle was holding the same white bag she had when she saw her yesterday coming out of the pharmacy. Now what? Was she going to pour a box of arsenic on the tree?

Maggie could bear it no more. She went outside.

"Hello," she said.

Noelle didn't answer. Why should she? Maggie thought. She was only standing on Maggie's front lawn, under an oak tree that her husband wanted to destroy.

"May I help you with something?"

Noelle didn't meet her eyes, but she shook her head. She was a slender woman, with a nice figure, as Maggie's mother would have put it. She wore a black dress for the funeral that would have worked just as well at a cocktail party. The skirt had swing to it. Her white blonde hair was tied back, but Maggie could see, when she turned around, that she'd put on a lot of make-up. Once, a very long time ago, in a home ec class, a cosmetician had come in and told the girls how to play up their assets. Maggie remembered how Winifred had laughed at that, though Maggie, studious as ever, jotted down notes. *Put contour on your nose if you want to slim it.*

Put liner around your lips to plump them up. Noelle must have gone to a similar class.

"Are you looking for something?" Maggie asked, her temper starting to rise. She hated being ignored.

"All he wanted was to paint his pictures. He loved the river." Again, there was that fluty baby doll voice that seemed so unnatural. Were people born speaking like that?

"I'm sorry, but he could have painted pictures of the Hudson with a tree in front. Think of the great Hudson River school of painters. There are plenty of trees in their paintings."

"Bender wasn't one to compromise his vision," his widow said.

She looked like she might sob, and Maggie took a step toward her, thinking to offer comfort, but at the first step Noelle whirled around and put up her hands.

"No," she said. "Don't you come near me."

"But you're on my lawn," Maggie said. She sounded so childish, even to herself. She wished she could be big about this, she wished she didn't care. But she did, she did.

"Where I grew up," Noelle said, "we were part of a real community. People didn't worry about boundaries. Children could go wherever they wanted. If you wanted to play on your neighbors' lawn, you just went there."

"Did you put lye on your neighbors' trees where you grew up?" Maggie snapped.

Noelle took a step back then, stumbling slightly, as she did so patting her stomach in the age-old way women do when they're pregnant. Oh, no. It was getting worse and worse. There had to be a way to connect with this woman. Maggie wanted to be the sort of person who could connect with her, or anyway she felt she should be that sort of person.

"Can I get you some water?"

"No," Noelle said.

"I'll bring you a folding chair," Maggie said.

She started toward her garage, but she hadn't gone far when Noelle called after her.

"I hear you're a writer."

Maggie stopped. "Yes, well I was."

"I need to make some money fast," Noelle said.

"Publishing's not a way to make money fast," Maggie said.

"I read about a woman who dreamed an idea, wrote it down and sold it for seven figures."

Why was she arguing about publishing with a woman on the day of her husband's funeral? "Of course," Maggie said. "It could happen."

Four helicopters flew overhead, in formation, heading south from West Point. Maggie wondered what they were doing, what was going on in the large world.

"I want to hire you to help me write it," Noelle said.

"I'm sorry, but I don't do that kind of thing anymore."

Noelle shook her head. Not a woman to hear what she didn't want to hear. "It's a mystery about an exotic dancer," she said. "I mean, the exotic dancer is the detective. Isn't that fabulous? One of her clients gets murdered and she's got to solve it. She knows all sorts of self-defense skills because she's used to having to defend herself from men. It's all sort of film noir," Noelle said. She looked more animated than Maggie'd ever seen. She looked sincere. For the first time Maggie felt she wasn't toying with her.

"It sounds like a good idea."

"I know," Noelle said. "It's a great idea. I even have the title. Strip and Search."

"It could be good."

"How much would you want?"

"Really. I just don't do it anymore. Quite honestly, if I were going to write, I'd write my own book. I just don't write anymore."

Noelle glared at her. "You just won't do anything, will you? People like you. Always judging. Looking at people like me with contempt."

A limousine pulled into her driveway. The driver beckoned to her, but Noelle held up her hand. "Coming," she called.

She opened up the little white bag then, and began opening up the package. She didn't make eye contact with Maggie, just began ripping away cardboard, shredding it onto the grass, and then an ornament emerged, and Noelle took it and hung it on the tree. It was an angel, sitting on a toilet.

"He loved these," Noelle said. "They always made him laugh."

Maggie wanted to point out that Noelle had a perfectly good cherry blossom tree on her own lawn that could host a multitude of angels on toilets, but something in Noelle's face stopped her. It was that look of defiance, that same look Peter always got, that look that touched Maggie's heart every time. There was something so vulnerable about that look. Something that made Maggie feel certain it would be crushed.

What was she fighting about?

Let the poor woman hang up her foolish angel and Maggie could get rid of it when she was gone. Or better yet, give it to Winifred, who she felt absolutely confident would love it.

Chapter Fourteen

"An angel on a toilet! Of course, I want it," Winifred said, when Maggie called and told her about the encounter with Noelle.

The phone felt warm in her hand. She'd made herself a cup of tea, and settled herself in her kitchen, a tidy little room built for a time when servants did the cooking and weren't expected to use much space. No island. Barely enough room for a refrigerator. She had chickens everywhere. Mugs in the shape of chickens and little chicken oven mitts and salt and pepper shakers. Maggie never had figured out where this love of chickens came from, given that she didn't like the living creatures particularly well. But for years, for Mother's Day and her birthday, people gave her chickens.

"Bring it over next time you come. I'll put it at the nurse's station."

"I wonder if I'd be considered stealing," Maggie said. "If I give you something that doesn't belong to me, but that someone else put on my tree."

"Did she tell you how she and Bender met?"

"No, we didn't get that far."

"She jumped out of a box on his 35th birthday," Winifred said. "It was love at first sight. Something similar happened with my second husband," she went on, "though there wasn't a box, and no poles were involved."

"You're making this up."

"I am not."

"So, she was an exotic dancer?"

"She was a stripper, Maggie." Winifred began cawing with laughter and Maggie wasn't sure she was telling the truth, though she suspected she was. She'd not known many strippers in her life, although one of her Sunday School students had found it an effective way to pay off student loans.

"I suppose there goes her invitation to join the church," Winifred said.

"We are all sinners," Maggie observed. Though only some of us are paid by the hour, she thought. But did not say. Because she'd known her best friend long enough to know she'd end up on the bad side of that argument.

"Bender didn't care. That was the only thing I liked about him. That he married her. He wasn't a prude. He didn't care about offending the nice church ladies."

"You know, my friend, your average church lady has seen more drama and ill behavior than just about any other person. Trust me when I say we are not so easily shocked."

Maggie noticed Mr. Cavanaugh walking by with his dog. So he hadn't gone to Bender's funeral either.

He paused for a moment in front of the tree, looked at the angel and then moved on. What if she should have moved the damn tree? Maggie thought. What if she had been unreasonable? Maybe she was one of those prudish church ladies.

"So now that you know she's a stripper, do you think she murdered Bender?" Winifred asked.

Maggie turned her attention back to the phone, which was becoming slippery under the heat of her emotion.

"I don't know that anyone murdered him, Winifred. Peter says he died of a heart attack and I believe him, but I just want a better sense of what's going on."

"In case Young Sherlock winds up being the murderer?"

"In case he's accused of it. Yes, all right, I'm concerned because I know Peter had a disagreement with Bender and he has a flare for getting into trouble and I assume you already know all about it since you seem to know everything."

"Peter Nelson is trouble."

"He's always been trouble," Maggie snapped. "That's part of his charm."

"No, it's gotten worse. You're so fixated on the boy he used to be that you don't see the man he is. You don't see what he's become."

Maggie began pacing around her kitchen, not that there was anywhere to go. On the refrigerator she had a picture of Juliet and Peter from back in third grade, when the nature counselor came to talk to the class, to tell them about all the birds and animals in the community and Maggie had raised her hand, because she was the parent of the day, and asked why it was that peepers make that high squeaking noise in the spring. "Because they're having sex," the counselor had said. Juliet didn't speak to her mom for a week, but Peter, dear Peter, laughed and hugged Maggie.

"If someone had run Bender down," Maggie said, "or shot at him, or stabbed him, I could believe that Peter was the culprit. But I simply do not see Peter as a poisoner. By God, that child barely passed biology and that with old Mr. Laws helping him cheat, tapping him on the back during the Regents test whenever he got something wrong. I simply do not see Peter committing that type of crime."

"They wouldn't have lasted, you know," Winifred said. "If Juliet were alive today, you probably wouldn't even remember who Peter is."

"How can you say that?"

"Because they wouldn't have. Because she was so different than him. Your daughter was a star. She would have soared, and he'd wind up exactly where is, doing a lousy job and drinking too much."

Again, Maggie pictured him as he had been that last night, the last truly happy night of her life. Juliet so full of life, and Peter so handsome. So strong.

"You're wrong. He would have been a star too. She would have pulled him up with her. But when she died, he lost the best part of his life." Her voice began to crack. She wasn't even sure what they were arguing about. "His life was destroyed because he loved my daughter. How can I let down someone like that?"

"So even if he killed Bender. Even then, you'd find some excuse?"

"He didn't do it, Winifred. I know that as surely as I know that I didn't do it. Or you didn't do it, for that matter."

"You're sure of me too?"

"Yes, because I know the people I love. I know who you are and what Peter is. And I also know what you're not."

Winifred began clearing her throat, raspy sounds coming across the phone. It sounded like Arthur was pounding her on the back, trying to bring her relief. When she finally spoke, her voice was husky.

"You're a fool, Maggie Dove."

"I must be, to have put up with you all these years."

Winifred laughed at that, a welcome sound.

"You've been a good friend."

"So have you, Winifred. You don't sound so good."

She wheezed deeply. "Old friends. Old hearts."

"You're right," Maggie said. "I am a prude."

"I know," Winifred said, and then her voice got serious. "And I'm a fool."

"Fair enough," Maggie said.

"No, I really am a fool. I think I've done something stupid, Maggie."

"Tell me what. Can I help?"

"I don't know," Winifred said. "I have to think. I've got to get my head straight."

The noon whistle sounded right then, a sound that always startled Maggie, mainly because it never sounded at noon. There was no way to prepare yourself for it. Sometimes it blared at five minutes to twelve and sometimes five minutes after, but whenever it blared, it always surprised her, and by the time the sirens finally stopped sounding, Winifred had hung up.

Chapter Fifteen

Maggie woke Sunday morning with a feeling of dread so heavy she could feel it pressing against her stomach. This went way beyond her nervousness at teaching Edgar Blake, though she was nervous about that. Surprising because there wasn't a lot to be nervous about when you were a Sunday School teacher. You couldn't be fired from the job. You couldn't go wrong, really, and yet she struggled to get out of bed. She felt like a storm was coming, felt it so surely that she looked out the window, but all she saw was a blue sky and some clouds.

Maybe it was time to retire as a Sunday School teacher, she thought. She'd been doing it for 30 years, which was a long time. The President of the United States could only serve eight years. No point in doing it if there was no joy to it. In fact, the whole purpose of teaching Sunday School was to communicate joy.

She decided not to show the vegetable movie. Better to do something crafty, something that would occupy Edgar's hands. Maggie got to church early and set up the class room. She put out five glue sticks, just to be on the safe side, though she doubted five students would show up. It was soccer season. They wouldn't have any students at all except that some of them did hockey and practiced on Saturdays.

Edgar burst into the class room two minutes ahead of everyone else. His hair had been shaved off, which resolved one problem, but soon enough another problem emerged. He roared right over to the glue sticks and grabbed them up in his hands. All five. In trooped Ambrosia Fletcher, on the verge of tears, as always, and the lovely Shu Chin, who, if past was any predictor, would sit quietly for the next hour.

"Share the glue sticks," Maggie said to Edgar.

He clutched them tightly to his chest. She didn't feel like arguing, and so she went to the supply closet and retrieved five more glue sticks, one of which she handed to Ambrosia and one to Shu Chin. Edgar paused, and then grabbed up Ambrosia's glue stick as well. She began to cry.

"Give that back," Maggie said. "You're being a bully."

He stared at her implacably, a little like a shark.

"Peter Nelson," she said, "or no, I mean Edgar Blake. Put down the glue stick."

She sat down so she could look more clearly into his eyes. There had to be a way to reach this boy. "You're being cruel."

The little chickadee began to sing, the class pet. Edgar gazed at her, and then threw all the glue sticks at Ambrosia. "Take them," he said.

She thought of a story her husband liked to tell about how President Kennedy handled Russian leader Khrushchev during the Cuban missile crisis. An agreement had been reached, but then Khrushchev sent a telegram saying he wanted to back out. Kennedy could have gone forward and launched an attack, but he chose to ignore the telegram. He allowed Khrushchev a face-saving moment, which many considered to be one of the triumphal decisions in American foreign policy. Maggie decided to allow Edgar a face-saving moment as well.

"Thank you, Edgar, for sharing, she said. "Now, let's talk about Adam and Eve."

"I don't want to glue anymore," Ambrosia said.

"You don't have to. Why don't you color?"

The girl looked at Edgar like a rabbit eyeing a snake. "I don't want to."

"You can color next to me," Maggie said, thanking God for Shu Chin, who throughout this whole fiasco, sat quietly, reading the children's Bible.

And then, in confirmation of the principle that no matter how bad a situation was, it could always get worse, Agnes appeared. She was the principal of the day. It was her job to remove unruly children from the Sunday School class. Never in all of Maggie's years had she sent a student to the principal of the day. It violated everything she felt about Sunday School, but now, watching the look that played across Edgar's face, a look of anger and triumph that reminded her of Peter in his prime, Maggie began to get a bad feeling.

"Trouble?" Agnes asked. She cocked her head.

"No trouble at all, Agnes," Maggie said.

Agnes looked around the room brightly. "Peter helping you today?"

"Peter? No?"

"He wasn't in church. I thought perhaps he was with you."

"No," Maggie said, and willed her to leave, which she did eventually, leaving Maggie once more along with Edgar, who had, while Maggie wasn't looking, taken all the crayons from Ambrosia. He looked at her. She looked back. She had given birth to a child. She had buried that child. She had buried her husband. She could face down this miserable child, spawn of Satan, Bender, she thought. Bender with his manicured hands stretched toward her house. Funny how some men got manicures.

Edgar lunged to take Shu Chin's Bible, which he succeeded in grabbing out of her hands and throwing onto the floor.

Everyone hushed at that. Maggie could hear the minister's voice projected through an intercom, talking about a tree and temptation. So much came back to trees. But she barely heard it as she swept forward and picked up the Bible and kissed it, an old tradition.

"Never throw the Bible on the floor," she hissed. "People have died for this book. This book matters."

She felt like all the anger she'd been carrying around her for years, ever since her daughter died, so cruelly, was about to erupt into a terrible plume that would sear right out of her like a dragon. She was so angry she felt afraid. What was she capable of?

"Who died?" Edgar asked.

"Juliet," she whispered.

"Who died?" he repeated, and she realized he was talking about the Bible. He wanted to know who had died for the Bible. Maggie couldn't think, she was so upset, and the only name that came to mind was Khrushchev, who most certainly had not died for the Bible.

"Well, Thomas Cranmer for one. Have you heard of him?"

Ambrosia sank onto Maggie's lap and began to suck her thumb.

"No."

"He lived a long time ago. In England," Maggie said, as she surreptitiously picked up all the glue sticks and put them away. "He worked very hard to translate the Bible into English because it used to be that regular people weren't able to read it. King Edward, a boy of about your age, supported him, but then he died. The new queen didn't agree with what Cranmer had done, and so she asked him to recant, which means to say he had to admit he was wrong. Then, he had to sign his signature to some papers, and he used his right hand."

"Why did he sign? I wouldn't sign."

"Probably not," Maggie said, "but I imagine he was scared. He knew the queen was very powerful, and very angry, and quite mean. Her nickname was Bloody Mary."

She looked out the window of the classroom, toward a little grove of magnolia trees. They were just starting to flower, the pinkish petals dewy, though Maggie knew within a week or so they would be blowsy. Nothing aged as quickly as a magnolia blossom. Some bedraggled forsythia huddled in a corner like teenagers from a party gone bad. Everything she thought about lately seemed to involve trees, Maggie realized, which brought her back, in her memory, to the sight of Marcus Bender lying dead under her oak tree.

"What happened then?" Edgar asked.

She wiped her eyes. "To Cranmer? Well. He wound up being sentenced to death anyway. The queen had no mercy. And then, on the day of his execution, he said he was wrong to have ever recanted. He loved to read the Bible in English. They tied him to the stake, and the flame began to burn and do you know what he did?"

"No."

Both Edgar and Ambrosia looked at her intently. Even Shu Chin seemed intrigued.

"He took his right hand and he put it in the flame, so that it would burn first and as it burned he said, 'that unworthy hand.' Though, of course, he wasn't unworthy at all. He was very, very brave."

The classroom was silent after that. Edgar surveyed his right hand. Ambrosia went over to the naptime rug and sat down, and they were sitting peaceably when the parents arrived to retrieve them. Ambrosia's parents were running off to soccer practice, but Edgar's mother stayed to help her clean up, though Maggie assured her it wasn't necessary. She was so tired she had no conversation left in her. She wanted to go home. But Helen Blake was not to be deterred. In her own way, she was just as stubborn as her son, and so she put away the Bibles and the remaining crayons, and set the chairs back on the table.

"We learned about Thomas Cranmer today," Edgar told her.

"Did you?" she said. She grinned at Maggie. "And here I thought you were going to learn some foolish thing about the twelve vegetables."

"It was a near miss," Maggie said.

Helen laughed. "He does love history. Thank you for taking the time with him. I know he's not always easy."

She looked exhausted. Her eyes had dark circles under them and her face was flushed, as though she'd just woken up, which Maggie suspected she had. Helen didn't go to church. Instead, she dropped Edgar off at Sunday School and then lay down on the couch in the church library and slept. There were some who felt she was using the church for free babysitting, but Maggie figured there were many different ways for a church to be a sanctuary.

"He wasn't too much?"

"Not at all."

"Well thank you, Ms. Dove. Sometimes I think you're the best part of this town. Quite honestly, I don't know why we moved here in the first place." At that, her glasses fell on to the ground. She scooped them back up and pressed them back on her nose.

"People might be a little reserved at first, but they'll come around. You'll see."

"We've lived here for five years," Helen said.

"Oh."

Maggie did one last check to see that everything was put away, then locked up the room.

"It's more than that," Helen said. "Well, I'll be honest. I think some of the people here are cruel. One of my best friends died here last week, and now they're saying he might have been murdered."

"Marcus Bender?"

"Did you know him?" Helen said. She rubbed her wrist against her pale face. "I still can't believe he's gone. He never would have moved here if it weren't for me. He would have stayed in the city, but then one day he came up to visit me and he saw the river and well, you know how Marcus was about the river."

"I do know."

"When he was passionate about something, he was passionate."

"Had you known him a long time?"

"We went to college together. Amherst. We were part of the Honor Society there, Marcus and his first wife, Char. I was so lost when I first got there, coming from Kansas, and they both took me under their wing. They were good friends to me."

They started up the steps, in the direction of the parlor, and coffee hour. "His daughter, Lorelei, is the same age as Edgar. She had a bunch of developmental issues and they wanted to put her in special ed classes, but Marcus wouldn't have it. He wanted her mainstreamed. He fought to get her tutors. He challenged them, wouldn't let them get away with taking the easy way out."

The church bells began to chime, a lovely sound. Automatically Helen reached for her son's hand as they made their way up the steps.

"He did everything," she said. "Met with the principal, the tutors, the special ed board. I don't know how he did it all."

Maggie couldn't even picture the Bender girl except for a distant memory of someone dressed up as a princess. Someone sparkly who she noticed dumping a whole bucket full of candy into her trick-or-treat bag. But now Maggie felt badly that she didn't know that about her father. That she didn't know his kids.

"When I heard he had a heart attack, I wasn't even that surprised. I thought it was because he was pushing himself so hard all the time. But now they're saying that he was poisoned."

"I think they have a ways to go before they can prove that."

"Who would want to murder Marcus?" Helen asked. "Everyone loved him."

Edgar just stared at Maggie, as though he knew all the secrets to her heart, and the one time she would have wished for the boy to be bad, to distract his mother, he was good as gold.

"One of the police officers had a grudge against him, they're saying. Some rogue officer who was selling drugs on the side."

"No," Maggie said. "No, you're wrong about that. I know that police officer and he's a good man."

Helen shrugged. "That's not what I hear."

Maggie made it through coffee hour, but afterwards she thought she'd better go see what was happening with Peter. His name was coming up in too many conversations. It was a bad sign.

For the first time she felt a twinge of doubt. What if he had gone bad? Would she know?

Maggie called Peter when she got home. "How are you doing?"

"Fine," he said. His voice sounded slushed.

"Didn't see you at church."

"I've got a cold; I took medicine."

She felt irritated with him, but that wasn't fair. Maybe he had taken medicine; maybe he was sick; maybe it would all turn out right. Maybe she was just being pessimistic. She crawled into bed, waiting for it to be five o'clock. A person shouldn't go to bed before five, she thought, but by three thirty she was asleep and slept right through until ten o'clock in the morning, right until five minutes past the moment that she was supposed to meet up with Iphigenia.

Chapter Sixteen

Maggie wasn't a fast runner, but she could get dressed quickly, so less than ten minutes passed between when she woke up, slid into her clothes and went power walking up Main Street.

Poor Iphigenia looked like a wilted fern, her normally vibrant hair flattened like a frightened dog's ears, lines appearing on her face that had never been there before.

"I'm sorry I'm late," Maggie said. "Let's go get this over with."

The breeze was surprisingly strong for April; winter hanging on for dear life. Already flowers that had bloomed only a week before were fluttering all over Main Street.

"Tscha," Iphigenia said. "I was hoping you wouldn't come. What's wrong with your hair? Let me fix it before we go."

"Don't put this off any longer," Maggie said. "Let's get this done and then we can go out and celebrate."

Doc Steinberg's office was only two blocks away. The doctor's office was in a large Victorian house, painted yellow, with a big American flag flying out front.

It had belonged to the Steinberg family for years. Maggie had gone there, her mother had gone there. Doc Steinberg had driven her to the hospital with her daughter's body. She'd stayed with Maggie through that entire terrible night, holding her hand when the ER doctor pronounced her dead, holding her when she called to donate her daughter's organs, driving her home, where Winifred and all the other members of her community were waiting for her, mourning.

The receptionist was a woman whose name Maggie could never remember, though she'd known her for years. That was the problem, that she'd known her for so long it would be embarrassing to call her by the wrong name. Victoria or Veronica?

Normally the wait for Doc Steinberg was excruciating, but they were the first appointment of the day and she swept out to see them. At the sight of her tall white-robed figure, the luxurious brown hair—because Doc Steinberg would not be pressured into highlights—Maggie felt a twinge of panic herself. Doc Steinberg was a good doctor, but she had no bedside manner at all. She believed in no sugar coating.

Iphigenia could barely stand.

"I'll just walk her in," Maggie said.

"Of course."

Poor Iphigenia clutched onto her arm, shivering with fear. "You can do this," Maggie said, though she was beginning to doubt it herself, and then she left her friend and went back into the waiting room.

Fifteen minutes passed. Then another fif
utes. Maggie talked to Veronica/Victoria
spring fling, which always took place the first week in
May. Then they talked about Bender's funeral, which Veronica/Victoria had gone to. "Humanist," she sniffed. "No mention of God, and no buffet." They put his cremated remains into a special tube, which they put into the river, though supposedly the widow had reserved some of them, which she was going to have made into a ring. "They crush the ashes, like a diamond."

Maggie thought she heard Iphigenia crying. For all she'd tried to reassure her, the thought of cancer terrified her. The body rebelling. Everything in disarray. Cells going after each other. But she also knew what she'd told Iphigenia was true, that it was survivable, and if Iphigenia had it, she'd beat it. Still, Maggie's hands were shaking when the receptionist began listing all the people who'd been at the funeral. More than she'd expected, but then his children were young. She was surprised to hear Joe Mangione was there. She was ruminating over that when suddenly Iphigenia erupted into the waiting room.

"I'm done," she squealed. She stamped her feet like a flamenco dancer. "There is nothing!"

"I'm so glad."

"I don't have to come back for a year."

"Thank you," she said, hugging Maggie. "Thank you for bringing me here."

Maggie whispered a prayer of thanks, waved good-bye to Victoria/Veronica.

"Good bye, Meredith," Iphigenia sang out to the receptionist. Meredith? Then they started, linked arms, toward the door and suddenly Doc Steinberg was there.

Maggie turned to smile, but before she could go further Doc Steinberg said, "Maggie, would you mind sticking around for a minute? I want to talk to you."

Automatically Maggie put her hand over her heart. Could Doc Steinberg tell just by looking at her that she was sick? Had this all been an elaborate ruse for Iphigenia to bring her in for a checkup? But she had no symptoms.

"I have to get back to the salon," Iphigenia said. "I'll see you later."

Doc Steinberg beckoned Maggie toward her inner office. Maggie had no choice but to follow, though she had the strongest possible feeling no good would come of this. Either there was something so physically wrong with her that it had struck Doc Steinberg between the eyes and she would be admitted to the hospital immediately, or something was wrong with Peter.

Hannah Steinberg had dated Peter a decade or so ago, as had many of the woman in town. Maggie had been hopeful about the relationship because it seemed to her that if anyone was strong enough to set Peter on the right course, it was Hannah. Unfortunately, they hadn't gone out for a month before Hannah dumped him and announced she was gay. After that he preferred women with less ambition and a good deal less sense.

"Sit down, Maggie," she said.

She was brusque, but that didn't mean anything bad, Maggie knew. That was just Hannah's manner.

A striking drawing hung on her wall, a beautiful gold- threaded piece, which reminded Maggie of what she'd forgotten; that Doc Steinberg had gone to India some months ago to do volunteer work. She was wearing dangling Indian earrings.

"I forgot you went to India. Did you like it?"

"It changed my life," Hannah said, sitting down. "Peter's told you about the toxicology report on Bender?"

"No."

"I talked to him yesterday and he said he was going to talk to you."

"He didn't," Maggie said. She had spoken to him yesterday after church, but thought him drunk. "I'm sorry; I'm not sure what you're talking about."

Doc Steinberg shook her head. "He is such a screw up."

Maggie flinched.

The words were so harsh. The office was harsh, the walls dank with all the bad news that had been spoken there. Doc Steinberg's diplomas bounced back the light. The wall hanging was beautiful but frightening, Maggie thought. She noticed a Rubik's Cube on the corner of the desk, pictured Hannah twisting it back and forth with her strong hands.

"I talked to him yesterday. Told him there was going to be trouble and he should hire a lawyer. Told him he should talk to you about it, Maggie. Figured he'd want some support. I don't think he can do this by himself and I can only get so involved. As it is, the medical examiner's going to give me hell for talking to him about the autopsy."

"Hannah, I'm still not sure what you're talking about."

Doc Steinberg frowned, punched some keys on her keyboard. Maggie smelled the faint trace of her floral perfume, a frilly aroma that belied her presence, a smell that reminded Maggie of her grandmother and home.

"Bender's tox report came back. It showed the presence of MDMA."

"What does that mean?"

"Ecstasy, Maggie. Bender died of an overdose of Ecstasy."

Maggie felt a chill sweep over her. Ecstasy, the drug Peter gave warnings about in his role as DARE officer, the drug he was in charge of confiscating, the drug he had gotten in trouble over when he was young. Almost derailed his whole career. A bunch of kids out in the woods, having a party, all of them arrested and brought into the police station, but his record was sealed because he was a juvenile. Juliet hadn't been with him that night, had been in Baltimore at a Model UN meeting.

"So Bender took drugs?"

She felt like she was in a fog. He didn't seem like the type, but what was the type? But then Doc Steinberg's voice cut across her mind.

"No," Doc Steinberg said. "He wouldn't have taken this much. Seven grams? Not if he were a recreational user. Not by mistake."

"So what are you saying?"

"Someone poisoned him, Maggie, and Peter's the prime suspect."

"Hannah."

Doc Steinberg shook her head, turned toward her computer screen and began tapping her finger again against the keyboard and Maggie thought what an exceedingly annoying sound that was, like teeth chattering. How she missed her old Olivetti and the dings and bangs and outright noise of a regular typewriter.

"You know Peter," Maggie protested.

"He had access and he certainly had motive. Bender wanted to put him in jail, and by the time he was done talking to Walter Campbell, he probably would have."

"All right, but half the town probably had access and motive," Maggie said. "What about Mr. Laws? He must have access to Ecstasy."

Doc Steinberg looked at her and Maggie flinched. She wondered how low she could go.

"Why did he try to cover it up, Maggie? Why didn't he cordon off the crime scene and call Walter Campbell right away? Why was he so sure it was a heart attack?"

"I never said he wasn't an idiot."

Maggie slumped back into her seat. She'd dressed up for her visit with Hannah Steinberg, because you always did. No one went to her in sweat pants and so she had on her slacks and leather shoes and a white silk blouse.

She thought of her dear friend, so impulsive. How Peter had once almost set the church on fire because he'd been so excited to light the communion candle that he hadn't noticed his sleeve was on fire. She thought of how he'd come running down to her house from the police station, all passion and heart. A dog with a badge. She'd known, hadn't she, that he shouldn't have swept her inside so quickly. She was as much at fault as he was, encouraging him to protect her.

"This is Walter Campbell's doing, isn't it?"

"I'm not going to lie," Doc Steinberg said. "Walter's the one driving this. He's the one who ordered that test. But if he hadn't done it, no one would ever have known Bender was poisoned. A murderer would have got away free. Bender would have been buried and that would be the end of it. It's a good thing Walter knew his stuff and ordered that gas chromatography test. And there's no question Walter hates Peter. But even so, you can't say that he's wrong. Peter screwed up and he better do something about it."

Doc Steinberg's face looked solemn. That was the thing about her, Maggie thought, that just when you thought she was brusque and uncaring, she'd do something to show you how much she cared. Really, she cared too much. Suddenly Maggie was back on the Saw Mill Parkway, lights flashing, car mangled beyond recognition, the little blue car she'd love to go toodling around in, the stretcher, her daughter, Doc Steinberg alongside her, holding her up. *"It's time to say goodbye, Maggie."*

"They're gunning for Peter," Doc Steinberg said. "You better go to him and tell him to pull his head out of his butt. You're the only one he'll listen to, Maggie. You're the only one who can save him from himself."

Maggie felt dazed when she left Doc Steinberg's office and started walking toward her house. The river loomed in front of her, gray and implacable. Four hundred years ago Henry Hudson had sailed down this river, four hundred years from now it would still flow. She felt more afraid than she'd felt in a very long time.

She desperately wanted to protect Peter, but it's not an easy thing to protect people who are self-destructive. She wished it were enough that she loved him, which she did. But she suspected that some more drastic action was called for, and she worried she wasn't strong enough.

She stumbled down the street in the direction of her house. People said hello and she nodded, but didn't hear. She turned the corner, onto the beautiful street on which she'd spent her life, and she paused for a moment on her lawn. In the stillness of the moment, she remembered how she'd sensed that night that there was something evil in her presence. She had breathed in that evil, and there was no way in this world that was Peter. Foolish boy. Misguided. Self-destructive. All of these things were true. But not evil. That she would stake her life on.

Chapter Seventeen

Maggie called Peter the moment she walked into her house, but he didn't answer his phone. She called his home phone, his cell phone, the police department. He'd taken the day off, they said. She left messages for him to call her back, but knew he wouldn't. Based on more than 30 years' worth of knowing and loving Peter Nelson, she suspected he was off doing something stupid. But how stupid and where? Where would he be at 11:30 on a chilly Monday morning?

He wouldn't go far, she knew. He preferred to contain his insanity to within the confines of the town. He might be over by the docks, or on the rocks that bordered the river, or in the woods. She hoped it wasn't the woods. That was a vast tract of land that stood on the eastern edge of the village. Acres and acres of forest filled with caves and streams and hidden places and hints of the old farmland this area used to be: crumbling stone walls and unexpected metal shovels and rakes that cropped up suddenly. He had certain favorite spots he liked to go to when he was a boy, but the prospect of her running around the woods screaming for Peter was not an appealing one.

Maggie tried his phone again. No answer.

Best place to start would be at his apartment. She'd find him, get him help. He was alive, after all. One thing she'd learned from her daughter was as long as you were alive, there was something you could do. Bender poisoned. Bender murdered. It seemed like something out of a book, a game. It didn't seem like something that could really happen. Already it seemed ridiculous to think she'd been so mad at a person about a tree. Anger dissipated quickly. But when she was in the grips of it, when it had hold of her, she couldn't break its hold. She'd been glad at that moment when she found Bender's body. She'd felt he'd received the retribution she couldn't give him. She'd assumed God struck him down, but what if it was Peter? Dear Peter, who devoted himself to her, who absorbed her love as his own. Her hatred as his own.

What would Peter do without his job?

He'd never wanted to do anything else, had never wanted to live anywhere but this village. Surely, they'd give him a second chance, even if he'd made a mistake. He'd earned it, hadn't he?

Peter lived in an apartment building at the bottom of Main Street. A brick building the village had restored some years ago so that people who worked for the village would have an affordable place to live. It was an elegant building, glass walls with ficus trees propped against them and beautiful river views. Peter's window was immediately visible because of the Yankee flag hanging in the middle of it. The builders had been hoping for potted plants in the window boxes, but they'd relented after a certain amount of arguing.

She rang the doorbell.

No answer.

She hoped he wasn't sitting in there purposely not answering the bell. She was beginning to get irritated when Mr. Cavanaugh and little Fidelio came walking out the door. Mr. Cavanaugh held a piano book under his arm. *Music for Millions, volume one.*

"Thank you," she said, when he held the door open for her.

"He's not there," Cavanaugh said. "He ran out."

"How long ago?"

His little dog barked, tried to paw at Maggie's leg. He was a soulful little friend with huge pleading eyes. Cavanaugh's eyes were less friendly, though the man himself was pleasant. He'd given Maggie lessons for years during a period of time she'd thought of using the pianist Alexander Scriabin as a character in one of her mysteries. She'd taken five years of lessons before she realized the idea wasn't going anywhere.

"Calma, Fidelio," he said. "Thirty-five minutes ago."

"Was he really running?" Maggie asked.

"Yes. Police business, I assumed."

That couldn't be good. Had Walter Campbell called and demanded he report to the police station? But he wouldn't run then. He'd dawdle. Peter made you wait if you were going to yell at him.

"He had on boots," Mr. Cavanaugh said.

"Are you sure?" she asked, though there was no need. The man had a photographic memory, remembered the birthdays of every one of his students. She hadn't taken lessons from him in years, but he still said happy birthday to her every October 4. It wasn't like he wrote it on a calendar either. He just remembered.

"Boots, a wind-breaker and jeans."

"He's going into the woods," she said. She looked down at her own shoes. They were comfortable and clean. For now.

She hesitated for just a moment. She wanted to ask Mr. Cavanaugh why he spit at her tree, but that would have to wait. She needed to find Peter.

Chapter Eighteen

Heading toward the woods. Heading toward a place that was dark, inaccessible and likely exceedingly muddy, Maggie thought. Oh joy. At least it was too early in the day for the coyotes to be out, wasn't it? Last time she'd gone up she'd been sure she heard one baying behind her, though it wound up being a deer, though quite a scary-looking deer. People thought deer were harmless because they were vegetarians, but they were big creatures and surprisingly testy. Maggie didn't want to mess with another one.

Driving to the woods would save her a few blocks walk, but then she'd only have to park the car, and it would take just as much time to walk to her house and get the car. Better to just do what she had to do, she thought, as she started up Main Street, each cross street in alphabetical order. Past Alcott and Bryer and Carson and so on, each street named for a family she had known.

Past the hair salon, Iphigenia waved. Past the police department. She was Sisyphus without the ball, a cranky lady going up a hill. She could actually imagine her fear as something separate from herself, something that weighted her down. The village smelled so sweet. There was always one day in April when spring erupted, when everything smelled alive and young. Past the bagel place and the dry cleaner, and the manicurist and the other manicurist and the real estate agent and a third manicurist, which reminded her that Bender had manicured nails. Her husband, who had not been the most macho of men, had always been disturbed by manicures.

She called Peter again on his cell phone as she trudged up Main Street in the direction of the woods. "Peter, this is ridiculous. We have to talk."

She imagined him sprawled on his couch, drinking, sulking. "It's not hopeless," she said.

Up past the Chinese restaurant and the yarn store and then across Broadway and into the development of homes built on what had once had been a cow pasture. Then further up to a point where she used to go sledding when she was young. Suicide Hill, they'd called it, and she'd used it as a title for one of her mysteries. Then up past the high school and finally up into the woods. Immediately the air changed, wet and promising. The ground was covered with dead leaves. A dog ran at her, closely followed by a man. "He's friendly. Sorry."

She kept going deeper into the woods. She heard peepers, coming from a pond a little bit further on. She used to love to try and sneak up on the peepers, but they always stopped right when you got there. You couldn't trick a frog. She used to love to walk around here when she wrote dialogue. People looked at you oddly when you spoke to yourself, particularly if you spoke in a French accent, as Inspector Benet did. But no one cared in the woods. The only other people who went there were dog walkers and they seemed accepting of foibles. She'd gone there for so many years she knew all the spots, the tulip tree cut in half by lightning, the shoe someone must have lost in the 1950s, the stream that went dry suddenly every summer, the weird bush that bit you with bristles when you went by.

She kept going, heading in the direction of the rock that she knew to be Peter's favorite place. It was a giant flat rock in the middle of a stream, and he loved to sit there and think. He'd gone there as a Boy Scout, before he got thrown out. He'd been on track to be an Eagle Scout, but there was one last badge he'd refused to get and although his mother'd begged him, he wouldn't do it. She'd come to Maggie then and asked her to try, though it did no good.

Because of the storm a few days ago, the trails were wet, lots of branches were down. There was a wild energy to the whole place that made her feel like a party had taken place. Off in the distance, Maggie thought she heard a gun fire, but then realized that it was a branch crashing to the ground. She smelled something unusual. Not fire, but gasoline. An unexpected smell. There were no cars allowed in the woods and no room for them. She made her way toward the smell, assuming it was Peter, up to no good. She didn't feel afraid. Not really. There was no danger in these woods beyond that of falling branches and the occasional deer hunter with a bow and arrow, and yet she felt unsettled.

"Peter," she said aloud.

Now she definitely heard an engine noise and she turned toward a small clearing and saw that someone was on a dirt bike and as she watched, horrified, the dirt biker rode right into a rock and crashed to a halt.

She yelled, started to run toward it, but then the driver turned to her, waved, walked his bike back a few yards, then got onto it and rode his bike back into the rock once again. It was the Asian boy from the river, the one who had been on a skateboard, and was now trying to kill himself with a dirt bike. Or so it seemed. Back again and again. He crashed into the rock ten times.

Maggie sat down on a large log and watched him, horrified and amazed by the battering he was taking, until finally it dawned on her that this must be how he was learning to ride. It made sense. Without something solid in front of him, he could go careening into the woods. Better to go slowly and be stopped by a rock.

The air was cold, but watching this boy was warming, and he seemed to take pleasure in having her there. His helmet was huge and red, but she could see his eyes sparkling, could see him turn and look at her every time he got himself up. She began clapping and laughing and, encouraged, after the twentieth crash, he began to put put in a circle. She'd never seen anything like it, such a concentration of power and grace. Such a perfect metaphor for life. Into the wall. Back on your feet. Into the wall. Back on your feet.

Finally, he began to ride in a broader circle, weaning himself off the security of the rock. He rode in a slow, careful circle, round and round until before her eyes she could see him gain confidence. His arms were bent forward at a difficult balletic angle. Then he began to speed up. The air smelled sweet with oil, the sound surprisingly gentle, an urgent hum. He was dressed like a bird, in patterns of blue and red with a number 126 patched onto his back. Circling more quickly, crunch of tire over stick, the beauty of power and youth and suddenly Peter came pounding into the clearing.

He looked like an insane person. His hair was all on end, his face red and wet with tears, and he clambered toward her. She stood up, confused, assuming he was going to yell at the boy, prepared to remind him that he himself had ridden dirt bikes in the forest. The boy went roaring off, but Peter didn't even look his way. His attention was on Maggie.

"Peter," she said. "Are you okay?

"Did you get my message?" she went on. "I met with Doc Steinberg and I was trying to reach you. I could help you find a lawyer. We'll be able to work this out," she said, though even as she walked toward him, she knew something terrible was coming. She flinched against bad news.

"I'm sorry, Dove," he said, voice breaking. "But I just got word about Winifred. She had a heart attack. She didn't suffer, but we've lost her."

She looked at him stupidly. She'd only just spoken to Winifred the other day and she sounded fine. There was a mistake. It was just like Winifred to play a joke, but death was no joke. Death was sudden and vicious and Maggie sank into Peter's arms and she sobbed against his chest and as she did, she heard the peepers singing around her. They must have begun singing while she was watching the boy. They had turned on, but she had missed them. She cried as she thought of her friend. Sadness and loneliness stretched out in front of her, but how grateful she was to have Peter's strong arms to lean on.

Chapter Nineteen

The town stopped for Winifred's funeral. Three of her four husbands came and spoke, which caused a palpitation in the community. So many men! They'd all known Winifred had been married a lot, but seeing all the men standing there, in their suits, was a lot to absorb. Winifred would have loved it, Maggie thought. She loved nothing more than to shock people.

The husbands clustered together after the service and Maggie said hello, though she hadn't been wild about any of them: Ned, the high school football star who Winifred had followed to college whereupon he immediately injured himself and ended his career. She'd had her daughter with him. Then there was Scottie, a jockey she met in Saratoga. After that divorce, she'd moved out to Fort Worth, where she married Jerry, the one who broke her heart, the one who hadn't come. And then finally there was Fred Melrose, who ran a catering business in Ardsley but got into some difficulties with his taxes. They'd got divorced a decade ago.

Winifred always made much of the fact that although she'd divorced her husbands, she'd never broken up anyone else's marriage and never had an affair.

Each one came "sui generis." Maggie'd never been sure why that was such a good thing, but it mattered to Winifred. She had ethics, if not a long attention span.

Winifred would have liked her funeral, Maggie thought. That was the only way to get through it. To distance herself a little. To laugh. Winifred would have been pleased at the turnout. The synagogue was packed, with people standing up in the back aisle. She would have liked the rabbi's speech and the way he spoke about her good works. She'd been involved in so many more causes than Maggie'd realized. She would have liked her daughter's speech too. Winifred and Amy hadn't always gotten along. Amy actually lived a mile south, but hadn't seen Winifred in five years. But she put that all aside for the funeral service and talked about her mother's bravery. How she was such an inspiration.

"You did good," Maggie said to her afterwards and Amy grinned one of her rare grins.

"Thanks, Auntie Mag. Isn't it amazing what thousands of dollars of therapy can do?"

The Dolan boys came then to play their bag pipes, which wasn't a traditional feature of a Jewish service, but Winifred had loved to hear them play. Watching them huff and puff to "Sunrise, Sunset," made Maggie tear up all over again, and she had just wiped her eyes dry when Agnes appeared, almost out of nowhere.

She was in fine form. Her hair was now a dusky shade of red, parted to the side, without bangs. She had on false eyelashes and dark lipstick and she wore a very nice white suit. She looked a little like a bride, in fact.

"I tried out a new hair dresser in the city," Agnes said, answering the question Maggie hadn't asked. "Thought I'd splurge."

"It looks very nice."

"Want a ride home?" Peter interrupted. He looked like he'd been punched. His face looked a decade older than it had when she'd met him in the park.

"No," Maggie said. "Thanks, but Winifred always got mad if I left a party too early."

"Is there going to be a party?" Agnes asked.

She looked so concerned that Maggie felt touched. She remembered Agnes as she had been, Agnes in high school, always on the outside of things, always left out. She was one of eight children, which you would think would make her sociable, but her family hadn't gone that way. They'd all stuck together, clannish, with the result that none of them had friends outside the family. Only Agnes seemed interested in making friends, but she was a homely girl. Not part of the popular set, which consisted of Maggie and Winifred and Shelly Lundeen and Patti Baker. They'd been cruel to Agnes.

"There's no party," Maggie said. "I just meant that Winifred would not want me to leave the funeral early.

"Oh," Agnes said, looking flustered for the first time in the years Maggie had known her. But then she rallied.

"Why didn't the third husband come?" she asked.

"I don't think she'd spoken to him in twenty-five years," Maggie said. "Plus, I don't think their break up was amicable. She never liked to talk about him."

Maggie hadn't even met him. The wedding was out in Fort Worth, where Winifred had gone after the break-up of her marriage to the jockey, her second husband. She'd moved to Fort Worth, got a job as an assistant to someone at an oil company, left her daughter back in Darby, with her parents. Maggie couldn't go to that third wedding. Juliet was young then, Maggie busy with her husband, they'd lost touch. She must have been married to him for five years. Maybe more, and then one day she showed up back in Darby. She could see Winifred was hurting. She knew she'd loved that husband and he broke her heart, but Winifred never liked to talk about him. He was like a bad dream.

"Maybe he killed her," Agnes said.

"Nobody killed her."

Agnes scanned the room. She was like a terrier, Maggie thought. Relentless.

"She was sick," Maggie felt compelled to add. "She told me herself she was worsening."

"For a mystery writer you have an unsuspicious mind."

"Winifred was an old woman. She was sick and her heart gave out." That's what Amy said anyway. Or that's what she said the doctor said.

"Only 62," Agnes said. "Not so old."

Maggie felt something cold encircle her heart. "What are you suggesting?"

"It's just that our small village seems to be suffering from a spate of sudden deaths. A suspicious mind, which I freely acknowledge having, might wonder if there weren't a serial murderer at work."

Maggie felt the ground underneath her shift, as though she'd been in an earthquake. The bagpipe music began to sounder louder, more grating.

"A serial murderer. You think Agnes' death is related to Bender's?"

"Is it impossible?"

"What do they have in common that anyone would want to kill them both? They didn't even know each other."

"On the contrary," Agnes said, eyeing Gretchen who seemed to be yelling at Hal. The world's most romantic couple were having an argument right in the middle of Winifred's funeral reception. Had the world gone mad? "There are more points of connection between them than you think. Including your young friend."

"Peter? Why on earth would Peter want to kill Winifred? They were friends."

"Were they?" Agnes said, looking at her so sadly that Maggie faltered, wondering what new horror was coming her way. But before she could pursue the conversation, Winifred's daughter Amy appeared by her side and started to cry and Maggie put her arm around her and guided her off to a secluded corner. They sat next to each other on a red couch. Maggie felt dizzy, concerned, exhausted. How desperately she wanted her friend right then! How much she wished she had Winifred there to talk to. But here was this girl. Girl, she was 45-years-old, but she still saw that sweet girl in front of her who spent so many years of her life crying. Even her father wasn't paying much attention to her. He'd married again, to a young, thin wife and his four daughters took after her.

"Now I'll never have a chance to make things right with her," she wept. Poor thing, Maggie thought. Poor girl, who had born with a football player's body and a pair of liquid brown eyes that could tear your heart right out.

"You were a good daughter. You have nothing to reproach yourself for."

"A good daughter." Amy wiped her hand across her nose. Maggie searched around for a handkerchief and gave it to her. "A good daughter who hadn't seen her mother for five years. I lived a mile away and I didn't see her for five years."

"She was a provoking woman," Maggie said.

"I thought she'd live forever. I always thought I'd have a chance to fix things with her. I figured she'd live to 105. I never thought she'd die so young."

She began to cry, large fat tears that actually bounced off her legs as they fell. Tears, Maggie suspected, that came from deep within her, from a little girl who cried because her mother wasn't there. Tears she'd been crying for a long time.

"She did love you," Maggie said. "I hope you know that. She didn't always show it as well as she should have. But she loved you and she was proud of you."

"Yeah," she sniffed. "Right."

"She was so pleased you were good with numbers. Remember that time you counted to 10,000 and wrote all the numbers down on a pad of paper? She talked about that for years. She couldn't believe she had a daughter who was such a math whiz. And I think," Maggie went on, "that even though she hadn't seen you in a while, she always knew you would come if she needed you."

Amy nodded. "I would have."

She blew her nose strongly into her handkerchief. "In fact," she said, "Mom did call me. Right before she, right before she passed."

"What for?"

"It was something insignificant. I thought she was calling to apologize, but she just had a question about something."

"What?"

"It was about Peter. She wanted to know if I was going out with him, which was ridiculous because he'd be the last person I'd go out with."

Why would Winifred ask a question like that? Maggie wondered.

"The funny thing is," Amy said. "I actually had news I wanted to tell her. I have started seeing someone, and

I'd planned to go by and tell her about him this week. I thought it might patch things up between us."

"That's wonderful news."

"I know. A miracle, right?" She laughed and cried at the same time.

"Well, she would have been happy, then. She always hoped you'd find someone."

"I don't know why. She didn't have much luck with romance."

"No, but she was always hopeful."

"Do you suppose I could bring him by to meet you sometimes. I suppose you're my surrogate mother now."

"Of course," Maggie said. "You don't even need to call first. Just come. Please. Better yet, let's pick a date, that way we'll be sure to meet."

The next day Maggie went over to the nursing home to clear out Winifred's things. Amy had offered to come, but she knew she had to work and Maggie was content to do it. She wanted time alone in her friend's place. She wanted to soak up whatever remained of her. There wasn't much though. Winifred had cleared away most of her things before she moved there. So, there were some clothes, some jewelry, which Maggie set aside for Amy, a bunch of books, mainly her own. The furniture she gave to Arthur, who came by looking sincerely grief-stricken.

Most of the day Maggie spent sitting on the bed, looking through the old photos and letters and bills before putting them in boxes or throwing them away. She came across a note from Juliet that she hadn't even known Winifred saved. It was a thank you note for a long-forgotten birthday present, but it touched Maggie that Winifred had hung on to it.

"Dear friend."

She folded it up and was putting it in her pocketbook, when she heard someone at the door.

Maggie looked up and almost laughed out loud. She couldn't believe who stood in front of her.

Chapter Twenty

It was Inspector Benet, just as she'd described him in her mysteries. "*His hair was silver, his lips wry, his cheekbones carved. A man who knew how to tell a joke. A Frenchman. Elegant, mocking.*"

"Not much stuff left," Inspector Benet said. Even his voice sounded right. Not quite French, but southern. Genteel.

Maggie smiled at him. She couldn't help herself. This was who Winifred wanted her to see, this was what she had been so excited about.

"I'm Frank Bowman," he said. "You must be Maggie Dove."

She felt herself blush. How foolish. She struggled to rise to her feet and he put out his hand. Strong hands, she thought. Inspector Benet had been a jujitsu master. He had strong hands too. Hard hands.

"I saw you at the funeral," he said. "But you were surrounded by a crowd and I didn't want to interrupt."

"Winifred had a lot of friends."

"Yes," he said. His eyes sparkled. They actually sparkled. "She was a pip. One of the most remarkable women I ever knew."

"Yes," Maggie said. "Me too."

He leaned against the bed, smoothed out his pants. "She told me you were the best writer who ever lived."

Maggie laughed. "Except for Shakespeare. Even Winifred had to bow down before the Bard."

"Shall I compare thee to a summer's day?" he quoted, which made her blush.

The sun was beginning to set. She'd spent the whole day cleaning and sorting. Surprising given that Winifred didn't have many things, but moving always took so much longer than expected. The sounds of the nursing home were becoming more insistent, the wheels of the food carts, the medicine being dispensed. Maggie's stomach rumbled loudly and automatically she crossed her arms.

"You must be hungry, Ms. Dove. And tired. Would it be presumptuous of me to invite you out for some dinner?"

Her first instinct was to say no. It was the day after her best friend's funeral. Less than a week since finding her neighbor dead on her lawn. She should find Peter. She should talk to him.

"You know she'd want you to go," he said, this man with the sparkling eyes and the hard hands and the soft white hair.

"She would, wouldn't she?" She could almost feel Winifred's hands at her back. *Go! Go!* "I'd like that."

She picked up the last of the things. The room was empty, and she wished it farewell, and then they walked together toward the front door. Maggie noticed a clustered of white-haired women sitting by the front entry way, eyeing her as she went past. She noticed they all held copies of *Crime and Punishment.* Book club, she suspected. They all smiled at Frank, then began whispering. It all came back to high school, she thought. But then he went off to retrieve his car, which was a sleek silver car with a door that swung open rakishly. A Mazda, and it had a stick shift, which she'd always found appealing. There was something competent about a man who could drive a stick shift.

"I know just the place," he said, and she sank back against the chair and let him drive. It felt so good to have someone in control. She'd felt so rudderless, and here was a man who knew exactly where she wanted to go, and he was right. He drove them to a charming restaurant, right on the Hudson, that served drinks with all sorts of spices mixed in and tasty little plates of food and delicious desserts and she wolfed it all down, surprised at her hunger.

He knew all about her, which was also nice. She didn't have to explain who she was or who Juliet had been. Sometimes she thought that part of why she stayed in her town was because everyone knew who she was. But mainly he talked and she ate and he told stories and she ate.

He told her stories about his childhood in New Orleans, and his mother, who was still alive, who was captain of her golf team somewhere in Florida. She'd been quite a character in his childhood. She'd been a smuggler and had taken them back and forth to Mexico City, stealing artifacts. "We had nasty encounters with customs, let me tell you. When they do a full body search…"

She laughed and laughed as he told one story after another, and when she was as full as could be, she sat and looked at the river for a bit. A group of kayakers went by, the rhythm of the paddles oddly comforting.

He put his hand on hers then. "Are you all right, Ms. Dove?"

"Please, call me Maggie. And I'm feeling more all right than I expected to be," she said. "Thank you."

She looked up into his face, so keen and interested. He reminded her a little bit of her husband, because of course Inspector Benet had reminded her of her husband too. She'd never liked macho men. She'd loved men who had command of their minds, who spoke with authority and had elegance. She liked that he didn't make a lot of noise when he ate.

"You have an expressive face, Maggie. I don't imagine you'd be a good liar."

"No, not much good at poker either. Every time I have a winning hand, I say yippee, no matter how hard I try not to."

He laughed. "And you, a Sunday School teacher. I didn't know you were allowed to play poker."

"When I was growing up I couldn't. Couldn't play any games on Sunday, or sing, or dance. My parents were very strict. But I never liked all those rules. I always felt like God wanted me to have fun. Maybe it's just my own projecting, but I have always liked the story of Jesus at the wedding, turning water into wine."

"I hope you're right," he said. "It would be nice to get to heaven and be offered a glass of wine."

"It would be." And to see her daughter she thought, and to see her parents, and her friends, and all the people she'd loved. She felt her eyes tearing up.

"I'm sorry," she said. "Not such good company."

"Don't apologize for your grief," he said, and Maggie, grateful, smiled into his eyes. He touched her hand lightly. "You've been struggling for a long time. You must be exhausted."

She felt like he was seeing into her soul. She felt the strangest feeling of release.

"You're not a psychiatrist, are you?"

"No," he laughed. "I'm in insurance.

"We should go," he said. "I don't want to wear you out. Let me take you back to your car and then you go home and try to rest."

He drove expertly, smoothly, and she was in front of her car before she knew it. He came over and opened the door, and walked her to her car.

"Can you make it home all right?"

"Yes, thank you. It's not far to go."

"I'll just follow you for a bit," he said.

"There's no need."

But he did. He followed her all the way back to her house, his lights in her rear-view mirror, a comfort, and when she pulled into her driveway, he tooted his horn and then drove away, and then she went in, to bed. That night Maggie dreamed of Winifred. She dreamed they were at a party in Mexico, and Frank was there too, and there was loud frantic music and laughter and then a gun shot, and when she woke Friday morning Maggie felt groggy, and she noticed the light on her answering machine blinking. It was Winifred, who must have left her a message on the day she died, that Maggie hadn't noticed because she'd been so busy running after Peter.

"Hey, Maggie," she said. "You'd better come by. I think I've done something stupid."

Chapter Twenty-One

Maggie needed to find Peter, which she didn't want to do because she knew whatever he had to say would be upsetting. She felt like a child. The day was so beautiful, the air so sweet and perhaps she should just drop the whole thing and let whatever happened take its course.

But she couldn't. She was a great believer in seeing things to the end. Which was why she was always being asked to chair committees.

Peter didn't answer the phone. Of course. So, she called the police station and the secretary told her he'd been suspended and Maggie's heart seemed to slingshot right into her throat.

"Why?"

"I shouldn't say," the secretary whispered.

"Please, Stephanie."

She spoke so quietly Maggie could barely hear. "They got the autopsy report on Mrs. Bell," she said. "That's all I can say."

"Winifred was murdered? Is that what they're saying?"

"I can't say," she whispered.

"Stephanie," Maggie said. "This is important. I need to know."

"I can't tell you. He's here."

"Peter?"

"No. Walter Campbell," and she hung up the phone.

Walter Campbell was everywhere. He was like fate or death, always looming, always larger than you thought it should be. Walter Campbell who left his wife and children behind in Manhattan so he could move to Darby-on-Hudson and destroy Maggie's life. Who had insisted on an autopsy for Bender, who was going to destroy Peter, who set this whole wretched thing in motion.

Peter had to be at home. Judging by the way he'd looked at Winifred's funeral, he hadn't been out much. She grabbed up her purse and head toward the door, startling Mr. Cavanaugh, who was staring at her tree. Had the whole town gone mad? she wondered. She was tempted to stop and ask him why he spit at the tree, but she didn't want to be distracted. Not now, not when she needed to find Peter.

She half walked, half ran, down to Peter's apartment. The school buses were out in force, and a huge black Yukon was behind one of them, the driver hammering on his horn. "Come on. Come on."

She turned to glare at him and he glared back. More anger. Hal Carter? Was that really his face?

Winifred murdered! How was that possible? Who would take her life? Maggie's eyes were tearing, her nose ran. She was an ugly crier, she knew it. She thought of what Frank Bowman had said last night, that she had an expressive face. She thought how she'd been laughing and smiling just last night. How was that possible? How had she gone from her best friend's funeral to going out with a man, and now to find out her friend was murdered.

She got to Peter's and rang the doorbell and he didn't answer. She was furious. She couldn't take this. He was a grown man. He had to meet her part way. She yelled his name. "Peter Nelson, open your door."

Was that her voice? she wondered. Was she that harridan? She felt like she was splitting in two and then the door was open and Peter was there, looking at her with an expression so haunted that she couldn't possibly yell. His face was pale. He held his head stiffly as though he had a migraine. She knew at once he hadn't slept all night. By the look on his face, he hadn't slept in a long time.

"They got the autopsy report," he said. "She was poisoned."

"With Ecstasy?"

He nodded.

"So the same person killed them both?" Maggie asked, trying to make sense of it.

"It came from the same lot," he said. "Same pills, it looks like."

Peter spoke as though he were drugged, though he didn't smell of beer. She had a terrible feeling that he was just shutting down. He smelled old, of dirty clothes.

"That makes no sense. I can see someone wanting to kill Bender, and I suppose I could see someone wanting to kill Winifred, but why would anyone want to kill both of them? They had nothing in common."

She wanted him to come up with an explanation, to be the same loud, vehement man she'd always known, but this Peter was someone different. Quiet, resigned.

"Think, Peter. Can you think of any connections between them?"

He walked carefully down the hallway. She was struck by how quiet everything was. No music blaring, no TV shouting. He must have been sitting in the quiet, which was so unusual as to be unnerving. He'd left his door open and she followed him inside, into his living room, and then she saw what he was doing, why he seemed so sad.

The room was filled with scrapbooks. Everywhere she looked, Maggie saw pictures of her daughter. Juliet and Peter graduating from kindergarten, both of them wearing mortarboards made out of construction paper. Juliet standing on Peter's shoulders, doing a flip at some long-ago birthday party. There'd been a huge parachute and they'd all jumped around on it. The two of them holding hands and walking on the beach, his handsome face tanned, his blonde hair bleached and Juliet fair, always, with her dark black hair.

"Oh, good grief, Peter," she said, as she sat down on the couch and put one of the albums on her lap. It was like tearing at her heart with an ice pick. It hurt, but it also felt so good, to see her face, to know that even twenty years later her daughter was still loved. As long as she was loved, she was still alive.

"I like to look at her pictures," he said. "I like to remember." He ran his hand over one especially loved picture, the two of them at the prom. They only got to go to the junior prom. She died before the senior one, and so they canceled it for her, the town coming together in their grief. No one could celebrate with Juliet dead.

"When she's with me, I feel like I'm better," he said.

"I know, chickie." She ran her finger over her daughter's face. So loved. So loved. She looked, startled, at a picture she hadn't seen in a long time, Juliet in shorts in front of a Christmas tree. Juliet had loved Christmas so much that Maggie used to love to surprise her on July 25. She'd wrap up a present and decorate one of the fir trees and her husband would dress up as Santa and they'd sing Christmas songs.

"I should have died that night."

"No," she cried out. "Never say that."

"I should have. My life hasn't meant anything since then. I was the one who didn't have my seatbelt on. I deserved to die. Why did God choose me to live?" Was this the same strong man who'd been with her only last week, who'd wanted nothing more than to protect her when she found a body on her lawn?

"You can't know what God was thinking. All you can know is that you are alive and you have to appreciate that. You have to be thankful for that."

"Thankful," he said.

"You can't just surrender, Peter. If not for yourself, think of Juliet. She would have wanted you to fight. She would have believed in you."

Such a passionate girl. Always so committed and so quick to fight injustice. She hated to see anyone bullied. She joined the Rainbow Coalition even though she wasn't gay, but because she didn't want those students to feel alone. "It's a terrible thing to be isolated, Mom."

"Did you get a lawyer?" she asked.

He nodded. "I got O'Connor."

The local real estate lawyer. "I thought he was dying."

"No, he's in remission."

"Do you think you might want someone a little more energetic?" she asked. Even when O'Connor was perfectly healthy, he didn't have all his wits about him. "Anyway, don't you want a criminal lawyer?"

"He's good people, Dove. Don't you fret."

"I'm not fretting. But it does seem to me that there are forces mobilizing against you and you might do well to fight them."

"They will never arrest me. Not here, Dove. There'd be a revolution."

"Peter, that sounds like the sort of thing people say right before the revolution. If they can prove you did it, they'll arrest you and it won't matter who you are what you've done or anything at all."

He pressed his lips tightly together. No point in telling him to be reasonable. She knew he wouldn't be. His whole life was predicated on not being reasonable. It was like when he'd played baseball. Peter had been a good player. He wasn't that big, but he was all heart, and you knew when he had his bat that he was going to swing it. When he made contact with the ball, it sailed. One time, she remembered, the ball stayed in the air, looping up like a kite, so far out of the field that the poor outfielder had almost run into the river to get it. Not long afterwards a scout came to town. Small college, but a good scholarship and it would have worked out except that Peter got mad at the umpire at the game and pushed him. He got tossed out. End of career. It was as though he'd rather throw something away than find out he couldn't be good at it.

"You don't need to make it easy for him, Peter."

He threw a bottle cap in the direction of the wall. On the window sill he had a stack of books from high school, the last ones he'd read, she suspected. *To Kill a Mockingbird*, *Of Mice and Men*, *The House on Mango Street*, *Leaves of Grass*, the last a gift from Juliet.

"How can I stand up to a man like that? He has millions of dollars in the bank and he has everyone in the village on his side. Campbell says this and Campbell says that. How am I supposed to fight that? "

"With facts. With other suspects. There are alternatives, you know. There are other people who wanted them dead. There have to be, because I know you didn't do it."

"Being a mystery writer isn't real life, Dove."

"It is though, I know about people. Listen I've done a lot of reading about poisoners. I've poisoned off all my victims, in fact, except for the third one and that was a cement block, but the thing is that poisoners are a specific type of person. They're patient. They're manipulative. They like playing games. You are the opposite of a poisoner, Peter. You're more of a meat cleaver kind of guy."

"You're just saying that because you love me," he said, though she could see a bit of a spark returning to his face.

"I do love you. I would defend you, quite honestly, even if I thought you were the murderer. But you're no poisoner, Peter. And I won't let Campbell pin this on you. But you have to help me. You can't just sit here and let them frame you."

"What do you want me to do?"

"Well, the thing I don't understand is why someone would use Ecstasy in the first place. It doesn't seem like a dangerous drug. I mean why not use cyanide or strychnine or belladonna, for matter," Maggie said, thinking of the shrub on her front lawn, thinking of all the various ways there were to kill someone.

"Maybe that's what the person had to hand. People usually use the substance they're familiar with."

"What sort of person would have Ecstasy in his possession?" she asked, feeling slightly foolish.

"A DARE officer." He grimaced, flicking another bottle top.

"Beyond that?"

He sighed. "A teenager. God knows there's enough Ecstasy in this town. Not as much as there used to be, but it's still pretty easy to get. And there's this new type that's supposed to be very lethal."

"Yeah, but I don't see why a teenager would want to kill Bender. Plus, how would they get to Winifred? Anyway, teenagers tend to be more impulsive. Who else?"

He leaned forward, Rodin's thinker on the couch. With Peter thinking was a physical process. He ran his hands through his hair. He chewed his lips.

"What other sort of person would use Ecstasy?"

He grinned at her then.

"Well, Dove, not to shock your tender sensibilities, but there is one class of people known for using Ecstasy."

"Who's that?" she said.

"Strippers," he said, "but there are no strippers in Darby-on-Hudson."

Chapter Twenty-Two

She had a clue! It wasn't much, but it was something. She'd actually done something, which was sort of amazing. Now Maggie just had to figure out what to do about it.

It was so easy to get people to do things in books. All you had to do was write a scene and Inspector Benet leapt into action. But in real life, it was not easy to knock on a grieving woman's door and try to interview her. Particularly when you knew that woman hated you, and when you were trying to ask her if she might have killed her husband.

Maggie had no authority. She had no badge. She considered going to Walter Campbell for help, but rejected it instantaneously. She could almost picture the expression on his rock-like face when she told him why she suspected Noelle. No, she had to do something else.

Maggie went home and changed her clothes. Put on a little more make-up and a V neck shirt. She wasn't sure what vibe she was going for, but thought she should look a little sophisticated. Not that it worked, because the moment Noelle opened the door to her house, she thrust out her hip and said, "What do you want?"

"I brought you a chicken casserole," Maggie said. She'd defrosted it; always kept one handy for the dinner brigade. You never knew when one of the elderly parishioners would twist an ankle.

"Oh," Noelle said. "You're the second person to drop off food today."

There was that same artificial voice, baby-like, and the same languid motion, as though she could hardly be bothered to reach for the casserole dish. Her eyes were large and slightly slanted, like a cat's.

"Really? Who else was here?" Maggie asked automatically, but Noelle didn't seem offended. Not a woman who kept secrets, it seemed. Not a woman who valued her privacy. "That other lady," she said. "The one who looks like you. Agnes."

"Agnes Jorgenson does not resemble me in the least," Maggie snapped. But Noelle just stared back blankly. She had a way of looking all innocent, Maggie realized, when she was about to stab you in the back. Agnes Jorgenson. She of the googly eyes and dour expression. She did not look like Maggie. Not that looks were important. Not that she was vain. Not that she looked as good as she used to, but still.

"Anyway, I wondered if I might talk to you."

"About what?"

This was not going to be easy, Maggie thought. She could hardly flat out ask if Noelle used Ecstasy and poisoned Winifred with it.

"You said you were working on a book. Is there anything I can help you with?"

"You'd help me?" Noelle asked. "Why? You hated my husband."

She looked like a martyr. She looked like she expected Maggie to tie her to a stake and light the wood. Honestly, Maggie didn't think she was that bad. She tried to smile. She tried to look like a normal, friendly person, which she hoped she was.

"I didn't hate him. I hated what he did to my tree."

Don't hate the person, she always said to her Sunday School students. Hate the act.

"You hated him from the moment he moved in. Me, too. You don't need to try and hide it. I've been dealing with people like you my whole life."

She tucked her head back at that. Maggie couldn't figure out if the woman was beautiful or not. Her skin was slightly pockmarked from acne, but the color of her skin was beautiful. Slightly tan. Her hair was thick, her eyes slightly close together. She had beautiful eyebrows and long lashes. She reminded Maggie a little bit of one of the Romanov princesses, girls who looked beautiful from some angles and homely from others.

"People like me how?" Maggie asked, feeling her heart beginning to pound, feeling like what she wanted to do was slam the door and leave, but she couldn't do that. She needed information. She needed to help Peter. That was worth a certain amount of humiliation.

Meanwhile, over Noelle's shoulder, Maggie could see the interior of the house was the color of a brothel, in so far as Maggie knew what the inside of a brothel looked like. Where there had once been colonial blue walls and soft white wainscoting, the room was now painted a color that reminded Maggie of inflamed tonsils. The walls were pink, plush, pulsating, unnerving. In the corner, where the Bells kept their piano, where Mr. Bell used to sit and play songs and Mrs. Bell would pull out her banjo and they would all sing Rambling Rose and Let Me Call You Sweetheart, in that corner was a picture of Noelle, in the nude, with a pinecone. It always came back to trees with that man, Maggie thought.

Noelle crossed her arms. Maggie stood there like an idiot, hanging on to the casserole, thinking she should have brought a bottle of scotch. "People like you," Noelle went on. "People who judge. People who lead your safe little lives. People who think they're better than people like me. Hypocrites."

"I don't think I am a hypocrite," Maggie said. "I was quite up front about disliking your husband. Whatever else I am, I'm not a liar."

Noelle stepped backward, brought her fingers to her lips, as though hoping desperately to find herself holding a cigarette. She smelled ripe, Maggie thought. She smelled like she'd been fermenting. She remembered reading once that Steve Jobs had a distinctive and unpleasant aroma because his diet was so strange. She wondered what sorts of food Noelle ate.

"Why did you come live in this village if you feel that way about us?" Maggie asked. "Why not stay in the city?"

"Why shouldn't we live where we want to live? On the river. Bender loved the river. It was his passion. He named his children after river gods. He was committed to the river. He loved it." Her voice broke.

"He said you were a Sunday School teacher," Noelle said.

"Yes," Maggie said, straightening up just a little bit. She was proud of her job.

"Then why couldn't you forgive him?"

"I couldn't forgive him because he never apologized. One of the very last things he did was try to poison my tree. How am I supposed to forgive that?"

Maggie suspected she had a point. She suspected her relationship with Bender had not been her finest moment. She knew for a fact that she'd forgiven people for far worse grievances. Peter, for example, who seemed hell-bent on destroying her life. And yet she loved him.

She should go home. She'd make no progress here, and yet, to her surprise, Noelle turned and began walking toward the staircase. It seemed like she wanted Maggie to follow, and so she did.

That at least looked familiar. Maggie could remember sledding down those steps on pillows. Winifred, she thought. Winifred. So much life. Winifred had wanted so much out of life, had been so determined to marry a prince, and she had tried so hard. Always expecting something magical to be underneath every man she went out with and always disappointed to find out it was just a man, after all. Yet still hopeful, still looking for that fifth husband. Was it possible this woman could be involved in her death?

Finally, they were up in the room that had been Winifred's. They'd torn down the walls between several of the bedrooms, turning them into one giant studio. At one end of the wall, near a window, was Bender's easel. On the other side was a desk with a computer on it and several neat shelves containing folders. Noelle walked over to the easel, and gestured to it. There was Bender's painting.

"He'd been working on it for months," Noelle said. "He loved the river."

Maggie looked at it. Perhaps not surprisingly, it looked very plush. Very sensual. Lots of brushstrokes. It was the blue of the river on a spring day, when the sun, as it did sometimes, turned a soft yellow and the houses on the river were whitewashed and the river itself was so blue it looked like the Mediterranean. In the lower corner of the painting was the tip of Maggie's house and next to it was a blank spot, where the tree should be. Bender hadn't even been able to bring himself to paint the tree. Her pretty little oak.

She could see how that wouldn't fit in with the tone of his painting, but why not just paint around it. Why not reimagine it as a tulip tree, for that matter. She was surprised at how much lower her house was than his. What must he have felt every day looking down on her like that? Maggie wondered. From this angle, she must have looked so small. From this angle, she realized, he had a clear view right into her house. He would have seen her glaring at him. He would have known, but he didn't care.

Well, that much she knew, though she felt herself start to get angry all over again. She couldn't even be in this man's house, now dead, without feeling annoyed. The fact was, if anyone in this area had the disposition of a poisoner it was Bender. He was manipulative, spoiled, vain. It would be easy to imagine him toying with a victim, pretending to be caring even as he slipped poison into her food. In fact, he had done that exact thing with her tree. Pretending to be concerned for what Maggie wanted even as he slipped lye onto its branches. But it was Bender who was dead, Bender who had been poisoned.

"This is who he was," Noelle said. "This was my Bender."

Maggie was touched by the sincerity in her voice, even though she objected strenuously. What could she say of seeing Bender's work beyond that he was exactly what he seemed? At the same time, it did seem like he loved Noelle and she loved him and that was something honest. She had to respect that.

"What do you want from me?" Noelle asked.

Maggie took a deep breath. She could do this.

"I don't know if you've heard, but there was another death in the village. The woman who used to live in this house, matter of fact. Her name was Winifred Bell."

Noelle shook her head.

"You probably met her when you bought this house."

"I wasn't there," she whispered in her fluty voice. "Bender took care of all that."

"Did he ever say anything about her?"

"That old lady?"

Maggie sighed. "Yes, the old lady who was my friend. Did he ever say anything about her?"

"Why?"

"Because they both seem to have been murdered in the same way and so there must have been some connection between them and I'm trying to figure out what that was."

"I thought that good-looking policeman did it," Noelle said. "Peter Nelson."

"No," Maggie said. The room was oppressively hot.

"He poisoned Bender. He hated him because Bender was going to get him fired."

"He hated your husband, but he didn't kill him, and he didn't kill Winifred either."

Noelle looked at her blankly.

"Winifred," Maggie said. "My friend. The lady who used to live in this house."

Noelle shrugged.

Maggie knew she needed to press on. She might not get another chance.

"I know this is going to sound tactless," Maggie said, "but I understand there's a lot of Ecstasy in your profession."

"The drug?" Noelle asked.

"Yes."

Noelle's eyes narrowed. "There was, but I left that all behind a long time ago."

She put her hand on her stomach protectively. A woman who was used to having her every action observed, Maggie thought. Not a woman who would make such a motion without knowing what it implied.

"I'm trying to think of why someone might have used Ecstasy to kill Bender and I wonder if it was a way to put suspicion on you."

"Me!" she cried out.

"Maybe as a way of framing you. Of making the police look into your background."

"No, I never would have hurt him."

"It's just that it's an unusual drug to use. It's not the first thing that comes to mind when you think of killing someone. I was reading up on it and it's very difficult to know how much Ecstasy could be lethal. It might be one pill or it might be 50. There had to be some reason the killer used this particular drug."

"But the policeman's the killer."

"Say he's not," Maggie snapped. "Say Peter Nelson's not the killer. Is there anyone else you can think that Bender might have known who would use Ecstasy?"

Noelle sank down onto a heart-shaped seat. There was no place for Maggie to sit, but she didn't want to. She crossed her arms. She wondered if Noelle was taking her question seriously, and then she spoke.

"His first wife uses Ecstasy," she said. "She uses it a lot."

"She's a drug addict?"

"No," Noelle said. "No, she has Parkinson's. She uses it to treat her Parkinson's. She always has a large supply. She gets it on the internet."

Parkinson's, Maggie thought. The same disease Winifred had. She didn't know whether this first Mrs. Bender knew Winifred, much less wanted to kill her, but it was something. Something new she hadn't known before; something she doubted Walter Campbell knew. It was time to go see him, she thought. She'd been putting it off, but finally she had something to tell him. Maybe she could go see the first wife too.

"Did that help?" Noelle asked, and suddenly she looked changed again, from angry to needy, and for a second, she saw what Bender had loved about her, the vulnerability that must have touched him, the softness beneath the armor.

"Yes," she said. "Thank you."

The phone was ringing when she walked into her house.

"Just wanted to see how you were doing," Frank Bowman said. "Did you recuperate from last night?"

"I had a wonderful time, thank you very much."

"You sound upbeat."

"I am, I just went to talk to Bender's widow and I think I got a clue."

She could hear him smiling over the phone. Funny how changing the shape of your lips made the sounds come out differently.

"A clue?"

"A little clue, but it's something."

"May I ask what it is?"

I've found out that Bender's first wife used Ecstasy to treat her Parkinson's. Well, you would be the person to ask. Did Winifred ever meet her?"

"What's her name?"

"Char. Char Bender."

"No," he said. "I don't recognize the name. But I can ask around if you like. Maybe someone else knows."

"That would be wonderful."

"Now I'll feel like the real Inspector Benet," he said. She started, wondering how he even knew who Inspector Benet was, and then she realized Winifred probably spent hours talking about her and Inspector Benet and her husband and his fingers. Good grief. She began to blush. "Perhaps we could discuss our findings over dinner," he said.

"I'd love that," she said.

Such a small step, she thought. But such an important one. So many small steps lately. But now for the next challenge. Now to see Walter Campbell.

Chapter Twenty-Three

It was 3:00 on a Thursday afternoon, which meant Walter Campbell would be at D'Amici's deli. Maggie knew that in the same way she knew that Agnes had her hair done at Iphigenia's every Friday, or that Allison Cooper had her nails done every Wednesday, or that the town drunk would be standing outside the marina around 4:00. Because part of the pleasure of living in a small town was knowing its patterns. Its rhythms. Like the tide. So many of the children of the village moved away because they craved adventure. But Maggie loved the order, loved the way everything made a sort of sense.

Maggie knew she needed to talk to Walter Campbell, but she didn't want to do anything as official as make an appointment. That would put too much on the line. But she figured she could stop by D'Amici's and grab a late lunch. She wasn't surprised to see Hal Carter there, and Joe Mangione, who had answered her call when she'd intended to call 911. And Walter, of course, and Agnes, which was surprising. Even more surprising was that Agnes seemed to be in the middle of laughing at a dirty joke. A surprising woman. Though they all quieted up the moment Maggie walked in. She had that effect on people, she supposed, because she'd been a Sunday School teacher for so long. Or because you're a prude, she could hear Winifred mutter.

"You're slumming," Agnes said to Maggie the moment she walked in.

"Hello dear," Joe said. He was still wearing his Darby-on-Hudson ambulance corps jacket. He was very proud of it; said he'd be buried in it and she believed him. "Let me get you a cup of coffee."

He didn't actually work at the deli, but when Mr. D'Amici was hung-over, which was quite often, Joe stepped in. Now he went behind the counter and poured her a cup.

"Sorry about your friend," he said, as he handed her the hot cup. He also set a corn muffin on a napkin. She knew he'd accept no money for either. Generous and kind. When her minister got sick last year, Joe'd brought her meals for a week, and he wasn't even religious. He just thought things should be done in a certain way.

"That Winifred. She was a pip," Hal said. "I had to fix her furnace right before her second wedding. Do you remember that?"

"She was one of a kind."

"I remember the time someone stole her pocketbook and she chased him down the street," Agnes threw out. "Doesn't seem like someone who would be poisoned."

They were quiet then. A poster of a naked woman hung in the corner. Two winning lottery tickets and an autographed picture of Clint Eastwood. Some muffins the size of pumpkins sat on a counter. Walter still hadn't said anything. From the moment she walked in, she noticed him standing in the corner, but he hadn't spoken, smiled or anything else. He just stood, watchfully. Which was unnerving because he was a big man. He seemed even larger up close than he did at church. He had a massive face, something that should be etched in a rock.

"I wonder if I might have a word with you, Walter," she said, after a while, when the conversation began to wind down. The deli closed at 4. They'd all been up since 4 a.m.

"Oh, oh," Hal said. "You're in trouble now, Walter."

"Of course," he said, as though he'd been expecting her to ask.

He was supposed to be a genius, she knew. He taught Sunday School too, though he preferred the older kids, grappling with the more serious issues. She'd heard him once leading a discussion on faith by action. One of the confirmands refused to write a faith statement and Walter kicked him out of the class. She'd protested because she didn't think anyone should be kicked out of Sunday School ever, but Walter had argued that if the church didn't believe in anything, there'd not be much point. She knew he was right, which made her dislike him anymore.

"Do you want to come to my office?" he asked.

"I'd rather just walk and talk, if you don't mind."

Going to the office would make it too official, she thought. Also, it would alert Peter's co-workers. She knew how visible she was walking on Main Street, but she thought her motive might seem more innocuous.

"I wanted to talk to you about Peter Nelson," she said. "I'm a friend of his."

"I know," Water said, his voice an ominous rumble. The good-natured persona he'd exhibited in D'Amici's seemed to have disappeared. "They tell me he's been like a son to you."

"That's true," she said, and felt a throb of emotion, though she forced it back. She didn't want to be sidetracked, didn't want to be pitied, in any event, by this man who had made his millions and then deposited them so he could toy with his life and throw away his family. She felt a crushing desire to explain Peter to this man. She knew Peter didn't like him and knew Peter well enough to know that where there was dislike, there was always impudence. How to mend that fence.

"His mother died young," he said.

"Yes, that's right. She was a gentle woman and her life became too harsh."

"She killed herself."

"No. Not intentionally. She lost hope. That's all it took."

"She overdosed."

A young couple walked past them, so fresh and neat, with a little plump baby swinging in a carrier.

"She mixed drugs and alcohol, but no one ever thought it was intentional. She was medicating herself, the best she knew. You know," she said to this man, who probably thought he had complete charge of his life, "I've never agreed with that proverb that God doesn't give you more than you can bear. It seems to me that quite often He does."

"And you a Sunday school teacher."

"I love God. But I'm not entirely sure I trust him. Or I do trust him, but I don't understand him. All I know is that Kelly Nelson was overwhelmed by her life. That's all."

"And then you stepped in?"

"Yes, that's right. I always saw something special in him, even when he was a little Sunday School student. He's one of those people who would be great in war time, who would hurtle himself in front of bullets in order to break through a barricade, but he had a terrible time with the law and order of a community. But he always tried to do the right thing. He's passionate about kids. He's very protective."

Campbell didn't speak. They continued to walk down Main Street, in the direction of the river. A boy shot by on a bicycle, without a helmet, his feet splayed wide as he soared down toward the river, his laugh a desperate cackle. Without thinking Maggie reached toward him, wanted to slow him down, though he was past before she could do anything about it.

"He was in the car when your daughter died."

"Yes, but that was hardly his fault."

"I just wanted to separate fact from fiction," Campbell said.

"She was seventeen years old. They went to a party. It was raining that night. They left early because she had a curfew. Eleven o'clock. They were at a stop light on the Saw Mill. A van, coming south, skidding, jumped over the island and rammed into her. She had on her seat belt. She was trapped. Peter didn't have his on and he was flung from the car."

"Why wasn't he driving?"

He said it gently, with just the same tone as a doctor might mention that, oh, that lump wasn't what it seemed to be and you might need some more tests. She thought of the way the snake whispered his temptations to Eve. She threw out her chest. She would not let this man make suggestions.

"He was high. But she wasn't. She was perfectly sober, the designated driver."

"She was driving his car. So it was unfamiliar to her."

"She was perfectly familiar with that car and they were stopped at a stoplight. No one could have got out of that."

"He had Ecstasy in his urine."

"Yes, he did. And he had to go to court and he lost his driver's license and after that he vowed he would go clean, which he did. He devoted himself to helping kids, which is how he came to be a DARE officer. It wasn't his fault, but he blamed himself."

"You didn't blame him."

"There was nothing to blame him for. He didn't do anything."

Campbell shrugged. "You're a good woman then. There would be many who would blame him, who might think had he been driving they wouldn't have been stopped right there."

"You could go crazy thinking about things like that. You reach a point in your life where you have to figure out if you want to be filled with hate or love.

They'd reached the park. He sat down on the bench and motioned for her to sit down as well, though she didn't. She gripped onto the metal edge of the bench for support. An empty Circle Line boat went past. Automatically she raised her hand to wave at it but there were no passengers aboard.

"I'm new to Darby, Ms. Dove. But I've learned quickly that a town like this has its own rhythm. Frankly, that's why I chose to work here and that's why I'm talking to you about this, though in any other context I'd consider it inappropriate. You say that Peter Nelson is a good man, but let me tell you the side of him I know. He's been on probation three times. He's the DARE officer in this town, and yet he oversaw a party at which children were drinking. I don't know whether he killed Bender, or Ms. Bell, although I can believe it. I understand they argued. About money. But the shock to my department is not one that I will soon forget. That man may go to jail or not, but he will not be a police officer here anymore. I can promise you that. And I can also promise you that we will do a most thorough investigation into these deaths. If Officer

Nelson is responsible, he will be prosecuted to the fullest extent of the law."

She stood still for a moment, heart pounding with anger. "You had your mind made up from the beginning. You dislike him and so you assume he's guilty," Maggie cried out. "But are you looking at anyone else?"

"Of course, we are checking out all suspects."

"Did you talk to Noelle Bender?"

"I will," Campbell said, faltering for just a moment.

"Did you happen to ask her about her background as a stripper, and the fact that Ecstasy is quite common in that community, and what about Bender's first wife, Char, who takes Ecstasy for Parkinson's? Do you know about any of that?"

He stood up, swaying slightly, reminding her of pictures she'd seen of statues being pulled to the ground. Lines from Ozymandias popped into her head. "Two vast and trunkless legs of stone stand in the desert…"

"This is not a game, Ms. Dove."

She pulled herself up to her full height, which wasn't much, but felt surprisingly powerful, under the circumstances. "No, it's not a game. We're talking about a man I love, who has devoted himself to me and to this town and I am damned if I will see you railroad him," and with that she turned and strode away from Walter Campbell, remembering, as she walked, an expression her mother used to say that summed up the situation perfectly. *Well, chuck you Farley,* her mother whispered in her ear.

Chapter Twenty-Four

Sanctimonious son of a gun. She hated Walter Campbell. He reminded her of Sir Thomas More, who had always annoyed her. A man who put faith before his family, rules before love. Who made his wife and daughters beg when what was at stake was his honor. As though anything was more important than love. Why did she think a man like Walter Campbell could even begin to understand what she was feeling?

One thing Maggie knew for sure. Campbell wasn't going to stop her. She would not be bullied into giving up her quest. He had nothing to hold over her. He was nothing to her. She wasn't going to leave Peter at the hands of someone like that.

Playing a game? If anyone was playing a game it was Walter Campbell, setting himself up in his ridiculous house. She'd heard all about it. He'd claimed he wanted a simple life, but then he bought Margery Rusk's old house and tore out the inside so that it would be environmentally correct, with a generator in case of storms and heated floors and screens that went up and down at the touch of a button. Two million dollars' worth of renovations so he could live simply.

The idea that Peter would have murdered Winifred. Or Ms. Bell, as he put it, as though anyone in this world had ever referred to Winifred that way. She was anything but Ms. Bell. She was always a Mrs. So what if Peter had argued with her. They were both argumentative people. They could each argue with a tree; it didn't mean anything. None of it made sense. And why would they argue about money? Peter knew she didn't have any. He could have come to Maggie if he needed money. He would have come to her. But someone had killed Winifred. With malice, someone had chosen to take her life, to put a tablet of poison into her food or medicine, with the intention of hurting her. Maggie shivered, feeling both afraid and angry. It was so wrong. So cruel.

Maggie trudged up Main Street, back in the direction of her house. The cherry blossoms had blown off after the last storm, leaving the trees almost embarrassingly naked, the green leaves struggling to make up for what had been lost. They bent toward her, haggard from the wind, apologizing, it seemed to her, for their shame. She knew she should ask Peter about the argument, but she couldn't bring herself to do it. She staggered forward, running everything through her mind, until she felt a car gliding behind her.

"Hey," she heard someone yelling. "Hey, Miss Maggie. How you?"

She looked over to see her favorite real estate agent cruising along in a Bentley.

"Want a ride?"

"No thank you, Sybil."

"Get in, Miss Maggie. You look like you're going to blow a fuse."

Maggie got into the car and sank into its plushness. "This is fabulous," she said. "I feel like I'm being laid out at my funeral."

Sybil laughed heartily at that, her whole body quivering with humor. She was a good-natured girl. Her laughter could be heard booming all over town. Her entire family laughed. Sometimes Maggie ran into them at Applebee's and the whole restaurant reverberated with the noise. They all argued and fought and swore with each other and then made up in dramatic fashion. She'd always thought if she could have voted to join a family, that would be the one she'd choose.

"You must have made a good sale."

She laughed again. She had three chins and a plump build, all of which made her look cheerful and young. She'd been a few years older than Juliet, in the fast crowd. Used to stand on street corners smoking. Always good natured though. Seeing her made Maggie wonder what Juliet would be like now. Would she have changed? Would they be close or would it be like Amy and Winifred, two people who just couldn't seem to find a way to connect.

"I sold the Blackwell house," Sibyl said.

"No kidding."

That house had been on the market for years. It was a strange property because although the house itself was beautiful, it was on the grounds of the elementary school, which meant whoever lived there would be surrounded by children laughing and playing. Not such a terrible penalty, Maggie thought, but it had been unoccupied for years.

"One of the hedge fund kings," she said. "He won't be home during the day so he doesn't care about the kids. He liked the bones of the house. I bet he won't ever be there."

"Good for you. You were patient."

"You planning on selling your place any time soon, Miss Maggie?"

"No, I'm in it for the duration," Maggie said. They had this conversation every six months. One of the downsides of being friends with a real estate agent.

"I could get you a nice two-bedroom condo. Right on the river. Or there's a nice unit up at Riverside, with a balcony and a pool. You wouldn't need to worry about anything, and it would be cheaper."

"I'm not worried about the money," Maggie said, which was true. Thanks to royalties from her late husband's works, and from her own mysteries, she was well-set financially. "But that house has been in my family for generations and I can't sell it, even though I know it's silly. It will pass out of the family when I die, but still, I'd like to keep it in the family as long as I can."

Sibyl took her hands off the wheel for a moment, held them up in the air. "It's okay. No judging here."

She'd ask her again in six months, Maggie knew.

They'd made it into her driveway at this point, and Maggie sat there, luxuriating. Not entirely ready to get out of the car.

In front of her loomed Bender's house, which looked deflated. Although only a week had passed since his death, it already looked overgrown. There were some ash trees in the corner, rolled-up leaves still clinging to the branches, having survived winter somehow and unwilling to let go, would not let go until the green leaves pushed them out and then their curled-up bodies would scatter everywhere, hunched up from their suffering.

"There's someone who's likely to need a real estate agent soon," Maggie said.

"I thought that too," Sibyl said. "But she doesn't own the house. It belongs to the first wife."

Again back to the first Mrs. Bender, Maggie thought. A woman with Parkinson's. A woman with more than enough reason to want to kill Marcus Bender. But not a woman who seemed to have a reason to kill Winifred.

"Isn't that unusual?"

"Nothing's unusual in real estate," Sibyl said. "I guess he wanted to make sure his young wife didn't have cause to murder him. So he arranged it so she wouldn't get anything if he died. Must not have trusted her much."

"She didn't get custody of the children either," Maggie said. "They must have gone back to the first wife. Did you meet her at the closing?" She remembered how excited Winifred was when she sold the house to Bender.

She'd made so much more money than she'd expected. Not a woman who looked backwards. Not a woman with nostalgia.

"Not at the closing, no. She had a proxy acting for her because she had a harp concert."

"She's a harpist?"

Sibyl shrugged. "I guess so. She told me that she'd practiced for years and finally was making progress, when she found out she had Parkinson's. She wouldn't be able to use her hands much longer, so she wanted as much time to herself as she could get. I guess that's why she didn't care that much about Bender moving on."

"That seems a little cold."

"I once went to a closing," Sibyl said. "Man and wife, married 30 years. He told her he wanted her to improve the house, so they'd get top-dollar. She spends a year fixing and caulking and painting. Goes to the closing, buyers write the check and he snatches it right away from her. Turned out he had another wife in mind. That was cold."

"Let me ask you this," Maggie said, "did Winifred have anything to do with Bender's first wife? Would she have talked to her during the sale?"

"I don't think so. Maybe. They might have talked together on the phone."

It made no sense, Maggie thought. Even if Winifred did talk to her, why would that make this first wife want to kill her? But somebody killed Winifred. And it wasn't Peter, and it didn't seem to be Noelle. This wife was as close as she had to a suspect. Maggie had to pursue it. She would call her and set up a meeting. She spent the night trying to come up with some reasonable excuse for wanting to talk to her, but then, late at night, she had a revelation. She would try the truth.

"I'm trying to figure out who killed my friend," she said to Char Bender the next morning, when she reached her. "Would you mind if I come by and ask you some questions?"

"I'm very busy," Char said.

But she relented.

For the rest of the afternoon, Maggie went through her library, trying to understand what she was up against. She read through books about poisoners. She read about how Ecstasy might be introduced. It could be a pill, she read, or it could be in liquid. Death would be preceded by palpitations, blurry vision, dry mouth, confusion, agitation, dehydration, liver failure. Not an easy way to die.

Suddenly the force of losing Winifred almost smacked Maggie in the face. How she wished her best friend was there, for her to talk to. She touched the window, cold and remorseless, and thought how she had stood by the window, thinking to throw a rock at Bender. Grief gnawed her. This was the terrible part of grief, that it throbbed. Never went away. She sank down on her couch and the phone rang and she lunged for it, hoping that it would be Frank, which surprised her. She hadn't realized until she picked up the phone how much she'd been hoping that he'd call. Foolishness. But it wasn't Frank. It was Harriet Evans from church calling to say that they'd called an impromptu meeting of the Women of the Church and they were going to take her out to dinner

"That's very sweet of you," Maggie said. "But it's not necessary."

"You've been through a hard time, Maggie Dove, and now's the time to have your friends around you. We won't take no for an answer." Harriet was not a forceful person and Maggie suspected someone else had written out the words.

"We're going to that new Thai place. Helen Blake says it's good and Penny's gout is better so we're going to risk it. Next Friday night. Six o'clock."

"Okay, thank you."

"And you can bring that man with you, if you want. The one you went out with the other night."

"Thank you," Maggie said, wondering, as she hung up the phone how on earth anyone in this town kept a secret. She hadn't even gone out with Frank in Darby-on-Hudson. They'd driven quite a bit north. She hadn't even run into someone she knew. Was she being followed? Was there a secret Darby-on-Hudson cabal who kept track of 62-year-old Sunday School teachers and who they ate dinner with? Feeling rebellious and impulsive, two emotions Maggie had not felt in a while, she decided to make a call.

Chapter Twenty-Five

Maggie had never called up a man to ask him out. She'd gone out with plenty of boys in her youth, but that was back in the time when a girl wouldn't dream of making the first call. Or she wouldn't anyway. Though she had pursued her husband.

Even now, many years after the fact, Maggie blushed to think how she'd hurled herself at Stuart Dove, but then she had to do something to get that man to look up from a book. She remembered a red dress, his office desk, sweeping papers onto the floor, the look on his face, the growl he emitted. She blushed.

She didn't plan on wearing a red dress to her dinner with Frank Bowman, but she did feel a bit of a temptress when she called his number. An elderly woman answered the phone, sounding aggrieved when Maggie asked to speak to Frank.

"He's not here."

"Could you find him?"

She smiled picturing an irritated elderly woman clutching her copy of *Crime & Punishment*, trooping around The Castle, seeking out Frank. She wondered why he lived there. It seemed an odd place for such a vibrant man to live.

About five minutes passed and then Frank answered.

"This is Maggie Dove," she said.

The warmth in his voice, the sound of pleasure. A cluster of robins hopped about on her front lawn, such fat little birds with their bright orange bellies. "Maggie Dove," he said. "As I live and breathe. I was just going to call you and see about our dinner."

"Actually, I'm calling to ask if you'd like to go on an expedition with me. I'm going into the city tomorrow, to meet Bender's first wife, and I thought perhaps you would want to come with me."

"You're sleuthing."

"Conversating anyway, but I have a suspicion things would go easier if someone charming came along. Plus, I'm no good at parallel parking."

He laughed. He had a nice laugh, throaty. "I would have said you're charming enough."

"I'm not fishing for a compliment," she said, though she supposed she was. "Would you like to come?"

"I would be delighted," he said.

"Wonderful. See you tomorrow then, around 4."

Maggie dreamed of Marcus Bender that night. She dreamed he installed an elevator on her side lawn, then tried to hide it by putting a tree on it, but when he drove onto the street, he pressed a button that made the elevator appear and then he drove his car into it. It was strange to see him so vivid and alive in her dream, even if it didn't make any sense. She'd forgotten, in only a few days, how vital the man was. The animal energy he had. Even Maggie, who hated him, wasn't immune to it and she woke up feeling somewhat unsettled.

She called Peter, who was usually happy enough to laugh with her over something, but his humor seemed to have deserted him.

"An elevator," he said. "What?"

"How are you doing?"

She could hear gunshots in the background. She pictured him lying on his couch, watching TV, chips and beer around him, though hopefully not beer, not this early in the morning. "Do you want to take a walk?" she said. "Do you want to get out?"

"No," he said. "I don't want to go outside right now."

"You should, Peter. The air will make you feel better."

"I don't want to."

"All right, well, I wanted to let you know I talked to Char Bender and I'm going to be going into the city to talk to her. Maybe she'll have some thoughts on who else might have wanted to kill Bender."

"Who?"

"Bender, the man who was dead on my lawn."

"Char?"

"His first wife. She lives in the city."

"Oh, good. Thanks."

"She takes Ecstasy, Peter. For Parkinson's. I know it's a long shot, but maybe she's the poisoner. I'm going to check it out. I'm going to see her later today."

"Thanks Dove."

He paused. She pictured that dear face and didn't want to cause him anymore anguish. She knew he'd be sitting in his apartment, scrapbooks lying around. He might well choose to sit that way for the rest of his life. Beautiful girl, she thought. Beautiful daughter to inspire such loyalty, and she felt an ache of pain run through her as sharp as a bullet. But she had to know.

"Peter, there's something I have to ask you about."

"Of course, Dove. Anything."

"I talked to Walter Campbell."

"Lucky you," he said, his voice a haunting mixture of hope and defeat. How badly he'd wanted to be a police officer and how he'd struggled at the academy, so disappointed when he found out they didn't hand out guns on the first day. They he would have to make it through a semester of classes before he got a gun.

"He told me you argued with Winifred about money."

"No," Peter burst out, in a tone that suggested he was telling the truth.

"But did you argue?"

"No," he said. This time more softly. She'd listened to that boy lying for most of his life. She could recognize all his different tones of voice; she knew this one.

"What did you argue about?"

"It was nothing, Dove."

"It must have been something." She remembered what Winifred had said, in her last conversation with her. *You don't see what he's become.*

"Trust me, Dove. It was nothing. Nothing that relates to this."

The air was silent between them. Trust him. Have faith in him. Have faith. Her minister had once told her that a Christian was someone who lived with hope. Was that what it was? Hope? Or fear? What if she pressed him too hard and found out it was all an illusion?

"I'm trying to help you, Peter. It would be easier if I knew all the facts."

Silence.

"You know," she said. "It would be nice if you had a little faith in me too."

But he clicked his phone shut, leaving her alone with her worries and her faith and her lack of it, and she paced around the house for a while, but it was impossible to sit still for wondering how the meeting with Char was going to go and what Peter had argued about and who could have killed Bender and Winifred and what was going to happen with Frank Bowman. When she'd paced around a sufficient number of times, she decided she had to get out of there. She'd walk up Main Street and down, which would kill some time, and maybe she'd stop in the stationery store and buy some cotton balls for a project about the parable of the lost sheep. Which she did, and then she stopped by the library and picked up her book club selection. She went to the hardware store and got picture hooks, waved at Iphigenia, waved at D'Amici, who was back at work with a large bandage over his eye.

Then she ran into Helen Blake and Edgar. She heard them first, before she saw them. "Don't bite that. How many times do I have to tell you? You'll get rabies."

Helen had the war-torn look of a woman who's spent the afternoon with a sociopath. Or a child. Maggie remembered how long Saturdays could seem, particularly if they started really early.

At the sight of her, Edgar flew over to hug her, which touched her. He was looking especially angelic, with his blonde hair starting to grow back. "I wanted to put my hand in the flame, but mommy wouldn't let me."

"She's a good mother," Maggie said.

"You're the only person in town he likes," Helen said. She looked so tired. Maggie couldn't help but think of Juliet, and what she would have been like at this age, and how she might have helped her.

"Listen," Maggie said. "If some day you want to drop him off for a bit, I'd be happy to watch him."

Helen gripped her wrist. "Really?"

"For a while," Maggie said, stepping backward, both physically and metaphorically.

"I should warn you that my babysitter just quit because he closed the garage door on her head."

"For an hour anyway," Maggie said.

"God bless you, Ms. Dove," Helen said, and then flew on after Edgar, who was hurling himself down the street, in pursuit of Mr. Cavanaugh's little dog.

After that, Maggie stopped at the bank to take out some money, and she was about to head home when she noticed a bit of a commotion on Main Street. Walking toward it, she saw it was the Arbor Day celebration, which consisted of the mayor, Walter Campbell and three women from the garden club holding shovels.

She loved Arbor Day. It was one of her favorite holidays. She loved the whole idea of it. Planting new trees and celebrating trees and reading proclamations, which the mayor did with a nice air of gravity. When did you ever hear proclamations anymore? "Whereso the village of Darby-on-Hudson" he started, and launched off onto a history of Arbor Day, which made her cry, for some odd reason, thinking of a million trees planted in Nebraska, thinking of Bender, thinking of life and history, which she supposed was the purpose of a tree, in so far as a tree had a purpose, thinking…

"I read that Lance Armstrong paid $200,000 to move a tree on his property." It was Agnes, of course. Who else but Agnes would be thinking of uprooting trees on Arbor Day? "There's a man with access to drugs too. Too bad he doesn't live in this village or you'd have the perfect suspect."

Maggie laughed. She couldn't help herself, though it seemed to her that strange times were coming when Agnes started to strike her funny. A Boy Scout ran up and asked if she'd like a tattoo.

"Sure," she said and held out her wrist.

"It's temporary," he said, as he pressed the etching of a tree onto her. When finished he looked up at Agnes, seemed about ready to ask her if she wanted a tattoo, and then ran off. Agnes watched him thoughtfully.

"Just so you know," Agnes said. "I don't think Peter did it either."

"Really?" Maggie said.

"He's too much of an idiot," Agnes said.

Maggie figured you had to take encouragement wherever you could get it. The fact was, encouragement was in short supply lately. She looked into Agnes's googly eyes, staring at her, always, so appraisingly.

"Well, thank you Agnes," she said, feeling surprisingly optimistic.

Chapter Twenty-Six

Frank Bowman sped down the West Side Highway, which was Maggie's favorite road in the world. She loved all its twists and turns, the steel lace of the George Washington Bridge, that weird bump in the road around 76th street that made you go flying into the air, the boat basin with its sailboats, the docks where the cruise ships pulled up. Today one of the big Carnival ships had pulled in, and she gaped at the floating city. Then they kept going, down past the congestion of midtown. Further and further, until they were downtown, in the village, on one of those pretty cobblestone streets that the tourists never go to because they're so preoccupied with seeing the insanity of Times Square.

He pulled up in front of a pretty brownstone with window boxes filled with geraniums and a vivid stained-glass window on the top floor. "Somebody has money," he said.

"I'm surprised. I thought she was down on her luck."

"So," he said, "give me my marching orders. What do I do?"

"I don't know," Maggie said. "I'm not sure what I'm going to do. I just have to figure out if it's true that she uses Ecstasy."

"And if she had a reason to kill her husband," Frank said, eyes twinkling. He was a very enthusiastic assistant sleuth.

Maggie smiled at him. Hard not to. He looked natty. He wore a tweed sports coat and had a scarf tied around his neck. She suspected he had ransacked his entire closet looking for an outfit appropriate for sleuthing.

The inside of the building was less impressive than the outside. Turned out they had to walk up four flights of stairs, and she couldn't help chuckling as she listened to Frank wheezing behind her. When they got to the landing, she saw his hair had flattened out. He peered into the metal plate on the door, fluffing up his hair, until the door creaked open and Char Bender stood before them.

Bender's first wife looked fragile. She looked like a bomb had gone off alongside of her and that she'd been dealing with the reverberations for some time. She was thin, the knobs of her neck stuck out. She looked gray. Grieving for Bender? Maggie wondered. Hard to imagine she was mother to a six-year-old and a nine-year-old.

Both girls popped out, but she shushed them away, back into their rooms. Maggie noticed that although the building was luxurious, the apartment itself was shabby. A cat lay on a puzzle in the middle of the kitchen table. There were unwashed dishes in the sink and a crack in the ceiling. A steam whistle started to blow and Char went to turn it off. The television was on. A cartoon was playing.

"This is Frank Bowman," Maggie said. "He's helping me with my research."

"And what sort of research was that? I'm not sure I understand what you want to know. You said that your friend was murdered by the same person who murdered Bender."

"Yes. My friend Winifred Bell." Her voice caught when she said her name. "The autopsy results showed that she was poisoned with a dose of Ecstasy similar to the type that was used to poison Bender. I thought perhaps you would know how they were connected."

She shrugged. "I don't know. Bender didn't tell me about his life."

Maggie looked over at Frank, who smiled at her helpfully. She wished she could sit down, but Char clearly didn't want her to. There was nothing to do but blurt it out. This was why she was here. She could ask.

"It seems strange to me that Ecstasy would be the poison used. It's not the first thing that comes to mind when you think of poisoning someone. I understand you sometimes use Ecstasy, and I wondered if you had any thoughts. If, maybe, you knew Winifred somehow?" She held out a picture of her friend, though Char just glanced at it. Then she seemed to realize what Maggie was asking.

"That bitch," Char said. "Did Noelle tell you I used Ecstasy?"

"Honestly, I don't care what you do," Maggie said. "I'm just trying to figure out if someone maybe was trying to implicate you by using that drug."

Char stared firmly into her eyes and Maggie forced herself to remember something she often thought before walking into a Sunday School classroom. *Never show fear no matter what they do.*

"Parkinson's causes a depletion in the brain's serotonin. Ecstasy seems to modulate that change. There are people who've used it and who've found dramatic cures, even if not permanent ones. I was hoping that if I used it before my concerts, it would help me control my tremors. But it didn't work. All it did was cause depression and hallucinations, and so I stopped using it. So you can tell that wife of his that I am not the one who poisoned Marcus."

Maggie cleared her throat and looked over to Frank, not certain what to say or do next, but Frank jumped into the fray.

"This must be your harp," he said, pointing toward a large object in the middle of the living room, covered with a red cloth. Maggie had glanced at it briefly and thought it was a sculpture.

"Yes," Char said, walking over to it and pulling off the sheet. There stood before them a beautiful golden harp. Maggie had never seen one up close.

"This is my life," Char said, strumming her fingers across the string, creating in that one movement a beautiful sound. "This is my joy."

"You're a professional," Frank asked. He had a way of directing his attention at a person as though every ounce of his personality was directed at them. It was fascinating to watch.

"Yes," Char said. "I was, anyway. When my hands worked. Now I'm nothing."

"You're a mother," Maggie felt obliged to point out.

She shrugged. "There are a lot of mothers out there. Not many harpists."

"Still," Maggie said. "It must be a comfort to have them here."

Char began to laugh at that. The sort of laugh that sounded like a machine gun, forced and harsh. "You think?" she said, and she fell, laughing, onto a chair which wobbled under her weight. The apartment smelled of pasta and tomato sauce, Maggie thought, and she noticed cans of Chef Boyardee in the corner.

"A comfort? I didn't want them here."

"Ssh," Maggie said, picturing the girls in the room next door. Two little girls who she'd lived next to for two years and hardly knew, but still.

"Believe me, they know I don't want them here. I never said I did. I never wanted children. Told Marcus that right from the start. My career, my music, was my priority, but he wanted to be a father so badly. He told me he'd take care of them and he did. He was a great father. He loved them."

She seemed so sincere. Maggie believed her, and felt for her. She'd loved being a mother, but never believed it was a calling for all women. She thought of Helen. She thought how horrible it would be to feel stuck with children and truly not want them. She thought how remarkable it was that Bender had this hidden goodness. She should have known that. She did know that. That's why it had tortured her so much that she hated him.

"I can't keep them. I told them that."

Maggie thought she could hear one of them whimpering. She felt like her heart was going to break.

"I found a boarding school. They'll be well-taken care of. He left money for them."

"You didn't want to leave them with Noelle?"

"I would have, sure, but Marcus put a codicil in his will saying she was not to get custody of them. He was insistent about that. Had been from the moment he met her. He loved her. Well, he desired her. But he didn't want her involved in raising the kids. That's why he was so insistent that she not get pregnant."

"What do you mean?" Maggie asked, thinking of Noelle with her hand over her stomach, thinking how confident she was that Noelle was pregnant.

"When Bender got an idea into his head there was no persuading him otherwise."

Tell me about it, Maggie thought, thinking of her innocent little oak tree.

"He had her sign a pre-nup. She had to agree not to become pregnant."

"People don't always have control over things like that," Maggie observed.

"Of course they do. Haven't you heard of birth control?"

"Even birth control is not always 100 percent. Mistakes happen."

She laughed. "Not with Marcus they don't. "

"Well," Maggie said. "Not to be disrespectful, but he must have felt he made a mistake with your marriage. If you got divorced."

Char drew her eyebrows together. She looked like one of those Roman goddesses about to spew fire from her mouth. Maggie couldn't help herself. She inched over toward Frank, hoping for protection.

"You think he divorced me because he didn't love me?"

"That's usually why it's done."

"I'm the one who wanted a divorce," Char said. "I wanted to protect our love. We had something really special, something magical. I didn't want him to watch it decay, to see my body disfigured. I didn't want him remembering me this way. I wish I could have just disappeared, but I couldn't, so I set him up with Noelle. Who do you think arranged that party when she jumped out of the cake? I knew he'd like her. She was exactly his type."

Maggie felt like such a prude, such a Sunday School teacher. She didn't understand this at all. She thought the whole point of marriage was to stay with someone for better or worse. She felt so sad for this woman, who would leave behind someone she loved because she worried so much about her looks. She also felt frightened by her ruthlessness, and by Bender's.

"What would he do if Noelle became pregnant?"

"She wouldn't."

"Say she did," Maggie said. "Say she was so darn fertile she'd managed to get pregnant. What would he do?"

"She'd have to end the pregnancy. That's what the contract said. She had promise to have an abortion if she got pregnant."

"And if she didn't?"

"Then she'd lose everything," Char said.

"But that's monstrous."

"She's a grown woman. She knew what she was agreeing to when she married him. You make your choices, don't you?"

Now that, Maggie thought, was a reason to murder. If Noelle found out she was pregnant and didn't want to give up the baby, she might have felt forced to kill Marcus. She didn't know why she would want to kill Winifred, but at least this was a motive that was as least as good as Peter's. Better, even. This was something new, something undiscovered.

"We found out something Walter Campbell doesn't know," she said to Frank, when they got back to his car. "I'd feel triumphant, if I didn't feel clinically depressed."

"She was tough," Frank agreed. He roared out of the parking spot, as eager as Maggie to get out of there, she imagined.

"What a family. She's looking to get rid of her kids while they're still mourning their father. He's trying to take control of Noelle's body. It's sort of discouraging that the only person behaving well is a stripper."

He laughed at that, flicked the shift. He had nice hands, she thought. A musician's hands, with long fingers.

"Now, how about we get some food to eat?" Frank said. "I'm famished."

"I don't think I should. I have to prepare a Sunday School lesson for tomorrow and I haven't done a blessed thing."

"Maggie Dove," he said, stepping on the engine. "Forgive me, but you're forcing me to kidnap you. I will take you out to dinner if it's the last thing I do."

"Oh well," she said, figuring that after 30 years of teaching Sunday School, it would probably be all right to slack off for one class. She did have that vegetable movie.

"I surrender."

Chapter Twenty-Seven

They wound up at the Metropolitan Museum of Art. Maggie hadn't been there in years, not since she was a fourth-grade class mother and Juliet's class was learning about tapestries. She loved it, kept meaning to go back. Time went by so fast.

"Have you ever been to the private dining room?" Frank Bowman asked.

"I didn't know there was a private dining room."

"Ah." He guided her through the entry way, past giant bouquets of dogwood branches and lilacs, past lines of tourists and then through the Medieval section, past all those solemn Madonnas, clutching so fiercely to their babies, and then into the sunshine of modern sculpture, and then into the private elevator, Frank showing his pass, up to the fourth floor. The door opened to the sort of hush Maggie had only experienced before in a church. A friendly gentleman came and sat them in a table in the corner, next to a huge glass window that looked out onto Central Park.

"I feel like Marie Antoinette," Maggie said.

Frank laughed at that. A man who appreciated her humor. A good sign.

"We'll have the prix-fixe dinner," he said to the waiter, which wound up being four separate courses all relating to the paintings of Goya. Each serving coming with its own wine pairing, each plate more wonderful than the next, a tomato crostata followed by squid.

"A day boat squid a la plancha," the waiter intoned, "with arros negre, saffron aioli and espelette pepper."

"Squid," she said. "I've never had it."

It was like a painting, the squid on its side with a dollop of green sauce.

"You'll try it?" he asked.

"Of course."

Wonderful, and Maggie, giddy with her triumph with Char, with having found out information about Noelle, with the excitement of this beautiful place, found herself talking much more than she ever did. She was so excited to have uncovered something Campbell hadn't. "I just can't wait to see what he says. I mean I know he'll dismiss it. He thinks I'm just an amateur, which is funny when you think about it because he's just an amateur.

"I would just love, just once, to see a look of uncertainty on that man's face. A moment of hesitation and doubt. He's just so sure all the time. So smug."

The waiter poured more wine. "A bodegas terra Sigillata Filon Real garnacha," he said. "2011."

"So how did you come up with Inspector Benet?" Frank asked. He leaned against his chair as relaxed and attentive as a talk show host. "Winifred made him sound like the perfect man."

Maggie laughed, sipped some of her wine. It tasted like rubies, she thought. And the sun. And Spain.

"She was always on my case about that. She felt he was too bland, he should have a flaw. Be an alcoholic or missing a leg or suffer from abuse as a child. She wanted him haunted, but I wanted him to be serene. He was my fantasy, after all."

"Your fantasy was to have a perfect man."

She blushed. "Not perfect in the sense of boring, or rigid. But I wanted him to be a sort of romantic hero. I suppose I pictured him as one of those Regency sorts with the thick thighs and riding crops." She moved away her wine, resolving not to have any more until the next course.

"You loved him?" His eyes smiled as he spoke, she felt like she was being interviewed.

"I did love him, isn't that weird? There were times he seemed quite real to me. Times I could almost see him, like a ghost. Times I could almost feel him." She blushed again, thinking of one particular time, calling her husband Claude, their faces merging together.

"I took jujitsu lessons," she added, "to understand him better."

"Jujitsu!"

"Yes, and not just ordinary jujitsu. Brazilian jujitsu. "

"Are you good?" he asked.

"To tell you the truth, the most important thing I learned is that if you're under attack you should make as much noise as possible. Scream. It won't get rid of everybody, but it will get rid of the ones looking for easy prey. Of course," she added, "Inspector Benet did not scream. He lunged. He was master of the most esoteric moves."

She felt herself sparkling as she spoke, looked out and saw the city sparkling too. Beautiful city. With the candlelight flickering, she felt like she was in a movie. So often these last few years she'd felt dislocated, as though she'd wound up in the wrong life. She was a happy, strong woman who wound up starring in a tragedy. This, in this place with this man, was more what she'd intended.

"My husband used to say I should just give my Inspector a gun," she said, and started blushing again, though then the waiter came by with a new set of plates.

"A spring lamb," the waiter said, "with artichoke, white asparagus, fava beans and piquillo pepper."

"My goodness," she said, ready to tuck in.

And then another wine, this one an even deeper red.

"Was your husband jealous of Inspector Benet?" Frank asked.

"This is the Bodegas Mano a Mano," the waiter murmured, "from the Castilla La Mancha. It accents the spring lamb." She sipped it and though how wonderful it tasted.

His eyes were so gray, Maggie thought. Gray like the Hudson on stormy days. She felt like she could live in those eyes. She felt like no one had ever looked at her quite as intently as he had and she felt the strangest feeling, something she hadn't felt in a long time, something unfolding inside her that might have been happiness or might have been desire.

"No," she said. "My husband never suffered from jealousy. He had a very strong ego. I suspect when you've been a professor for as long as he had, when you're used to so much adulation, you develop a fairly strong sense of yourself."

"He sounds intimidating."

"No, he was very warm. He had a lot of friends, from all over the world, and they'd show up at our house when you'd least expect it. Three in the morning and the doorbell would ring and there would be some Russian poet with a chapbook, and then we would all sit in the kitchen and I'd make borscht. The one thing I learned how to do." She took a deep sip of her wine. "He was a professor of Russian poetry."

"You loved him."

"Yes," she said, "I did love him, but he's been gone for a long time."

Twenty-one years, she thought. Twenty-one years since he went to Russia to do research, or the Soviet Union, as it was then. The heart attack, the call, Maggie frantically getting over there, Juliet by her side, unable to find his body because they cremated him, and only a year later Juliet gone. Maggie's first thought gratitude that Stuart had not lived to see that.

She looked into Frank's eyes, which seemed to burn with an intense emotion. He was so handsome, she thought. His hair so thick, his gray eyes so arresting, his nose that sort of sharp, straight nose that always made her think of princes and kings.

"Dessert?" the waiter said.

"Please."

"A torta des tres leches," the waiter said. "With a salted marcona almond brittle and a Valencia Orange confit, accompanied by some Jerez sherry."

She gulped the sherry right down.

Tell me about you," she said, flustered and slightly dizzy and somewhat happy. "Why are you living in an old age home?"

He laughed at that. "It's not an old age home. It's assisted living."

"Even so. You seem like you could be on your own."

He shrugged, a Gallic gesture, so much like Inspector Benet. "I don't want to have to go to any trouble. I like having all my things looked after. Don't need to cook, don't need to do the laundry. I'm just lazy."

"But don't you find it a little depressing?"

He paused for a moment. She liked the way he always seemed to think about his answers. He took what she said seriously.

"I want to be able to enjoy my life," he said. "I want to do what I want to do, without worrying about details. To take a beautiful woman to dinner and not have to worry about mowing the lawn."

She laughed at that because in truth, nothing was harder to imagine than Frank Bowman mowing a lawn.

By the time they left, the restaurant was empty. They'd talked for hours, and she leaned on his arm as they walked out the door, slightly unsteady. When she sat down in the front seat, she closed her eyes and didn't wake up until Frank was pulling into her driveway. He walked her to her door, and she stood there, on her veranda, for just a moment, enveloped by his presence, the sweet smell of him, the solid weight of him, so much more solid than he appeared. Up close he was larger than he seemed.

"Good night, Maggie Dove," he said, as he leaned forward and gently kissed her on the lips, and she found herself kissing him back, harder, though he pulled away. "This has been an enchanting evening."

"It has been," she said, as she floated back into her home. "It has been."

Chapter Twenty-Eight

The next morning was a bad one. Some were like that. Sometimes the better the time the night before, the worse the morning. Payment. Maggie woke up, clawing for air. She felt Juliet close to her, as though she'd been with her in her sleep. She couldn't remember her dream, but she felt like she'd been falling. The sensation stayed with her, a feeling of panic, terror. She grabbed onto her bed. She cried out her daughter's name. "Oh, Juliet."

Maggie closed her eyes, tried to pull herself together. She thought of the 77th psalm, which had been such a comfort to her in the terrible days after her daughter's death. "In the day of my trouble I sought the Lord." She had to get out of bed. It was Sunday morning. She had to teach. That was a blessing.

She'd learned the only way to feel better was to be out, to be with people, and church helped. Being in that beautiful building, surrounded by kind people and bolstered by the presence of something larger than herself, that helped. If she could but get there.

But not yet. She had time. She put on the radio and there was Mahler. Ninth Symphony. The answer to a prayer. Thank God for Mahler. Did anyone understand grief the way Mahler did? She lay back on her bed and let the music soothe her, Mahler's great farewell to the world, written after he lost his own daughter. The music wept for her. She closed her eyes and let Mahler carry her along, the wail of the trombones, the French horns, the ominous pounding of the bass drums. The harp, which made her think of Char Bender. She waited for her favorite part, which came in the last movement, when it seemed like Mahler let everything in the world pour through him. When it was over, she closed her eyes and slept for a while and when she woke up she felt better, though tender.

She took a shower and made her way to the kitchen and sat down in her small sunny room, and had some tea and toast and looked out at her oak tree. Pretty little tree, and then she took out her Bible, and turned, as she always did, to the front of it, where the family tree was. There were her grandparents' names, written in their patchy old ink, there her parents' names and then her own name. Margaret Rose Leigh, born October 4, 1959 and next to her, her husband's name, Stuart Dove and then Juliet's name, born September 1, 1984. Died on May 18, 2001. She'd planned to give the Bible to Peter when she died. She'd sketched his name in, one desperate night, when she thought she couldn't bear to see the end of the line, and she thought that love was as strong as genetics.

She thought about all that had transpired. He had got in trouble for working at a party at which teenagers were drinking and Bender found out and wanted him fired. He'd had some sort of argument with Winifred about something, maybe money or something else. He'd rushed to help Maggie when she found Bender, dead, and in the process, he hadn't been as careful as he should have been. Had Walter Campbell not stepped in with his expensive test, no one would ever have known Bender was murdered. And then Winifred was murdered. All the facts swam in front of her. So much anger. She would tell Walter today about what she'd found out about Noelle's pregnancy clause. That was important. A true reason for murdering Bender.

But what she was missing was a link with Winifred.

That was what kept tripping her up. She could think of a million perfectly good reasons for killing Bender, but she couldn't think of any for killing Winifred, and certainly none that linked them. They knew each other through a real estate transaction, but there was no hint of trouble surrounding that. Winifred and Bender's first wife had Parkinson's. She sensed that must be important, but wasn't sure how. She wished she was smarter. She wished she could see what seemed to hover right outside her view, but she was a plodder. She needed to keep looking for links.

Maggie felt sure that someone in the village knew the answer to the questions she had. She just needed to find that person, which brought her back to church. She needed to get dressed, get ready.

She took a shower and put on her dress. Somehow it never seemed right to wear anything casual to church, though people did. She put on some make-up because her face was so pale. A beautiful woman, Frank Bowman had called her. All right, she was flattered. She looked into her eyes, rubbed some cream onto the wrinkles that sprung up after a late night. She put on her pearl earrings, and started to go toward the door when her phone rang.

"I wanted to see how you were." Frank's voice soft and smiling. She imagined his harem trying to ensnare him.

"A little hung over, but otherwise all right."

She could hear him smile. "Oh dear, I hope I haven't compromised a Sunday School teacher."

"Not yet," she said, which didn't come out quite like she was hoping. "But that reminds me, I'm supposed to invite you to our Dining Out Club. It meets on Friday night, if you'd like to come."

"What on earth is a Dining Out Club?"

Maggie laughed. "A bunch of us from church get together once a month and go to a local restaurant, usually one that's in financial difficulty, and then we all eat there, except the problem is that the food's not always so good. Hence the financial difficulty."

"I don't see how I could miss it."

"You would be most welcome I assure you. At the moment it consists of Agnes Jorgenson, who is a piece of work, and the Faraday sisters. There are three of them. One can't hear and one can't see and the other one collects coupons. She's the organizer of the club, you might say. Then there's Helen Blake, our newest member, with the little hellion of a child. Peter Nelson goes, and so does our minister. She's very nice, ethereal. And then there are assorted special guests. That would be you."

"That would be me," he said.

"We're meeting at a Thai restaurant this time. At 6:30."

"Would you like me to drive you there?" he asked.

"That would be fabulous," she said, and felt ridiculously cheerful, which was a good thing because she needed to get ready for Sunday School. She only had ten minutes to prepare, as opposed to her usual two hours, but she prayed that attendance would be low, as it usually was in April, because all the kids went to soccer practice, and she had actually settled on the vegetable movie, because why not? There was always something to learn, and she was curious to see what vegetable would represent Judas and she was humming when she went into the classroom and saw her faithful three students and Walter Campbell. Walter Campbell, wearing a kilt and standing next to a girl who could only be his daughter, and Maggie knew, at that moment, that she was in a great deal of trouble.

Chapter Twenty-Nine

Walter Campbell in a kilt. Dear God. It was as though Frankenstein were Scottish. Maggie could hear her best friend cackling in her ear. *Be quiet, Winifred*, she muttered, hoping she hadn't said it out loud. But Walter Campbell, for the first time in her acquaintance with him, did not seem to be mad at her.

"This is my daughter," he said, gesturing toward that tree-like girl with such reverence and adoration that Maggie actually felt pinpricks of affection for the man, at least until he looked at her and spoke: "I hope you've planned something good for today," he said. "She's 10-years-old, so she's a little old for your class, but I told Jane you were the best."

She felt flattered and oddly annoyed. Now she couldn't show the vegetable movie. Any other Sunday he could have come and she would have something well-planned. But today, for the first time in her career as a Sunday School teacher, she didn't have anything planned and her head hurt from her night out with Frank Bowman and she still felt a lingering sense of doom from her restless sleep that night.

Any other Sunday, she thought. Any other Sunday.

Still, Maggie recognized she had to do something impressive. Something remarkable, something that would blow Walter Campbell's socks off, a horrifying image if ever there was one. She would have to do something that would engage his daughter, and impress him, and so she decided to go to her default best project. She would bake pretzels.

It was project that had a teeny bit of religious significance, but it came with a wonderful story, and Maggie did love stories. Sometimes she thought she loved Jesus so much because he was always telling stories.

"Back in medieval times," she explained to the children, after Campbell had left and she was alone with the four of them, "people used to give up meat and fish for Lent. That meant they would eat a lot of bread, and it probably meant they were sort of hungry. One day a monk noticed some leftover pieces of dough in the kitchen and he decided to do something special with them.

"He took them and molded them into the shape of crossed arms, because that's how the people prayed then." She crossed her arms, to illustrate. Dear Edgar also crossed his arms and bowed. Shu Chin giggled at him. Ambrosia looked around wildly, as though a kidnapper was about to make his way through the door and Jane nodded. Her father's child, she thought. No smiles, just nods. She wondered what dinner at the family table was like.

"These little pieces of dough were so popular, people began giving them to children as treats when they learned their lessons, and they began to call them 'pretiola,' which means little reward in Latin."

Then she lined up the children, all four of them, and they marched from the classroom into the kitchen. Maggie buzzed with excitement but tried to contain herself because the last thing she wanted was to get Edgar worked up. He was being so good. Poor Ambrosia just kept asking where her mother was.

"She's in church, dear," Maggie whispered, holding the little girl's hand.

Jane looked all about her, not speaking much, but observing. Her father's daughter, and then they were in the kitchen and Maggie was pulling out the trays and finding the flour and other ingredients. She didn't have a recipe with ingredients in front of her, but she felt fairly sure she remembered what was required. Sea salt, which she found in one of the upper cabinets, undoubtedly left over from the last time she'd done it. Sea salt didn't go bad, surely. No yeast. Well, they would have to make do without, though that was going to be tricky. They would be flat pretzels. Flour. Then an egg. There were some in the refrigerator, marked "Do not touch! These belong to Agnes Jorgenson." Well. Tough tootsies, Maggie thought as she swiped one. Desperate times call for desperate measures.

Everything seemed to go well. Edgar did not spill flour all over the floor. They did not shun Jane. In fact, they were quite nice to her and included her in their mixing and it turned out that Jane had quite a knack for doing a Scottish imitation. Either that or she was Scottish. Hard to tell because she didn't speak that much, but they were all enjoying themselves and then they put the pretzels in the oven and waited for them to cook, and she sent the children to the sink to clean everything up, and as they were all washing and scrubbing, she found her attention wandering back to the connections between Winifred and Bender.

She wondered if Doc Steinberg knew Bender. She must. Even if Bender didn't go to her, she would certainly know him, or his children. She hadn't said anything about it, but then Maggie hadn't asked. Was it possible that Doc Steinberg was the murderer?

She was an upright woman. Unflinchingly honest. But one thing Maggie remembered from her research on poisoners was that many of them were doctors. She remembered reading a textbook for police officers that said, when investigating a poisoning, pay special attention to the person who prepares the victim's food and to doctors. Encyclopedias of poisoners were full of doctors. Look at Robert Clements, who poisoned four wives and only happened to be discovered when a coroner noticed the tiny pupils of the last one, making him think that morphine was involved. Or Michael Swango, who poisoned 60 or so people with arsenic, many of them his patients. He had no particular reason for wanting to kill them; he just took joy in their deaths. He was evil. Was it possible to imagine someone as upright as Doc Steinberg doing something like that? It was impossible to say. How could Maggie possibly look at someone she'd known her whole life and say they were a murderer? Easy enough to do in a book, but in real life, what sort of person took another's life?

That was when Maggie felt someone tugging at her arm. Looking down she saw all four children smiling at her, pointing toward the glass window of the oven, at the pretzels, which looked absolutely beautiful. She took them out and set them each on a little paper plate and then they sat around the table, said a prayer and began to eat them and they were doing that when Walter Campbell reappeared. The service was over.

Jane ran at him and showed him the pretzel. "I saved you some, Daddy. This is for you."

He placed a small piece into his mouth, chewing it so slowly Maggie wondered if he thought she was the poisoner.

"So," he said. "What did you learn today?"

"We learned how to make pretzels," Jane said.

"But what about scripture? What scripture did you learn?"

Jane looked at Maggie, who looked at Walter, in his kilt. Why did he always make her so off balance, she thought. What was it about that man that made her act like a foolish child? Her temper began to get hold of her. She could hear her mother. *Margaret, that temper of yours is going to get you in trouble.* But she couldn't help herself and she stood in front of him. "There was no scripture today, but we learned about friendship and community and nourishment. That's a good day's lesson, I think."

He shrugged. "I was hoping she would learn the essentials of her faith."

"There's plenty of time for that. But sometimes it's good to think about Sunday School as a fun place to go. However," she couldn't resist adding, "if you don't like the way I teach class, you're more than welcome to sign up and take over for me."

For just a moment she thought he smiled, which startled her. Then he looked at her closely, doing his wretched Sherlock Holmes imitation. She suspected she had a mark on her sleeve which would tell him she'd been out with Frank Bowman last night, or perhaps he could tell from the circles under her eyes, though what business of it was his if she should go to a museum with Frank Bowman, or if she should talk to Char Bender.

Char Bender.

"Actually, I need to talk to you about something," Maggie said. "Could I have a minute?"

"Not now," he said, looking at Jane, poor girl standing rooted to the spot, not wanting to give offense.

"Edgar will take her up to coffee hour, won't he? We'll meet you there in a minute," Maggie said.

The children waited while Walter thought and then he nodded his head imperceptibly and they all tore off. Leaving Maggie alone with him, in the kitchen. She went over to the table and sat, to even up their height a little bit. She could not have an argument with a man's knees and she suspected an argument was coming. He maneuvered himself onto the chair and sat down across from her.

"I spoke to Char Bender yesterday."

He looked like steam would come out of his ears. "I told you…"

She cut him off. "Last time I looked you were not my father. I found out some information. Would you like to hear it?"

He crossed his arms. She could almost see him counting to ten. He still wore a wedding ring, she noticed. Boy, she would love to hear the details of that breakup. She wondered what his wife was like, she wondered what would propel a man as pompous as this one to abandon his family.

"This relates to the murders. Do you seriously not want to hear it just because I found it out and you didn't?"

"What did you find out, Ms. Dove?"

She told him about Char then, and what Bender's wife had told her about the arrangement with Noelle, and how Noelle might well be pregnant. If Bender had lived, he would have forced her to give up the baby. "That's a pretty compelling reason for murder, I would say."

"And what about Mrs. Bell?" he asked.

"I don't know why Noelle would have wanted to kill her, but that doesn't mean there isn't a reason. I just haven't found it yet. There's also the consideration that she did prepare Bender's food. Who would be in a better position to kill him?"

"You've done a lot of research on the psychology of poisoners, have you?"

"I've read a book or two."

"And written one or two."

"Yes, it's not a crime," she said.

"So you fancy yourself Jessica Fletcher, do you?"

"I fancy myself a woman who does not want to see someone railroaded because the chief of police is so obsessed with one suspect that he will not consider any others."

Walter Campbell snapped one of the pretzels in half. The damn noon whistle blew, startling Maggie.

"All right. I've listened to you. Now I'd like you to listen to me. I want to propose an alternative scenario. Do you think it's possible that Ms. Bell took her own life?"

"Winifred?" she said. "No."

Winifred a suicide? Maggie thought. Easier to see her as a killer.

"Is it so impossible to believe?" Walter said. "She had found out that her disease was getting worse. Perhaps she couldn't bear to suffer any more."

He gazed at her with a surgeon's implacable look. Was she getting worse? Maggie wondered. She didn't really know and Winifred never complained about it. She prided herself on her toughness, or maybe, Maggie thought, Winifred didn't tell her about her fears because she didn't think Maggie wanted to know. Was that possible?

"What are you suggesting?" Maggie asked.

"She knew that Marcus Bender died of an overdose of Ecstasy. Maybe that showed her a way out. She couldn't get her hands on a lot of other drugs, but she could get hold of Ecstasy."

Immediately Maggie saw the connection he was making. "So now you've got Peter giving her poison?"

"He might not have known what she was going to do with it. Maybe she told him it would help her with her Parkinson's. Like Char Bender. Maybe he thought he was helping her. He could have a perfectly innocent reason for giving her the Ecstasy."

From the kitchen window, Maggie could see the Memorial Garden. The young Sunday School students were clambering all over it, jumping on the graves. Soon someone would come and pull them off, complain.

"Next you'll be telling me Peter supplies Char Bender. Look, I'm not holding Peter up as a paragon of virtue, but I do think he'd draw the line at handing over Ecstasy to a sick person."

"Do you?" Walter said.

She stopped. Did she? The truth was she could see the whole thing with agonizing clarity. Winifred wheedling, Peter trying to say no, the two of them vowing to keep the information from her as though she were a school marm, or a Sunday School teacher.

"He has gotten in trouble in the past for selling Ecstasy."

"When he was 16, and his records were sealed." Foolishness, foolishness, Peter swept up with a bad crowd, getting into trouble. Oh her husband was so mad about that, wanted her to insist Juliet not hang out with him anymore, but Maggie insisted. She knew he was good. He needed help, not condemnation, and she still believed that. She looked in his eyes and saw goodness, and she knew she wasn't irrational. He had been her lifeline for these past twenty years. She loved him.

Campbell grimaced. There was something monumental about the man that made her want to pound on him and scream. He was too big, too implacable. He had a way of sucking the life out of everything. The kitchen which had, only half an earlier, been a place of joy and happiness was now as cold as a morgue.

"So then, what are you saying? Are you writing this whole thing off? You're saying that Winifred Bell killed herself and that Peter got her the drugs, and so that's the end of the story? One tawdry little episode in the Darby-on-Hudson history and that's the end of it."

"I'm not giving up, Mrs. Dove, and I never said I was. I'm just trying to understand what happened."

"Why don't you try understanding this? My friend is dead. My courageous, irritating, wonderful friend Winifred is dead and I find it hard to believe that after fighting this disease for so many years, she would just give up. I believe someone killed her, and instead of looking at Peter, who seems to be front and center in your giant radar vision since the moment you arrived in this town, I would advise looking around at other people, because I can tell you that there seem to me to be several people in town with motives." How easy it would be for Doc Steinberg to get hold of Ecstasy, she thought. She didn't want the murderer to be Doc Steinberg, but if she had to choose.

"May I give you some advice, Mrs. Dove?" He cleared his throat. "We are up against a man who has taken two lives, and maybe more. He's ruthless. If you get in his way, he'll kill and there's nothing I can do to protect you. Please, let the professionals deal with it. You are inhibited by your affections."

"You mean because I love people, I can't see them clearly. Well perhaps you're right. Perhaps love does blind you. But the blind have a gift for seeing things that we sighted people can't see."

She turned around ready to stalk away and ran smack into Agnes Jorgenson, standing on the outskirts with a cheese platter. "Would you like some?" she asked. "You could do with a bit of protein. You're looking peaked."

"Oh, good Lord," Maggie muttered, and she walked out of the room, leaving them both behind. But Walter's words stung. She hoped they weren't true.

Chapter Thirty

Maggie found Peter in the midst of a marathon viewing of Law & Order. He was up to the end of season 4. Poor Ben Stone was having a terrible time getting a woman to testify against a Russian mobster. Maggie'd always liked Ben Stone. He looked so tortured. She could imagine him as one of the monks making pretzels.

"Want to watch?" Peter asked. "It's his last episode."

"Sure."

She sat down alongside him on the couch, jumping up when she felt something bite into her, which fortunately was just the tip of a Dorito. That would explain the cheesy smell in the room, which almost, but not quite, overpowered the smell of sweat. Peter looked like he hadn't showered in a while and he certainly hadn't cleaned. Maggie took off her sweater and sat down on it. The alternative was to clean his apartment, but she didn't feel like doing that. She noticed he'd put most of the pictures of Juliet away, though his favorite one remained in the middle of the table, the one that showed the two of them at the prom.

She wasn't a big TV watcher, but she'd loved watching shows with her daughter. They tried to watch the silliest ones possible, shows with people eating spiders and trying to survive on desert islands or trying to lose 300 pounds in two weeks. Stuart had never understood how she could waste her mind on such things when all of Shakespeare's sonnets were there to be pored over, but she thought it was fun. It was a form of communion.

"I did my pretzel thing today," she told Peter.

"How'd it go?"

"Surprisingly well. Nothing burned."

"Did you remember the eggs?"

"No, I stole them from Agnes."

"Ha!" he said.

There was a Russian mobster on TV and you could see by his piggy little eyes that he was evil. He could be a poisoner. There was that poor woman, who had been in some other TV show surely. She was so scared and Ben Stone was pressing her and you could see the poor thing was going to die. He offered her witness protection and she didn't want it and he was going to send her to jail and then he played on her guilt and she surrendered and took the stand and there was that beady-eyed man looking at her. Maggie looked into his eyes. Thought how afraid she'd be having those eyes looking at her. Thought of what Walter Campbell said. About someone evil being after her. In the presence of evil. She'd always wondered what she'd do if she were confronted by true evil. Would her faith give her strength or would it desert her? Would she be able to stand up to someone like that?

The jury found the mobster guilty, but it didn't end there. They did kill the girl, who was the tall one from West Wing, the one who was so scared, and Ben Stone repented and quit so that Sam Waterston could take his place.

They were both still after it was over.

"He shouldn't have pressed her so hard," Maggie said. "He knew she was going to get killed."

"This was an evil guy. He had to put him away."

"I hope I'm never asked to do something like that. Imagine if just out of innocence you wind up seeing something terrible. Would you speak up?"

"Yes." He shrugged. "You'd have to."

She believed him. Whatever his flaws, she'd never doubted his courage. He would always be the first one running into a burning building, running towards trouble.

The day was still. Sundays. Maggie always found them the hardest day of the week, even with church to look forward to. There was always a pause on Sundays, a moment where it was impossible not to reflect.

"Peter," she said. "What went on between you and Winifred?"

"Nothing," he said.

"I know you had an argument with her, Peter. I know it was more serious than usual. She told me herself that things were bad between you."

The sunlight made him look older. It wasn't fair that the people you loved got older. She wished she could stop him in time. But then her daughter had escaped aging and such foolishness by dying. She was forever a young woman laughing in a picture.

"Peter, I will love you no matter what on earth you did, but I need to know. Things are getting really intense and I can't help you if I don't know what was going on and everywhere I turn, it's always something to do with you. I wish you would just trust me and tell me."

He stared resolutely at the TV, which had moved onto season 5. A woman was brought to the hospital and the fumes from her were so bad that several of the nurses fell over. She'd been poisoned, they thought. Perhaps with radioactive material. She was dangerous. Maggie clicked off the TV.

"Peter, I love you. I know you didn't kill Winifred. I don't have a moment's hesitation. But something was going on and I have to know what it was."

He slumped down, put his hand on hers. Just so had they sat at the hospital together, side by side, waiting for the results, waiting to see if Juliet could live.

"She changed, Dove. Maybe you didn't see it, but Winifred changed."

"How do you mean?"

"She was really angry about living there, at the Castle, and it made her kind of crazy. She got bored and she wanted to have some fun."

"So what did she do?"

"It started with Hal Carter."

"Hal? What did Hal do?" Hal, the most romantic man in town. The man who took care of his mother for all those years and then married the beautiful young Gretchen.

"You know Gretchen's mother lives at the Castle."

"I didn't know that."

He nodded. "She's lived there for a long time. She lives in one of the nice units, on the river."

"Okay." Maggie began to get a bad feeling.

"One day, Winifred noticed Hal Carter leaving her room. Late at night. She became curious, began watching, one thing led to another."

"Hal Carter was visiting Gretchen's mother?"

"He was more than visiting her, Dove. Turns out he'd always loved her. They'd been having an affair all the years his mother was alive, but after she died, he got swept up with Gretchen, but he never stopped loving the mother. That's what it all turned out to be."

"That's awful." Hal Carter, she thought.

"So Winifred, you know Winifred, she had to say something to him. And then the next day, Hal came back with a bouquet of flowers and a bunch of steaks."

"Steaks?"

"You know how Winifred liked a good steak. After that, every few weeks or so he'd show up with some steak."

"Did she ask him for the steak?"

"No, but she sort of made it known that if she had the steak, she wouldn't talk. Then she realized that a nursing home was a place where there were a lot of secrets, particularly if she had Arthur to help her."

"Arthur was involved?"

"People talk when you're massaging them. They tell you things. She had a whole list of things going. Small things. She didn't ask for money, but she liked things."

Maggie thought of the new couch and the new rug. She'd never thought to ask how she'd paid for it.

"It became an obsession with her, Dove. She began looking into everybody. Not just people in the Castle, but people in the village too. She got something on Doc Steinberg, but Hannah wouldn't play along. Told her she could say whatever she wanted."

"And what about Marcus Bender?"

"She was crazy about him, desperate to find out something about him. Because of you, Dove. She wanted to bring him down. That's what we were arguing about. She wanted me to use the police computer to see if he had any history. You know how she could be if she thought someone had wounded you in any way. She wanted him to go to jail. I thought, Dove, when I first heard he was murdered, that she had killed him, to be perfectly honest. I thought maybe she'd had Arthur do it somehow."

Gentle Arthur. Winifred.

What shocked Maggie was how little shocked she was. So much made sense then. Winifred's glittering eyes. How she always seemed to know everything. She must have known about Bender's murder before Maggie even called her.

How had Maggie not known? Was everything between them a lie? Maggie remembered how happy she'd been when Winifred returned to Darby after having been away for a decade. She'd looked defeated and wary when she first returned, following her disastrous divorce from Jerry, but soon enough she rebounded. She got involved with Fred Melrose and everything went back to normal. She was who she had been. She was who Maggie wanted her to be.

Winifred a blackmailer. But that changed everything, didn't it? It broadened the field. Now there were so many possible suspects. Maggie felt like her head was spinning. She felt ashamed of Winifred. She felt pity for her too, poor Winifred who wound up alone in a nursing home, unloved after all those husbands, so desperate for attention, and she must have turned her attention to the wrong person. Someone who didn't trust that she'd be able to keep a secret. Someone with a secret so dangerous he couldn't risk being found out.

"I never did it, Dove. She asked me a bunch of times and I always said no. I knew you wouldn't approve."

"Forget about me, Peter. It was wrong. You knew that all on your own."

She felt sad for Winifred, sad for the people involved. She thought of her friend as she'd been as a young girl, so vibrant and wild, so willing to risk everything. Then she thought of herself, and how this whole horrible thing had begun with her anger at Marcus Bender. Maybe Noelle was right that she should have just let him move the tree. Or she should have tried harder to talk to him, anyway. She should have laughed with him.

"I'm sorry, Dove," Peter said.

"Me too."

"Are you going to tell Walter Campbell?"

"I have to Peter. Frankly, I think we all need to grow up a little bit about this. But first," she said, "first I think I'm going to go and talk to Arthur. Maybe he has a list of names. Maybe if we go through them, I can figure out how big a thing this is."

He sank back in his chair. Sam Waterston pounced onto the screen; the first episode in which he appeared, so different from the later, ponderous man he became. This earlier iteration of Sam Waterston was flirtatious, boyish, handsome.

"I should have died that night," Peter said. "Why did God save me and not her?"

There was only night, as far as Maggie and Peter were concerned. She knew exactly what he was talking about. Maggie didn't answer. She didn't answer because there was nothing to say. She didn't answer because who understood God's reasoning. She couldn't believe God had chosen for her daughter to die. Nowhere in her imagination could see God being so cruel. But she also didn't answer because she was tired of talking about it. For twenty years they'd been going over the same territory and for the first time she felt like she was drowning in a swamp.

"I can't talk about that now," she said, and she left. She had to get to the Castle and talk to Arthur.

Chapter Thirty-One

But Arthur wasn't there. Gentle, laughing Arthur had skipped town, or so the nurse said, taking some of the residents' jewels with him. He wasn't at the home address he had given. No one knew where he was.

"What a shock," the nurse said.

It was a shock.

Dispirited Maggie planned to turn back, but then she heard someone laughing and felt herself drawn toward it, as she'd known she would be the moment she got there. She followed the laughter toward an airy salon and there she found Frank Bowman in front of an easel, surrounded by his coterie of women, each of them in front of an easel. In front of them stood a man with a black beret, standing next to yet another easel, on which was pinned a postcard. A tranquil Hudson valley scene that they were all in the midst of reproducing.

"Why hello," Frank Bowman called out at the sight of her. Eight women glared and Maggie couldn't help but feel a bit of pride that this man was so obviously glad to see her, this handsome man with his cool gray eyes, now crinkling up into a smile. He had on a plastic smock, and under that a striped long-sleeved shirt and khakis. She imagined a pencil behind his ear, but then that was Inspector Benet she was thinking of, who had that particular affectation. So that whenever he had an idea, he could write it down. Benet didn't trust technology, though it would have been helpful for him with his crime solving. Also, he didn't have any scars. Winifred had wanted him to be missing a leg, but Maggie'd fought her off.

"I didn't expect to see you today," Frank said.

He took off his white smock and walked toward her.

"Should we wait, Frankie?" one of the women called out.

"Better not," he said. "Carry on without me."

He tucked his hand into Maggie's arm, and guided her toward the hallway. Behind her she could hear hissing, like so many balloons giving up air.

"But you look upset," he said to Maggie. "What's bothering you?"

Funny how quickly you can grow to care for someone, she thought. Funny how important it can be to have a pair of sympathetic eyes looking at you and to know that he would be willing to drop anything he was in the middle of to talk with you. She'd forgotten how special that feeling was. She had held herself away from the world for too long, Maggie thought. Winifred was right, in that one particular instance.

"Is there somewhere private we could talk?" she asked.

"Of course," he said. "This way."

She followed him past a nurse's station, into an elevator that took them downstairs, to her surprise. Somehow, she thought it would be up, but it turned out this wing was set closer to the river. The whole tone of the place changed. Here the Castle was like a regular apartment building, with amenities. People were reading newspapers and laughing. They kept walking, down a muted hallway, and then deeper and deeper into the building. They passed by a pool, a gym and a quiet couple playing chess and then around another corner and then they were in front of his apartment. She almost cried out when they went inside, it was so magnificent.

A huge window faced out onto the Hudson River. Maggie couldn't help but notice a willow tree slightly blocking his view and felt a sudden tenderness for Frank for not insisting that tree be cut down. The room itself was somewhat impersonal, like an upscale hotel, but there was a picture of an old lady in the corner. His mother, she assumed.

The kitchen was twice the size of her own, though he had as few things in it as she did. Not a cook, she thought.

"I'm just going to wash my hands," he said. "I'll be right back."

She sat down at the couch and noticed, on the coffee table, copies of all her books. Winifred would have given them to him, she felt sure. She felt both flattered and exposed. What had she written?

She hadn't been alone in a room with a man in a long time, if you didn't count Peter, which she didn't. She'd forgotten how different a man's room smelled, without the floral scents with which she was so familiar. Frank's room smelled of toothpaste and she remembered reading once how there was coal in toothpaste. That's how Colgate got its name, and she thought about her husband then, about the way his room had smelled, which was of old books. She'd been so sure of herself when she seduced him. She knew he desired her. She could remember how powerful she felt when she draped herself across that desk. "Oh my dear," he'd whispered, but then he'd surprised her with his strength.

She had no power now. No one had seen her naked in years, except for Doc Steinberg. She was 62 and yet people did marry at her age. She knew several. And there was Gretchen's mother, who had to be Maggie's age. Was that why she had come here, she wondered. At the back of her mind, was she hoping Frank Bowman would sweep her up in her arms and carry her away from all these troubles? Would that be so wrong? Maybe Walter Campbell was right. Maybe she shouldn't be involved.

"Now," Frank said, walking back into the room, sitting down at the chair across from her, so close their knees were almost touching. "Would you like some tea?"

"No thank you," she said. "I just really need to talk."

"Of course."

She told him everything. His eyes turned dark as she spoke, like storm clouds, especially when she got to the part about the blackmail.

"I know about that," he said.

"You do?"

He smiled slightly. "I'm afraid Winifred went after me too."

"Oh dear. I'm sorry."

"I'm afraid that I was not completely honest about my sources of income when I filed my report with the Castle. As Winifred discovered, some of my investments come from places that are not, shall we say, Triple A rated."

"You're a crook?"

"No, I'm an aggressive investor, I would say. Nothing illegal. But close. To answer the question you want to ask, I gave her free accounting advice. She was harmless, Maggie. She was just bored."

"Not everyone might have found her harmless. She might have come across someone who didn't want to pay up. That fact is, I can't make excuses for her. I don't know what possessed her to go around blackmailing people. Nothing makes sense. I can see why someone might have wanted to kill Winifred. I can see why someone wanted to kill Bender. But I can't see why anyone would want to kill both of them. There can't be two separate murderers running around."

She looked out the window, at the river, which had darkened. The waves looked like little sharks, swimming around in front of her.

"I feel so stupid," she said. "I feel like someone's laughing at me."

He held her hand then. "Maybe Walter Campbell's right. Why don't you go to him and tell him everything and let him take over?"

"Maybe I should," she said.

Why was she even fighting this battle, she wondered. She hated Bender, Winifred had brought destruction down on herself and Peter would be in trouble no matter what she did. Maybe she should just give up. Hand it all over to Walter Campbell and devote herself to Frank Bowman. She finally had a moment of peace in her life. Why not enjoy it, and yet, when Frank invited her out to dinner, she said no. She wasn't ready to surrender just yet. She couldn't give up, because there was someone out there killing people and she didn't trust Walter Campbell to stop him and the fact was, it was wrong. Even if the people deserved to die, it was wrong. It was evil.

She got back into her car.

"You sure you don't want dinner?"

"I'll see you Friday," she said. "At the Dining Out Club." She headed out, but was so distracted she wound up on the other side of the county, near Rye Playland. She parked her car and wandered around there for a bit, strolling across the beach and picking up shells. Being outside cleared her head, and after a few hours she got back in her car and drove home, where she found, on her front lawn, a body lying under her oak tree in the same exact position in which Bender had been.

Chapter Thirty-Two

Another body. Maggie looked around, prepared to make a U-turn and leave the street behind, possibly forever. This time there would be no Peter to run to her rescue, but Walter Campbell, who would loom over her and ask questions. Was this some terrible loop of time forcing her to go over her sins over and over again, she wondered. And then the body moved. Sat up. And shook out her hair.

"Oh," Noelle said. "You startled me."

Was it so wrong that Maggie didn't want any of the Bender family on her lawn? Was it so much to ask? It wasn't a big lawn, and neither was it such a big tree, which she noticed, now hung with two little angels sitting on toilets. Maggie felt herself surge with aggravation.

It was like living next to Communists. They had no sense of personal ownership. What would Noelle do, Maggie wondered, if she went over to her lawn and lay down? But the discouraging answer was she probably wouldn't care. Would hand her a blanket and say, Enjoy.

"May I sit with you?" Maggie asked.

Noelle shrugged and Maggie crouched down alongside of her. It was less than two weeks ago that she found the body and yet it seemed much longer. Even the oak tree seemed vastly different, now plumped up with the lushness of spring, two times its previous size. And yet, on this very spot Bender had lain, poisoned.

"This is a nice tree," Noelle said. "It provides so much shade."

The woman had no sense of irony, Maggie thought. It was almost admirable.

"Did you plant it?"

"No," Maggie said. "My father did."

Noelle nodded. "I thought it seemed old."

She sighed, stretched out. Like a cat.

"I feel closer to Bender here."

"I can understand that," Maggie said. "There's something about trees that's eternal. I suppose that's why I love them so much."

Noelle smiled. "You gave him a hard time. He admired that, you know."

"I had no idea."

She laughed softly. "I think he was a little afraid of you."

"I didn't want him to die," Maggie said. "I was angry at him, but I didn't want him to get hurt."

Noelle shrugged. Off in the distance Maggie thought she heard a dirt bike. A woodpecker was frantically hammering at a tree. The grass felt dry and prickly.

"Almost two weeks," Noelle said. "And no arrests yet. I went to see that Walter Campbell and he said they were close. Why haven't they arrested that policeman? I thought everyone was sure he did it."

"There are other suspects. The police have to be sure."

"He was selling Ecstasy."

"No he wasn't," Maggie said. "He was at a party, he was trying to protect the children there. He was foolish. Stupid. But he's not a killer."

"Char said you came to see her."

"Yes," Maggie said, sort of startled. She hadn't realized the two women had a phone-calling relationship, but she supposed it made sense. Clearly it had been an amicable divorce.

"How'd she look? Can she still move?"

"She's having a tough time," Maggie said. "She told me about that contract you had with Bender. She said it was impossible for you to have a baby with him."

Noelle didn't seem the least bit put out by the question.

"He would have changed his mind. Men always do."

She put her hand over her abdomen. She was beginning to show. How had Bender ever thought to keep this woman barren, Maggie thought. She was a monument to fertility. She was life, in all its selfishness, Maggie supposed. Survival of the fittest. Evolution. Her children would be tall and strong, assuming she fed them.

"But what if he didn't?" Maggie pressed. "What if he insisted you follow the terms of the contract?" Would she have gone ahead and had the baby, Maggie wondered. Would she be willing to give up Bender and all the things he provided her with?

"He loved me. He would have changed his mind." She looked at Maggie. "I knew him. I knew his fears, I knew what he wanted. He would have wanted this baby and he would have loved her."

"I knocked on your door the night he died. You didn't answer."

For the first time, a shade of something crossed Noelle's face, whether it was anger or guilt or fear Maggie wasn't sure. But she sensed she'd touched a nerve.

"I was in the attic, writing."

"You didn't hear me?"

Noelle stared at Maggie with her huge brown eyes. A butterfly fluttered near her stomach, but she waved it away. Maggie fought to understand. "Or you did hear me, but you didn't want to answer the door?"

Maggie looked down at her wedding ring, and remembered an argument she'd had with her husband on a similar topic. When he was so sure he wasn't equipped to be a father and she was so exasperated at time going by.

"You thought it was Bender knocking. Not me. And you didn't want to talk to him."

"He yelled at me. At me!" Noelle said. She puffed up her cheeks, blew out. "Who did he think he was talking to? Who did he think he was? How dare he tell me what I could do with my body!"

"And then he went out for a run?"

"The doctor told him he should run. It was good for his heart."

Maggie tried to piece it together. The two of them had a fight. Neither one of them would give in. Bender left the house to cool off.

"And you locked the door."

"Yes. And I didn't plan to open it until he changed his mind."

He would have felt sick. He would have tried to go back home. He would have pounded on the door, but Noelle wouldn't open it. So he ran over to Maggie's lawn. It would have been ridiculous if it wasn't so tragic. Bender died on her lawn because he and his wife couldn't agree on family planning.

Maggie looked around her, then across to the house that loomed next door. She considered the vastness of it, the four floors, the windows and balconies and looked further up. Toward the small window at the top that had stayed lit all these weeks. She could see perfectly into that window. So that's why he ran to the tree, she thought. Because he hoped to see his wife there. But she wasn't looking out the window, but down at her computer. So he died waving at a wife who paid no attention, with a neighbor who was looking out yet another window, waiting to throw a rock at him.

Was that justice? Maggie wondered. Was that what he deserved?

Chapter Thirty-Three

Finally, Maggie thought. Finally, she had an answer to one question. It wasn't much, but it was the first positive thing she'd managed to accomplish. Now she knew why Noelle hadn't answered the door. She knew why Bender ran to her tree.

She also knew why Winifred was murdered. In a general sense, anyway. Winifred must have discovered some information pertaining to Bender's murder and, being Winifred, she hadn't reported it to the police, but neither had she kept silent. She had confronted the murderer. That made much more sense to Maggie than Walter Campbell's suggestion that her friend killed herself. She could see Winifred doing something brave and foolish; she couldn't see her passively surrendering.

The question was, what did Winifred know? Why was she killed?

She needed to call Walter Campbell and tell him what she'd learned, but when she called the police station they told her he was off with his daughter. Of course, she'd forgotten it was Sunday afternoon. She left a message and then paced around her house for a bit, waiting for him to call back. After several hours went by, she figured Walter wasn't calling. He'd probably dismissed her as a busybody. Well, too bad for him. She decided to go to the park. She called Peter and left a message. Maybe he would meet her there.

There was enough light left in the park that the girls' softball teams were still out. It was early in the season, the girls unscarred by defeat, and she laughed as she watched them all chattering and laughing and occasionally hitting the ball. She smiled at some of the parents, who she recognized from Sunday School. One of the garbage men was there. His daughter was built like a linebacker and had a great arm and she suspected she'd get a scholarship down the road. Would she come back then, Maggie wondered, or would she move away?

So many of the children moved away. It was expensive to live in Darby. She wondered if Peter wanted to leave. He'd always said not, but now, in this park, she wondered if she had coerced him into staying here. She'd wanted him so badly. Had he felt trapped? Should she have freed him long ago to live his life? Instead, he was a grown man living like a teenager.

She needed to talk to him, but then she noticed her cellphone was out of batteries. She'd forgotten to charge it in all her running around. She stuck it back inside her bag. She knew she should go home, but she wasn't ready yet. She watched the girls play softball and she took out her notebook, began jotting thoughts into it the way she used to when she was writing mysteries. Who had a motive? Who had the most at stake?

She wrote for quite a while, so absorbed in her task that she didn't realize night had fallen. She was alone in the park. She looked at her watch. It was 9:00 on a Sunday night. Not that late, but the village was quiet. Restaurants closed. Bars closed.

She wasn't sure what made her feel afraid, but suddenly she sensed she wasn't alone. The Mario Cuomo new Tappan Zee Bridge bloomed right in front of her, the streets of her town were a scream away. Yet suddenly, as she sat there on her bench, she felt as though someone were watching. Maggie turned around. Nothing was there except for the playground, now deserted. She stared at it for a moment. There were so many places to hide in a playground. She remembered how her daughter once climbed into a tunnel and didn't come out. Maggie didn't know where she was and had been on the verge of calling the police when one of the children found Juliet.

"Hello," Maggie called out. "Anyone there?"

Something in the stillness reminded her of the night on her front lawn. A memory she must have repressed because it jumped up at her now full throttle. The sensation of being watched, the smell of honeysuckle, the prickle of danger. She started to walk to the entry gate of the park, which was, unfortunately, a narrow spot, easily blockaded. But there was no one there, no one to block her way, she thought, as she picked up her pace.

This was a poisoner, not a mugger, she consoled herself as she trotted past the gate and found herself in a nest of old warehouses, an area that during the day thrived with artists and designers, but now was quiet. An elderly woman had died near here, a year ago. A woman with dementia who'd wandered away from her daughter and slipped on the rocks.

Was that a step?

An owl hooted. The moon winked. Maggie could hear traffic from Broadway. She was so close to safety, she thought, and then stumbled and scrambled back up to her feet. She felt dizzy. She felt alone. She remembered suddenly the story of one of the poisoners she'd investigated. A woman who told her husband that she was taking her son to visit family; the husband then, by himself in the house, looking to find some money he'd misplaced, looking under the mattress and finding there the body of his son. Horrors. Her stomach twisted with horrors, as Maggie kept walking forward and now was almost certain that she heard someone behind her. She thought of the 23rd psalm. "Though I shall walk through the valley of death, I shall fear no evil." She kept whispering the words. "Fear no evil."

She smelled something bitter, the smell of hate, sweat and hormones, which she recognized from her anger with Bender. She started to walk faster, but she felt exposed. Surely he wouldn't attack her. He. Did she assume it was Peter?

"Peter," she said. "Not Peter."

No, this hate couldn't come from him. Her eyes filled with tears. She didn't know what was worse, the sense of fear or betrayal. No, it wasn't Peter and she wouldn't allow herself to be attacked.

She crept forward, every nerve anticipating a blow. One of the warehouse lights flickered off. Then on. Was that a step? She couldn't take it, turned around to face whatever was coming toward her. It was enough. She would meet her fate head on and if this was the end, so be it. She couldn't take one more moment of this terror, and she thought she saw a foot just about to break into her circle of vision, when she heard a most welcome sound.

A dirt bike. She smelled oil, heard its buzzing whine, and then around the bend came her young man, ripping over the bumpy road. He rode right toward her, then slowed as he caught sight of her. Slowed down even more. Then stopped. She'd never been so close to him. His eyes stared at her curiously. She watched him take in her disheveled state. She suspected she smelled of fear, salty and dank. Beyond her she heard the slightest of movements.

He took off his helmet and handed it to her, nodded.

"Thank you," she said. This was no time for argument, and then she climbed behind him. He stood up against the bike, then pressed down and it jerked forward. Maggie almost flew over his head, but she held on. Her arms circled his strong chest. She felt the most amazing sense of security. Here was youth and strength and hope. Here was the future.

When he pulled up in front of her house, Mr. Cavanaugh was out with Fidelio, and he jolted as Maggie got off the bike.

"Can I get you some cookies?" she asked the young man.

"No, thank you," he replied, in a surprisingly deep voice.

She put her hand on his. "Did you see anyone there?"

"No. I don't think so."

"Maybe I'm losing my mind, but I thought I heard someone. It scared me. Thank you for coming along."

"You're welcome, he said, and she thought of a line from Paradise Lost that she'd always liked about reluctant angels. She thought of him like that, glorious and bold and rebellious, and she was about to tell him so when he got back on his bike, revved the engine, and tilting all the way back, like the Lone Ranger, he arced into the air and was gone.

"Nice boy," Mr. Cavanaugh said.

"You know him?"

"Yes," he said. "That's Billy Kim. He studies with me. You must know his mother."

"I don't think so."

"She owns the manicure salon on Main Street. He's giving a recital next Sunday. You're welcome to come. Calmate, Fidelio," he whispered. "Calmate."

The dog looked puzzled, as well he might, Maggie thought. For the first time Maggie wondered why

Mr. Cavanaugh always spoke to the dog in Italian. Or Spanish.

"Mr. Cavanaugh," Maggie said, "I wonder if I might ask you a question?"

It turned out that Cavanaugh was spitting at her oak tree because he hated Bender for what he'd done to his daughter. Lorelei Bender was Cavanaugh's most promising piano student and the first student he'd ever had who could have had a musical career. Cavanaugh went to far as to rent recital space at Steinway Hall to showcase her talents, but at the last-minute Bender pulled out. If she was that good she needed a better teacher, he said.

Cavanaugh pleaded. He would teach her for free. A talent such as hers needed to be nurtured. Bender switched her over to some high-priced charlatan in Manhattan.

"She's in the marching band now," he sniffed. "Plays the saxophone."

Yet another reason for hatred, Maggie thought. Yet another example of the anger that seemed to swirl around her dead neighbor.

That night Maggie locked up carefully. She didn't have a gun, but she did have a set of sharp steak knives. She took one and put it under her pillow. Not much defense against a poisoner perhaps, but it was something. Off in the distance she could hear the coyotes howl. She thought of them in the woods. Once she'd seen a coyote pup separate from its mother and it was one of the few times in her life, she felt actual physical danger. She felt the presence of evil. Someone was toying with her. Something dark was out there, and it frightened her. She looked out her window that night, watching, waiting, but nothing came. She looked out to the brightest of the stars and prayed for guidance. She felt weighed down by all she had to do. Everything kept coming back to Peter, but she knew it wasn't him.

Suddenly she remembered something that had been swirling around her consciousness all afternoon; something Agnes had said. She needed to talk to Agnes and her last thought, before she drifted off to sleep, was that she'd find Agnes somewhere on Main Street in the morning. She'd ask her then.

Chapter Thirty-Four

Of course, Agnes was not on Main Street, though she practically lived there. But Maggie did find Iphigenia, who looked surprisingly droopy. Far different than the cheerful Iphigenia she had seen only days earlier, when they went to Doc Steinberg's.

"Hello old friend, how are you?"

"Good," Iphigenia said, though she was no liar. She looked like an unwatered plant. Her dark eyes glistened with tears. Her hands shook.

They'd only gone to the doctor seven days ago. Life seemed to be speeding up, slowing down. Time playing such tricks.

"You got a good report from the doctor, didn't you? That was a relief."

"Yes, a good report," Iphigenia said, automatically guiding Maggie over to the chair. She was one of those people who couldn't speak unless her hands were busy. She looked upon Maggie as though she were an overgrown yew and began to hack. *It will grow back," her mother whispered. "Kindness is always more important."*

"That's easy for you to say."

"Are you feeling okay?" Maggie asked. She closed her eyes.

"Yes, I feel great. I'm in good health. This is what the doctor said."

"Tell me what's wrong. I thought seeing the doctor would make you feel better."

"Hush," Iphigenia said, and resumed clipping. She did it for a while. Maggie had no idea what was going on because her eyes were closed. Better that way. She listened to the snipping and made believe it was happening to someone else.

"There!" Iphigenia said, and smacked Maggie on the back of her head, which caused her to open her eyes and gaze upon her reflection incredulously. She looked like a movie star. An old movie star, but still. She'd always worn her hair casually, but Iphigenia had done something to bring out cheekbones she didn't know she had.

"Finally," Iphigenia said. "If I do nothing else before I die, I do this. My work is complete."

Maggie looked into her friend's eyes. Iphigenia sank into the chair next to her. "What is it? Why are you completing your work?"

"I didn't tell the doctor everything."

"Why?"

"Because if I tell her everything, I know she'll want me to go get tests and I can't handle that." She began shaking her head no.

"What didn't you tell her?" Iphigenia looked like she was boiling inside.

"I feel a lump."

"Didn't she examine you? Didn't the doctor feel it too?"

"Yes, but I turned so she wouldn't feel it. I'm scared. I'm not like you, Miss Maggie I'm not brave."

"I'm not brave either," she said.

"Yes you are. Look at all the things you do. You lose your daughter and your husband and you keep on going. You have the courage of a lion, and me, I am a mouse. I am less than a mouse."

"Iphigenia, I don't know where courage comes from, but I know this: it flourishes among people who love you. It's possible to do things you'd never do when someone believes you're capable of it. I suppose living in this village, and being part of this church, I've grown used to having people believe in me, and so I've come to believe in me too. If Doc Steinberg said you were fine, you probably are. But if you're not, you can deal with it, and I'll be there to help you."

Iphigenia nodded vehemently. "Yes, of course, you are right."

"Should we go to the doctor now?"

Iphigenia seemed about to sink to her knees, but then she pulled herself together, tossed her hair, locked the door to the shop and the two of them walked up to Doc Steinberg's. So many people waved at them as they walked by. Some she didn't even know, and it struck Maggie that it was hard to think that someone in this village was a murderer. Someone she probably knew, probably loved, was killing people. Someone might have tried to kill her last night, and the thought made her angry, and when she felt angry it brought up the emotion she'd felt toward Bender. She couldn't get past the feeling that although he was the victim, he was also the person who had set this whole thing in motion.

Doc Steinberg brought Iphigenia into her office and within five minutes she emerged.

"It was a mosquito bite," she cried out. Maggie noticed she was holding a little piece of white paper. "The doctor wrote me a prescription for Xanax."

She flew out the door then, and Doc Steinberg remained. "Did you want to talk to me Maggie?" she asked.

Maggie looked at her. She had been thinking of her as a suspect. She had been hoping Doc Steinberg was the killer because, somehow, if she had to pick someone, Doc Steinberg felt the most disposable, and she knew many poisoners were doctors. Yet now, looking at her, at those firm, competent eyes, at the red shoes she always liked to wear, at the tired, pale face, she could not believe that this committed doctor would hurt anyone. She loved Doc Steinberg. What was she even thinking about?

"Do you want to come into my office?" Doc Steinberg said.

"No thank you," Maggie replied. "I have someone I have to talk to," because she did need to see Agnes. She felt guilty about it, but Agnes was the only person she knew who she hoped would be the murderer. Though even Agnes, carted off to jail, would tug at Maggie's heart. But it had to be someone.

Chapter Thirty-Five

Agnes lived in a new development called Sheep's Meadow, so named because, in building the houses, the developer had torn up a sheep's meadow. Now it was a massive enclave of massive houses. In every driveway there was a Lexus or two. In front of every garage was a built-in basketball court, every mailbox announced the house was protected by a security system. On this late Monday afternoon, the whole area vibrated with the sound of leaf-blowers and lawnmowers.

"I never realized you lived here," Maggie said, after walking up from Doc Steinberg's office. She'd gambled that Agnes would be home, and willing to receive her, which she was.

"I've come a long way," Agnes said, and she spoke the truth. Maggie vividly remembered the apartment Agnes had grown up in. It was a squalid space over the video store, which had then been the candy store. Agnes lived there with her seven siblings, her exhausted mother and her father, who couldn't keep his hands to himself. Maggie's mother wouldn't let her go over there. That was how you handled a man like that in those days.

You didn't report him to the police. You didn't complain to his wife, and you certainly didn't try to remove his daughters from his care. You simply told your own daughter to avoid him, and if he had daughters of his own, well that was too bad.

"Seven thousand square feet," Agnes said. "One of the biggest units in the development. Have you ever seen anything like it?"

Not since Tara, Maggie was tempted to say, but forbore.

"I know you disapprove," Agnes said, pursing her lips. She seemed different here, on her home turf, Maggie thought. She looked more confident, more normal.

"Not at all," Maggie said. "I'm glad you got here, Agnes. You deserve it."

Agnes cleared her throat, beckoned for Maggie to come in. "Well, I suppose you'll want a tour."

They walked into the entry way, which was built in the shape of a rotunda. Maggie couldn't help herself, she thought of Abraham Lincoln laid out at his funeral. Why did this house keep conjuring up images of the Civil War? In the center of this particular rotunda was a nude, carved out of black stone, contorted in what seemed to be a very uncomfortable position.

"Me," Agnes said. "In my salad days."

Maggie looked at the nude more carefully. She'd never been sure when Agnes was joking, which she supposed was part of why she didn't like her that much. She made her feel off balance.

"This way," Agnes said, leading Maggie down a long hallway. She caught sight of a media room with a gigantic TV screen, then another room filled with leather-bound books, and they were in the kitchen and Maggie laughed out loud. She'd never seen anything like it. There was a huge granite island in the middle that was long enough to land an air craft carrier. All the appliances matched color. Everything gleamed silver. Maggie noticed Agnes eyeing herself in the refrigerator, smiling at her reflection.

"Fabulous," Maggie said.

"Isn't it?"

"No wonder you like to cook so much. Here I was picturing you slaving away over hot stove."

"Yes," Agnes said. "That's how everyone pictures me. Like the witch in Hansel and Gretel."

"I wouldn't put it like that."

"No," she said. "You've always been so tactful, Maggie Dove."

It was going to be a long afternoon.

Agnes gestured to her to sit down on one of the chairs around the island, which Maggie did and immediately felt enveloped in a plush warmth that molded itself like a hand to her back. It was a little like being held in God's hands, she supposed. If God were in the kitchen, and why shouldn't He be?

Agnes shrugged on an apron that had an image on it of one of the Disney princesses, and then she began bustling around with an Espresso maker.

"So what did you do out there in Oregon?" Maggie asked.

Agnes laughed. "Where did I get the money for this, you mean?"

"Exactly."

Agnes tugged opened the freezer, which was crammed full of pans of what Maggie assumed were her famous bread pudding. No wonder she was always first on the scene for the dinner brigade.

"Have you ever heard of Nancy Straub?"

"No."

Agnes put the bread pudding in a microwave that looked like it had the capability of launching a space ship. "She was a genius. A pioneer. She had an idea for a website where people could go to get their eyes examined, on-line, and then it would make up glasses for them. Simple actually, the difficulty was in getting the funding, but that's where Nancy excelled. She was a real wheeler and dealer. She built up a very successful business."

"And you were her assistant?" Maggie asked, trying to reconcile the image of this mover and shaker with the Agnes she knew. With the girl that lived with that creepy father and haunted their cheerleading practices, always trying to make the team, always the butt of jokes. Always about twenty pounds overweight and so eager. Always so eager.

"No. I was her wife."

"Oh."

"You're shocked?" Agnes said. She peered at her as though from a great distance, a scientist looking at a specimen under a microscope.

"Agnes, I wish you'd get it out of your head that I'm such a prude. Just because I'm a Sunday School teacher doesn't mean I don't know there are gay people in the world. I am an intelligent and fairly liberal member of the 21st century. I just didn't realize you were gay. I'm processing the information."

Agnes laughed, spurting air like a whale. Then she grew thoughtful.

"I didn't realize it either," she said. "I thought I was just miserable because of this town. I thought I hated men because of my father. I thought the reason I wanted to be with you so much was because I wanted a friend. Nancy saw something in me that no one had ever seen before. She saved me." Agnes' eyes glistened. "She opened up a whole new world for me."

Maggie remembered the sense of wonder she'd felt when Stuart loved her. The way he made everything seem possible.

"What happened?" she asked. "What happened to Nancy?"

Agnes cleared her throat. The microwave began to chime. "She died. Brain cancer. It was a hard death. I was by her side for every minute of it. She left me everything. Her family fought it, but there was nothing they could do. She was an outsider, like me. She made sure they didn't get any of her money."

Maggie knew she and Winifred had been cruel to her. They had, in some respects, formed the woman she had become. Maggie had been beautiful and she knew it and she loved it and she had devoted parents and she'd thought that life was good and people were good and God was good and how different would she have been had life been less generous to her. How differently would she have handled the hard times had she not had that cushion to fall back on.

"I'm sorry," Maggie said.

Agnes turned her back to her, retrieved the bread pudding and brought it over to the table.

"You were always the best of them," she said.

"I'm afraid that's not saying much," Maggie said, remembering all the times she'd laughed at Agnes' expense.

"No, but it's something."

Agnes set the platter in front of Maggie. The bread pudding smelled of eggs and vanilla; it was Maggie's favorite thing in the world, and now it bubbled and spat in front of her.

"Why did you come back here?" she asked Agnes. "You were so successful there, why did you want to come back to Darby?"

A cloud seemed to pass in front of Agnes. Her whole demeanor changed. Maggie had a terrible feeling her own face had changed in just that way when she spoke to Bender. It was the transformation of anger.

"I dreamed of coming back here. I dreamed of buying the biggest house I could, of showing everyone what

I had become. When I got back and saw Winifred in that nursing home, her legs bent up, her hands like claws…"

Of the seven deadly sins, anger is possibly the most fun, Maggie thought. One of Frederick Buchner's most famous lines.

"How I laughed," Agnes said, "to see her bowed down who had been so cruel to me."

To lick your wounds, to smack your lips over grievances long past, to roll over your tongue the prospect of bitter confrontations yet to come.

"When I think how she used to make fun of the way I looked in a cheerleading outfit. Which of us looks better now?" she said.

The chief drawback is that what you are wolfing down is yourself. The skeleton at the feast is you.

Of course, Agnes hated Winifred, Maggie realized. She'd always known it. How could she not after how cruelly Winifred had treated her, but the intensity of her emotion shocked her. For her to speak so openly about it.

How difficult would it have been to poison one of Winifred's pills? Agnes was always in and out of the Castle, visiting someone. She could have stopped by Winifred's room, could have put something in one of Winifred's pill bottles, and Winifred wouldn't have noticed. Agnes worked at the traffic court, so she was near the police station. Maybe she had come across some Ecstasy there.

But why would she have killed Bender? What grudge did she have against him, and how would she have killed him?

Maggie looked into Agnes triumphant eyes. *The skeleton at the feast is you.*

"But enough of that," Agnes said. "Won't you have some bread pudding?"

The bread pudding bubbled ominously. It looked alive. Maggie smelled nutmeg and remembered then a fact she'd discovered in researching her mysteries. That nutmeg could mimic Ecstasy. That you could poison someone with nutmeg.

"Come, you know you're hungry."

Maggie wondered if Agnes intended to poison her. Was that what this whole meal was about? She looked carefully at Agnes' face, at her arched eyebrows, at her all-knowing expression. She was a manipulative woman. She liked to play games. She had the exact disposition of a poisoner, or of a person mimicking a poisoner.

"What are you afraid of?" Agnes asked, pushing the plate a little closer to Maggie.

She was either intending to poison her, or joking about poisoning her. Either way, Maggie didn't want to be part of it. She shoved the plate toward Agnes and left.

Agnes's laughter saw her out.

Maggie was halfway home before she remembered that she'd wanted to ask Agnes a question. She wanted to ask her if she'd ever met Winifred's third husband, because it seemed like from something she said at the funeral that she might have. But she was damned if she was going to go back there and talk to that woman. She had other avenues to pursue.

Chapter Thirty-Six

"So was there poison in that bread pudding?" Frank Bowman asked. "Was Agnes trying to kill you?" Maggie had called him as soon as she got home. She needed to vent and could think of no better candidate.

Maggie settled into her couch in the living room. She looked at her desk, and the rock she kept on top of it, as a reminder. She didn't want to wind up like Agnes.

"I don't know whether there was real poison in it or not, but there was certainly a lot of hatred," she said.

"Don't have any more to do with her," Frank said. "I don't like her, Maggie. She's dangerous."

Maggie looked over at her oak tree, which looked different after the poison attempt. The leaves were still starting to come out, but some of the buds had hardened. They'd turned into little rocks.

Suddenly Maggie felt so tired. Agnes could have killed her, or hit her over the head, or shot her. She'd known that, hadn't she, when she went up there, to her house.

"I'll tell you the truth," she said. "There was a moment there, when I looked at that bread pudding and

I wanted to taste it. I think I wanted it to be poisoned. I figured I'd probably go quickly. It would all be over. Is there such a thing as killing yourself because you didn't have the energy for protection."

"You've suffered," Frank said. She liked the way he didn't offer reassurance, didn't say everything was going to be okay. She always found that ridiculous when things were so obviously not going to be okay, and yet everyone seemed to feel obliged to say it.

"But for all that, I don't think there was poison in that bread pudding. Agnes had no reason to kill Winifred. If anything, she would have been happier having Winifred live. She wanted her to suffer. She took enjoyment out of it, and God bless her, I can't even blame her. The hatred she felt was born out of the teasing that we gave her. It just seems like hatred twists everything around. Me going after Bender, and Agnes going after Winifred and Peter going after Walter Campbell."

"Why don't I come over?" Frank said. "Let me keep you company."

"No, thank you. I'm not good for much right now, but I'll see you Friday night. At the Dining Out club."

He laughed softly at that. "Of course. My debut."

"They'll love you," she said.

"I will be on my best behavior."

Maggie had a vision of all the ladies of the church circling him the way they did at The Castle.

"But after that," he said, "after the dinner, perhaps we could spend some time together. Alone."

She heard something in his voice she hadn't heard before, something that ran like a hot current underneath the gentility.

"Yes," she said, remembering the press of her lips against his. "Yes."

She felt so strange. So excited. So odd, and when the phone rang again, she grabbed it up, thinking it was Frank Bowman, but it was Helen Blake's distinctive Kansas twang on the other end.

"Do you remember how you said you'd be willing to watch Edgar for an hour or two?" she asked. Her voice was always unnaturally high, as though someone was stepping on her foot, a likely scenario.

"Yes," Maggie said. "I think so."

"Do you suppose, would it be an imposition, if I were to bring him over now?"

"Now!" Maggie looked at the clock. It was almost 3:00. Two hours until dinner and six hours until bed. Not that she was regimented.

"It's too much, isn't it? I knew I shouldn't ask."

"Hold on," Maggie said. "It's just I was surprised."

"You'll do it then," Helen Blake gushed. "Would you really? That would be such a help. I would owe you for the rest of my life."

"Well, when you put it like that, how can I say no?"

"Thank you, thank you dear Ms. Dove. And please, don't worry about that mark he has on his arm. I took him to the pediatrician and she assured me Edgar doesn't have rabies."

Chapter Thirty-Seven

Within seconds of putting down her phone, Maggie's doorbell rang, and there was Helen Blake with Edgar in tow. He seemed to be frothing, though perhaps that was the lollipop.

"Thank you so much," Helen said. Edgar hesitated, but she lifted him up off the ground and deposited him on the other side of the door, and then she squeezed him tight and said, "You are my heart. And now I must go."

And she did, leaving Edgar blinking in Maggie's direction.

"I have to pee," he said. Tufts of downy blonde curls made him look like an angel.

"All rightie," she said, and she brought him inside and showed him to the bathroom. Then he emerged and she showed him the hole under the stair case that used to be a hide-out for runaway slaves. She told him about how there used to be slaves in Westchester, but how her ancestors, the Leighs, had been involved in helping them escape.

"They hid in here."

"Can I hide in there?" Edgar asked.

"Yes," she said, and so he did, for an hour, and when he came out, she asked him if he knew how to play chess, which he didn't, and so she showed him some moves and they did that for an hour, and then she thought perhaps he'd like to walk around Main Street. So they popped into Iphigenia's and said hello and then stopped by D'Amici's, and she got him a bagel. Then she remembered how she'd been wanting to stop by the nail salon and ask about Marcus Bender's hands, which for some reason had stayed vividly in her mind.

There were four nail salons in Darby, and they stopped by each one, until finally they got to the one owned by Billy Kim's mother, which Maggie recognized because she had a picture of Billy up on the wall. She was an elegant woman, dark hair pulled back into a bun. Even Edgar seemed impressed by her. Or perhaps he was just tired. But he clutched onto Maggie's hand and didn't move.

"Your son helped me out the other night," Maggie said.

"Yes," she said, eyes crinkling. "He told me you like dirt bikes."

"Yes," Maggie said. "Matter of fact, I do. More than I would have expected."

Edgar began to gnaw on his knuckles and Maggie knew she only had so much time before he started to gnaw on her knuckles.

"I wonder if I might ask you a question, Ms. Kim, and I know this is nosy. But did Marcus Bender come here?"

Immediately she scowled. So Bender had worked his magic here too, Maggie thought.

"Not a nice man." Ms. Kim grimaced and shook her head. "Scared to die."

Maggie wasn't sure she heard her right. "He was worried about dying? But he wasn't that old."

"Worried about his heart. Always asking for secret medicine. I'm not a witch doctor. I give manicures. Always waving money in front of my face."

"Did he wind up buying anything?"

"I don't have anything," she cried out. "Nothing. He thought I knew a secret formula, but I don't. Not for him."

After that, Maggie and Edgar returned to her house. She remembered that Noelle too had said something about Bender being afraid to die young. He was vulnerable in ways he hadn't seemed. Could that have been how the poison was given to him? Someone, knowing he was afraid to die had given him a potion, which he had taken, because his fear blinded him. Maybe the poisoner told him it was a vitamin supplement. Or a special granola bar.

Again, she had the sense of a malicious mind at work, playing with her, playing with his victims.

When she got back to the house, Edgar began sucking his thumb. Poor chick was tired, she realized, and so was she, although it was only early evening. She sat him down on the couch and brought out one of her husband's old books. She opened to a map of tsarist Russia, and began showing him where the cities were, and what the various Cyrillic letters were, and they hadn't gone too far when he leaned his head against her shoulder and fell asleep. She closed her eyes, for just a moment, and she woke up to find Helen Blake sitting across from her, eating a sandwich stuffed with roast beef, provolone cheese, lettuce and tomatoes.

"I brought food," she said, holding out a sandwich to Maggie, who grabbed it, hoping she wouldn't gnaw it to shreds like a wolf. But Edgar hurled himself at his mother, showing her the book.

"Look at this Mommy. Look at this Mommy. Look at this Mommy."

"I see," Helen said, running her fingers over the page, turning the book to see it better. "Stuart Dove," she read. Then looked over to Maggie. "Maggie Dove," she said. "Did you know Professor Dove?"

"He was my husband," she said.

Helen jumped to her feet, which caused her sandwich to fall toward the carpet, though she dove quickly and recovered it. Then she flung herself down next to Maggie and grabbed her hands. "You are Margaret Dove. I didn't make the connection. I studied with your husband. His work was a genius. He taught me everything I know. I got my Ph.D. in Russian studies thanks to him."

"I had no idea," Maggie said. She actually did have no idea. She'd never even stopped to think about what sort of job this girl might have; she figured it as enough of a job keeping track of Edgar.

"You had a daughter, didn't you? He used to talk about her all the time. He said she was a genius. What's she doing now? Running the State Department?"

Maggie looked at her dumbstruck. She assumed everyone knew what happened to Juliet. Everyone did know, in her little town, but Helen was new and clearly, she didn't gossip.

"What happened?" she whispered, and Maggie told her, and Helen started to cry and Edgar started to cry and then Helen jumped up and said they should have some vodka, which she just happened to have in her bag. They put on a movie for Edgar and then they drank and talked and reminisced and Maggie felt a little like she was back in her past, with her husband and daughter, and as she looked at this crazy drunken girl in front of her, she thought how odd it was that blessings could come in the most unlikely ways.

When it was way later than Maggie had been up in a very long time, Helen swooped up Edgar and tiptoed out of the house. She hugged Maggie goodbye and Edgar opened his eyes briefly and said, "I love you, Maggie Dove."

"I love you too," she whispered, surprised to realize she meant it.

"Hey," Helen said, as Maggie leaned against the door, thinking if she didn't go to bed soon, she'd collapse, "are you going to the Dining Out club on Friday? Why don't I drive you?"

"It's not necessary," Maggie said.

"Nonsense," Helen replied. "It will be a pleasure."

"No, thank you," Maggie said. "The fact is a gentleman is going to drive me."

It felt so strange to say, given that she'd just spent the evening talking about her husband, but Helen's face lit up. "Oh how wonderful," she said. "Oh, how wonderful. What fun we'll have."

Chapter Thirty-Eight

Frank Bowman showed up Friday night looking surprisingly nervous, Maggie thought. He was dressed flawlessly. He wore gray pants, a checked shirt and a pale blue sweater. His gray hair was neatly brushed. He smelled of aftershave.

"You look like you're applying for a job," she said, feeling touched that he'd gone to so much effort for her. She was finally feeling better. It took two days to cleanse all the vodka out of her system. She swore she would not have one drop of alcohol at dinner.

"I hope you'll hire me," he said, a gentle grin returning to his face. Her own Inspector Benet, but a little courtlier than her imagined version.

"Absolutely."

He drove carefully, north on Broadway, north of Tarrytown, to the restaurant in question, that was tucked away in a spot that used to belong to General Motors. All the factories had been torn down, and lots of new apartments had sprung up, and with them little restaurants, among them this Thai one. He found a parking spot, looked at his watch.

"Right on time."

"They're going to love you," she said, putting her hand on his arm. "They're very nice people. They really are."

He leaned over, kissed her softly, and then pulled away.

"Come on," he said. "Let's do this."

They were exactly on time, and yet the entire Dining Out Club was already there. Walter Campbell sat in the middle of the table, somewhat like Jesus at the Last Supper, assuming Jesus played football. He loomed over everyone. To his left sat Noelle, which was a surprise. Then there were the three Faraday sisters, the core of the Dining Out club, the core of the church. Faradays had been attending the Darby Presbyterian church since it was first built, back in the days when Darby-on-Hudson had been a summer home for the rich and famous and the Tiffanys and Goulds and everyone else of their circuit built their summer mansions in balmy Westchester. They lived on Faraday Street in the Faraday compound.

Sibyl the real estate agent sat next to the Faradays. She'd been trying to get them to sell the compound for years. On the other side of Sybil were Agnes and Doc Steinberg, wearing a Spanish cape and red shoes, and Mr. Cavanaugh, his eyes slightly closed. Listening to whatever music played in his mind. Next to him was the minister, who also had her eyes slightly closed. She too always seemed to be listening to another world. Quite often Maggie would find her around the village, lost in prayer. She had what Maggie thought of as liquid eyes. Whenever anything bad happened to one of the congregation, it was as though she could actually feel their pain.

Then there was Peter, gazing up at her warily, and two empty seats by his side, and then Helen Blake, dear Helen Blake and Edgar, who at the sight of her ran forward and grabbed her by the hand. "Come on, Ms. Dove. Sit down."

Immediately the Faraday hearing aids clicked on. Three high pitched squeals burst into the room and Maggie suspected dogs in the vicinity collapsed.

"Am I late?" she said, though she knew she wasn't. They'd all gathered early because they were so excited about meeting Frank. She was surprised at how quiet Frank was, but she could see how the situation could be overwhelming. She'd only ever seen him surrounded by a circle of women; she'd never stopped to think he might be shy.

"This is my friend, Frank Bowman," she said.

"Welcome," Helen sang out.

"Why hello Frank Bowman," Agnes said. She tittered. Maggie'd heard that word a hundred times and never knew what it meant until she heard Agnes do it. She wondered if she had misheard what Agnes said about having a wife.

"Drink order?" the waitress said, a tall young woman with legs like stilts and hair turned up into a complicated style.

"Why don't we get some wine?" Walter Campbell said, the first agreeable words he'd ever said in Maggie's hearing. She immediately abandoned her plan to give up drinking.

"Why don't we order a bottle?" the minister asked.

"One bottle?" Walter said.

"Haven't you ever heard of the story of the loaves and fishes?" Agnes said. She seemed to be boiling over with excitement. Her face was dark red.

"I don't drink," Noelle said.

"Of course you don't," Agnes said.

"What's that supposed to mean?" Peter said, and Maggie's heart sunk at the tone in his voice, that aggressive bull-headed tone he got whenever he was about to make a complete ass of himself. "What are you implying, Agnes? If you have something to say to this woman, say it."

Noelle eyed him appreciatively, Maggie noticed. She had such long lashes.

Walter took out his gold American Express card. "Bring out five bottles."

"Oh my," the eldest Faraday sister said. "Who is he?"

"He's very big," the middle sister said.

"He's the police chief."

"The one who has it in for Peter?"

"Ssh," Maggie said. "He's right here and his hearing's quite good."

"Maggie's looking well. I hear she has a boyfriend."

"So," Walter said, looking at Peter, "Mrs. Dove tells me you were one of the first responders at 9/11."

"That's right," Peter said. Maggie noticed he hadn't waited for the wine to arrive. He'd already had a beer. Probably two.

"You must have been right out of Police Academy."

"That's right," Peter said. "That's right. I'd never even handled a crime. Only wrote traffic tickets, but when we heard the news, we all got into the car and went down there. Had to help."

"He went inside," Maggie said.

"Couldn't do anything much. But I had to help."

His whole face changed at the memory of it. It was, she believed, the finest moment of his life. On that day he'd been tested and not found wanting, but the reverberations from that day had shaken him. Between that and Juliet's death, he'd never quite recovered. Sometimes she wondered what sort of man he'd be had his life not taken such turns.

"You must be very brave," Noelle said.

Peter blushed furiously. "I…I…I just had a job to do."

"You have courage," Noelle said, her baby doll voice turning huskier.

Maggie thought she saw something gold flash under the table, wondered if Noelle wore a toe ring, wondered if she was rubbing her bare foot against Peter's leg. Whatever was happening, Peter looked like he was going to explode, and he turned to Walter and all but yelled, "Where were you on that day?"

Walter Campbell didn't respond right away. He pressed his lips together, seemed to be weighing his options.

"I was on the 87th floor of the north tower. I was sitting at my desk, talking to a trader in Japan, when the plane hit. The time was 8:46:30. The impact blew me off my seat. I thought it was a bomb. Next thing I knew I was covered in ceiling tiles. I could feel the building bend. I thought it would snap right then. But eventually it recoiled back to center. We didn't know what to do. We started to head down, they said the way was closed. We had been fire marshals. My best friend, Stan McGuire, he wanted to check on some people one floor up, but the way was blocked. But he had a crowbar and so we went up, and we cleared the way."

"You were those guys," Peter said. "I heard about you."

Walter nodded. "There were five people on that floor. Then we went up another flight. There was a woman there who was pregnant. Her water broke. She needed help going down the stairs. We were so sure the towers would be fine. We thought there would be rescue teams. We thought a helicopter would come. Stan told me to take her out. You talk about moments when your life changes," he said to Maggie. "Decisions that define your life. I knew what Stan was giving me, and I took it. Often I've regretted not insisting that he go."

"Shit," Peter said. "Pardon my French."

Peter began grilling Walter Campbell with questions. He was hypnotized. He loved nothing more than a tale of bravery. He didn't care that he'd hated Walter Campbell all these months; now Campbell was a hero to him. Maggie could see what would happen. He would devote himself to Campbell now. He was like a dog, Maggie thought, always looking for a master to love. She felt touched, and a little frightened, and she jumped when Frank's hand brushed against hers. She'd been so absorbed she forgot he was there.

"My world had changed in an instant," Walter said. "It took me a while to recognize it, though. I had to help build the firm back up. Made my money, and then one day, I was standing on Fifth Avenue and a plane went overhead and I quit my job, went to the Police Academy and here I am. In Darby-on-Hudson. Among you good folks."

Maggie had the sensation of being off balance. She thought of something her jujitsu teacher used to say, that jujitsu was the art of manipulating an opponent's force against himself rather than confronting it with your own force.

"I wonder if his wife is big too," the oldest Faraday sister said.

"What about you?" Walter asked Frank, gaze friendly. "Where were you on that day?"

"Nowhere nearby," he said. "I was in Mexico at the time. Doing some business."

And then the conversation moved on to the Faraday sisters to the stories they had to tell and then Noelle told a story about some traders she had known that had nothing to do with the World Trade Center but involved a large cake.

"I don't understand what she just said," Leona Faraday said. "Did she jump out of a cake?"

Agnes started to laugh so hard she began to choke and the minister, Walter and Peter all jumped up to help her and then the waitress came over, looking slightly aggrieved, Maggie suspected, that they'd been sitting for too long without ordering, and the Faraday sisters wanted to know if they could get something that wasn't spicy and Agnes said, "Oh no. We're at a Thai restaurant. We have to have spices." Sibyl began talking about a Thai banker who was buying a house on Main Street and Agnes said she wanted a pupu platter, which made Noelle start to laugh and Maggie thought how much she loved all these people, even Noelle, after a fashion, and at that moment Walter's phone buzzed and he answered it.

"Campbell here."

The whole restaurant seemed to quiet. Walter pressed the phone against his ear, grunted and then looked at Peter.

"Arthur Malone's body was just recovered."

"Who?"

"Winifred's assistant?" Maggie said, remembering the man who'd massaged Winifred's arms, the gentle man she assumed had helped Winifred get her blackmailing information. The man who everyone said skipped town, but he must not have. She remembered how he wept after Winifred's funeral.

"He seems to have been poisoned," Walter said.

"I tried to see him just the other day," Maggie said. "But they told me he was gone."

"No, he was in the Castle, on the grounds. Covered up with dirt and leaves. He might not have been found for years except that one of the residents got lost and everyone was out looking for her. Why did you want to see him?"

Maggie felt as if a spotlight was shining on her. "I called you," she said. "I wanted to talk to you about this. But not at this moment."

"You and he were friends, weren't you?" he asked, and she thought Walter was talking to her, but then realized he was speaking to Peter. Who had said nothing. Who sat there gripping the table as though he might float away.

"It's not possible," he said. "I thought Arthur…"

"Yes?" Walter Campbell said, but then Peter seemed to come to his senses. He looked around wildly and then jumped to his feet, and before Maggie could stop him, he went tearing out of the restaurant.

Chapter Thirty-Nine

For a moment, everyone just sat stunned, and then Walter Campbell went striding toward the front door, Maggie chasing after him. "This doesn't mean anything. It's not an admission of guilt," she said.

Walter stopped and looked at her for a moment. "Go home."

"No. I have to find him."

"It's not safe," Walter said.

"I'll go with her," Frank said. "We'll look for him together."

Walter nodded. Maggie felt irritated at being treated like a child, but it wasn't the moment to argue. She started out the door when her minister called to her. "We'll pray for him," she said.

"Thank you."

She always felt a slight thrill when she heard those words. Made her feel like she had a superpower.

"Where do you want to go?" Frank said.

"Down to the park," she said. "If he's anywhere, that's where he would be."

Frank got into his car, clicked on his seat belt, and assumed a look of grim determination.

"Thank you for driving me," she said. "I have to find him before Walter does. He's going to do something foolish, I just feel it, and he'll wind up getting shot and it will all be because he's angry. He's so angry and he's been like that for years."

She brushed away tears. The landscape looked blurry as though in a dream. They were driving down Broadway, there were streetlamps, and yet her tears smudged everything.

"He really was something special, something fine. A golden boy. He would have been a great soldier. He should have gone to war, but he'd never leave Juliet, you see. And then he wouldn't leave me. It's almost as though our love for him has been toxic."

Past the statue of Major Andre, the traitor hung during the Revolutionary War, past a playground Juliet used to love that she called Circle Square Park, past Lyndhurst with its concerts and roses and then further south and past her church.

"I'll tell you something I've never told anyway. I've always believed that something happened that night, in the car. Between Peter and Juliet. Something must have happened for the guilt to have stayed with him for so long, because really, it wasn't like it was his fault. The car was parked. They were at a stoplight. How could he have possibly known that a car was coming from the opposite direction, and yet he's blaming himself for something. I feel it."

"You can't blame yourself," Frank Bowman said, hand on the stick shift, slowing as they approached the park. No one was there. Even as they approached it, Maggie could see no one was there. The park was empty, deserted. Past 9:00 at night. Even the lights were out.

"No, I don't blame myself, and yet I suppose I do because if I could have figured out what was wrong, maybe I could have helped him. And if he's done something wrong, not that I think he has, but I suppose he might have, then I have to blame myself for a part of it because the man he's become is in part due to me." She felt like her eyes were swollen, and Frank handed her a handkerchief.

"Come on," he said. "Let's get out of the car. Let's see if he's here. We could use some air."

"I should call Walter Campbell," she said. But her phone wasn't charged. She was losing her mind.

"Oh, for heaven's sake," she said. "Can I borrow your phone?"

"I don't have one," he said. "Never use them."

She scanned the park, which seemed empty and yet she was sure Peter would head this way. He loved the river. "Do you mind waiting?" she asked Frank.

"Of course not."

They walked around the path, a broad oval that she knew from an ancient attempt at fitness was half a mile. It felt good to walk. They walked to the farthest point, at which you could see the tip of Manhattan. You used to be able to see the Twin Towers rising up from that point, and after they fell, the beams of light shining up, and now the Freedom Tower, though that always looked lopsided to Maggie. And there was the spruce that she had planted so long ago for her daughter, such a pretty little tree, so dainty compared to her oak.

"This is my favorite place," she said. "Isn't it funny how some spots just feel special. Even the air seems special here. I'm glad to have you here with me."

She looked up, expecting to see his warm eyes gazing on her, but saw instead that he was covering up a yawn.

"I'm so sorry," he said. "All the excitement of the last few days is catching up with me. I'm not as young as I was."

"No, I'm sorry. Here I am, going on and on and I barely know you. You must be ready to tear your hair out."

He held her hand for a moment. "I wouldn't say I barely know you. I feel like I've gotten to know you quite well in these last few weeks."

His grip was stronger than she'd expected; his expression more intense. She remembered how she'd felt the night he dropped her off home, the weird sensations that swirled inside of her. Desire? Was it possible?

The air was so still. The river quiet except for some waves that periodically smacked the shore. Even the bridge seemed subdued, the moon covered by cloud, a vast white shadow covering the sky. A cluster of hydrangeas stood right near here, their bluish blooms also phosphorescent in the night light.

He ran his thumb down her cheek. She heard his heart beating, felt her own heart beating with the same syncopation.

"Maggie Dove," he whispered. His eyes looked so dark. "Winifred loved talking about you, you know? She was so sure I would love you. She loved you. You and your mysteries, you and your husband, you and Darby, you and your daughter."

Maggie felt her eyes tear, not sure why.

"She wanted me to call you, and I did one day, but you weren't home, and I wasn't sure I was ready for what Winifred was suggesting. I'm not a serious man, as you can see." He laughed then, more of a bark than a laugh. "But then I saw you and I knew what she said was true. You were beautiful. You were what I was looking for. You were exactly what I was looking for."

"I know we haven't known each other that long," he whispered, but she found herself distracted by the hydrangeas, thinking about the night she'd stood out on her lawn, about how she'd thought about their poison, about how something so beautiful could cause death, about the heartbeat she thought she heard.

She stepped back, but his face was just as it always was, just as calm and friendly and kind, except surely his teeth had not always glistened so white. Surely there was something different about his smile. She wanted to take a step back but realized she was standing at the very tip of the park, that beyond her was a sharp drop off into the Hudson. There was no way back and no way forward.

"You were there that night, weren't you? In my garden. Watching."

"What are you talking about?" Head tipped, smile even larger.

"You were there the night Bender died. You were watching him, watching me. I heard your heart beating. You have a loud heartbeat."

He raised his hand to his heart. Laughed softly. "A birth defect," he said. "Which I control with medicine."

"Except in moments of excitement, I imagine. Seeing a dead man. Or being with a woman."

He laughed at that, and now his features did change. Lines appeared that had not been there before. It was as though the picture of Dorian Gray suddenly aged in front of her.

"I've been with many women," he said. "You are not that exciting."

She knew she should yell. The first rule of self-defense. Make noise. And yet she couldn't; she felt overcome with helplessness. They were so alone; the park so deserted.

"But why?" she asked, trying to understand. "Did you even know Bender?"

"Yes," he said. "I knew Bender. How could I not know him? Winifred talked about him all the time. Bender did this and Bender did that. Poor Maggie Dove and her tree. She sent me to talk to him. To try and persuade him to leave you alone."

"But you didn't have a quarrel with him?"

Maggie sensed him pushing her even closer to the edge. How far down was the drop, she wondered. Steep enough. How sharp all the rocks were. Even if the fall didn't kill her, the water would. She would disappear into the Hudson. Still, even frightened as she was, her mind kept working, trying to puzzle it out, and suddenly she felt something shift inside her. She understood.

"All along I thought that Winifred was killed because she knew something about Bender, but it was the other way around, wasn't it? Winifred was the one you wanted to kill. Bender was just a sideshow. You must not have been sure the Ecstasy would work. You weren't sure how much of a dose to give, and you wanted to practice and who better to go after than my neighbor, a man you knew was disliked, was hated, by so many people. But you needed to watch him die, you needed to know how long it would take."

He snorted softly, in a sound she thought of as agreement.

"He was vulnerable because he was so worried about dying. I imagine you gave him some vitamins. Told them they would help him live longer. Or maybe you just put some poison in his food when you were at his house."

"In his Gatorade, actually."

She looked again into his handsome eyes and thought of what Winifred had said. *There's someone I want you to meet.* She'd assumed Winifred was trying to set her up on a date because Winifred was always doing that, but what if she'd meant it quite literally? What if she really did just want Maggie to meet Frank because he was someone she already knew?

"Were you her husband?" she asked. The third husband, the one who didn't come to the funeral, the only one Winifred really loved. That's what she said. But then there'd only ever been Winifred's word for that and Winifred was an awful liar.

"You're good," he said. "Too bad your mysteries with Inspector Benet have been your only place to use those logic skills."

A train roared past, a bullet on its way from Connecticut.

"You needed money," she said, because it always seemed to come back to money. "It costs a lot of money to live the life you're living and you told me yourself how unethical your mother was, how you grew up making money on scams. You must have tracked down Winifred, which wasn't so hard to do. She must have spoken about the village. She must have been surprised to see you, but happy too.

"Her life had changed quite a bit. She was a prisoner of her body. It must have been nice to have you show up, interested in her again. Maybe she knew you weren't really interested in her, but she was flattered, and she'd have liked the secret. But something you did made her uneasy. She wouldn't remarry you, and then you got a different idea. She must have kept talking about me. Me and my successful late husband. Me and my widow's benefits. You could get the money from me, and I must have seemed ripe for the picking."

He yawned again, this time not even bothering to cover his mouth. "Yes, but now it's all a great waste of time. Two months wasted, and it's time to move on, Maggie Dove. I'm sorry, but it's time to go."

His heart began to beat louder. He took a flask out of his pocket. He poured some liquid into a cup and held it out to her. "It won't hurt," he said. "It never does. It's a blessing really, to go to sleep. Here, in this park that you love so much. Right near your daughter's tree. How peaceful it would be. No more fear and upset. It will all be over."

He put a finger in the cup and tapped it to her lips. She tasted wine. Communion. She felt her own heart beating in rhythm with his and she thought of Juliet, in the car, her face twisted at an angle that was so wrong. A tear slipped down her cheek.

"You told me yourself that you were getting tired of life," he said. "You were tempted to eat the bread pudding Agnes gave you. No one should have to suffer as you have." His eyes were so tender, lips so close. "Juliet's waiting for you."

She was, too, Maggie thought. She could see her, her beautiful daughter and her husband and her best friend. How desperately she wanted to see them.

"It's so fast," he whispered, and he leaned so close she could have kissed him, and at that moment, remembering the words of her jujitsu instructor, Maggie raised her hand up and smacked him as hard as she could under his nose, and then she ran. He staggered behind her, swearing, but she ran, in her heels, her poor middle-aged body wheezing for breath, running, hearing him behind her. Now she yelled as loudly as she could. And ran, and ran, but she wasn't fast enough, he was gaining on her, yelling for her and then she heard a sound that was the best sound she'd ever heard in her life.

It was the roar of a dirt bike, and it was coming right at her, and behind it was a phalanx of villagers, led by Walter Campbell, striding forward, Maggie thought, as though Frankenstein were leading the villagers and not the other way around, and they ran towards her, Walter Campbell faster even than the dirt bike, grabbing her up off her feet and crushing her in his grip.

"My dear," he said. "My dear, are you all right?"

"Yes," she said, leaning her head against his chest for just a moment, thinking how surprising the turns in her life were becoming. His own heart beat softly against her ear, a warm and sympathetic sound. "But I believe Frank Bowman has a broken nose."

He laughed at that, his giant face creasing into a smile, and then he strode off to help Joe Mangione who'd already put handcuffs on Frank and was leading him off.

Then they all surged past and only Agnes was there, the two of them watching the commotion and Agnes said, "Maggie Dove, would you like me to take you home?"

"Yes," Maggie said. "That would be very nice."

Chapter Forty

"I never liked him," Peter said. He was lying in a hospital bed. Turned out he'd run out of the restaurant, and drove toward the Saw Mill Parkway, toward the very spot where Juliet had died. He'd parked his car on the side of the road, got out, tripped and knocked himself unconscious. He was lucky he'd fallen onto the small grassy patch of land instead of onto the road or he likely would have been run over. Instead, some Good Samaritan found him, called an ambulance, and, for the second time in his life, he was transported from that particular spot to the hospital. "I always knew something was wrong with him."

"That would have been good to mention before he tried to kill me," Maggie pointed out.

"I still can't believe he was married to Winifred."

"She was always so mysterious about him," Maggie said. "She dropped off the radar during those years. I always thought it was because she loved him so much, and I assumed, when she came home, that she was heart-broken. But now I wonder if perhaps she was scared. She'd had a close call with him and she'd managed to get away. Maybe she just wanted to forget about him."

"Why didn't she say anything?"

"I think she was going to. That's what she called me about, but I think at first, after not having seen him for so long, it must have been a delicious feeling to have him there. He was a charming man and he was attentive, and she wasn't quite who she had been. She was so vulnerable."

Maggie thought of her foolish friend, so eager for love, and she thought of herself. She must have looked like an open wound, she thought. How he must have laughed to see how easily she fell for him. Peter, looking at her, seemed to read her mind.

"I hear you broke his nose."

"I did," Maggie said, with some satisfaction.

"Agnes told me once that Winifred had terrible taste in men, and she did. But I think it was when he turned his attention to me that she realized how dangerous he was. Poor friend, I do think her last act was to try and protect me."

"He wanted to marry her again," Peter asked. "He wanted her money."

"That's what drew him to her, but Winifred had run through most of her money. There wasn't much to tempt him with, and then she began talking about a much more promising candidate," Maggie said. "Someone who had a good pension from her husband. Someone who had enough royalties to live on. Someone trusting, and so he got rid of Winifred and went after me."

The room was quiet then, save for the inevitable noises of a hospital, the padded footsteps, the beeping, the announcements.

"I would have married him," she said. She looked down at the slim gold band she'd worn ever since she married Stuart Dove. It felt hot to the touch. "Had he asked me, I would have said yes. I loved him, or I thought I did. I felt so swept away by him." She thought of the night at the museum, how pretty she'd felt. She blushed as she remembered how hyper she'd been that night, how aroused and she wondered if he'd amused himself by putting some Ecstasy in her drink.

"You were vulnerable," Peter said.

"That was his skill, wasn't it? To know who was vulnerable. Walter Campbell told me that when they looked at nursing homes near where he lived, they found a number of unexplained deaths." Walter Campbell, who was back to being his brusque, annoying self. Who had barely deigned to look at her when she'd asked him for information, though she knew his secret, Maggie thought. *My dear.* "They don't even know yet how many women he might have killed. I guess a nursing home is a good feeding ground for a man like that."

"Yeah," Peter said, grinning. "But you're one tough Dove. You beat him off."

"It was close," Maggie said. She was sitting alongside him, waiting for him to be discharged. Doc Steinberg would be by soon.

"There was a moment, Peter, when I didn't think I had the energy to fight him. When I thought of surrendering. He was talking about Juliet and how she was waiting for me in heaven, and I thought how easy it would be to die, to be with her, to have all this over. I wonder if Winifred felt something similar. She'd left me a message, telling me she'd done something stupid. When he came to her with that flask, when he handed it to her poor twisted hands, I wonder if she decided to surrender as well."

Peter nodded. Poor face so bruised. Eyes filling with tears. He was the one person, she thought, who she could talk to about this, who understood exactly how she felt, who felt Juliet's loss as desperately as she did. Something within her twisted. Would she never feel better? Would this eat at her for her entire life? She couldn't let it. She owed it to Juliet and to Peter.

"We've had a tough time, you and I."

The hospital gown gave Peter's face a green cast. He looked middle aged. One of his teeth was chipped. She wished she could stop him in time. But then her daughter had escaped aging and such foolishness by dying. She was forever young, forever a young woman on the brink.

She heard the sounds of trays rolling on the aisles. She smelled chicken. Hospitals always smelled of chicken, she thought. Chicken and sweat and fear.

"You've been a devoted friend to me, Peter. You've been like a son. More than a son, really. But I realize that I haven't been fair to you."

"You, Dove? You've been more than fair to me."

"No. You have your life to live. You should have a wife and children." Her eyes started to tear up, but she forced herself to stay calm, to keep her voice steady. This boy, this man, needed to hear strength from her.

"Much as I love this village, Peter, I think it's toxic for you. I think I'm toxic for you."

"No."

"It's true. When I'm around, you can't help but remember the past, and you're young enough to move on. I think you should leave. Move away. Your career here is over. You're going to need to make a new start."

"I'm almost forty years old."

She laughed. "I know that seems old to you, but it's not. There are so many things you could do. I suspect you'll have some money to help you. I was talking to Winifred's daughter and she told me there was a bequest for you in the will. You could travel. You could see the world. You can take the time to figure out whatever you want to do."

He wiped tears away from his own eyes. "I don't want to leave you, Dove. I don't want to leave Juliet."

Maggie could hear Doc Steinberg's voice in the hall. She'd be here soon.

"She would have wanted you to. She was so excited about the new life that was opening up in front of her. I suspect she would have flown away from both of us. She would have soared to some wonderful height, because that's what you're supposed to do. Life isn't about staying safe and living in the past. Life is about adventure and joy and love."

He looked away from her. "I won't leave you, Dove. I won't leave you alone."

"But I'm not alone," she said, thinking of the parade of people running at her from the park, thinking of Joe Mangione, and Helen Blake and young Edgar, and Agnes, even Agnes, and Doc Steinberg and all her friends from the church, and the guys at D'Amici's deli, and even Walter Campbell. *My dear.*

"I'm surrounded by people I love," she said. "And who love me."

She gripped his hand. "Please Peter. Take this opportunity. I've already lost one person who I loved more than life. I can't bear to lose you. I can't bear to see you so unhappy."

He looked toward the river, which they could see from the hospital room. It looked so peaceful from here. Almost like a painting, with each small wave a tiny brushstroke.

He turned toward her then, his poor bloodshot eyes. "She broke up with me that night. At the party. I found her crying. Didn't know what was wrong. She'd been so quiet the last few weeks. Not herself. She said that she loved me, but that we weren't right for each other. We would make each other unhappy. That I would be bored by the life she hoped to live, that we were so different. I couldn't take it. Had too much to drink and she was going to drive me home. I had to change her mind.

We were arguing. She got to the light, and it turned red, and she stopped. Then it turned green, but I wouldn't let her go. I wanted to talk more. There were no other cars around. I thought we were safe. I kissed her. I told her I would always love her. The light turned red.

"She would have been safe," he said, "if I hadn't made her stop."

So much guilt, she thought.

"Listen to me, you didn't kill her. She didn't do anything wrong either. There was an accident. It was a terrible thing. But it wasn't your fault. You loved her and you loved me, and whatever guilt you have, you've long since paid for it. Please Peter, please. It's time to move on."

He looked away from her. She grabbed his hand and squeezed it, met his eyes.

"Please Peter. Do this for me. Do it for Juliet. Live your life. Be happy. Promise."

He nodded, and they were both weeping into tissues when Doc Steinberg swept into the room and told him he could go.

Chapter Forty-One

Several weeks later, Maggie ran into Agnes at the attic sale, sorting. It was the big push of the church, a time when everyone in the community dropped off all the garbage in their attics, the church sorted it and sold it and raised money for charity. Maggie was in charge of the toy department, and Edgar had volunteered to help her, which meant he spent most of his time attacking her with a plastic sword, but she loved it. Maggie loved the whole sale. She loved imposing order on confusion. She had tons of plastic boxes and she was absorbed in putting Barbies in one box and soldiers in another.

Agnes was holding a dinosaur when she came into Maggie's room. "For your department," she said.

"Thank you."

Maggie had a special section set aside for dinosaurs, and she put it there. She was trying to keep the meat-eaters separate from the vegetarians, though that wasn't working especially well because Edgar kept feeding them all into a giant plastic snake.

"How are you doing now that he's left?" Agnes asked.

Peter had moved out as soon as he was released from the hospital. He'd left that very afternoon.

"I had a note from him. He's already in California. He thinks he has a job lined up working as a private security officer for some actor out there."

Agnes looked a little softer, Maggie thought. Maybe because Maggie no longer thought her a murderer. Her hair wasn't so severely blow dried, her eyes didn't look like they were going to pop out of her head. She was smiling, Maggie realized, and she had nice teeth.

"How's Noelle?" Agnes asked.

Because Noelle had accompanied Peter out of town. Who knew? To go from Juliet to Noelle Bender.

"He's taking care of her. He's excited about the baby. I hope he has a pile of them. He'll love being a father."

Agnes began sorting through a pile of baseball cards. "Mind if I help?"

"Not at all. Many hands make light work," Maggie quoted.

Agnes smiled. They worked companionably for a bit, sorting and sweeping and occasionally pulling Edgar out of a box.

"I hear they've extradited Frank Bowman to Texas."

"He's wanted for several murders," Maggie said. She thought of those gray eyes, the way they changed when he looked at her.

"Agnes, there's something I've been wanting to ask. How did you all know to come for me that night? How did you know I was at the park?"

"Billy Kim told me."

"Who?"

"The boy on the dirt bike."

"But why would he tell you?"

Agnes blushed a little, looked quizzically at a dinosaur with a ruffle around his neck. "Because I paid him to follow you. Didn't you notice he was always around?"

"Well yes, but I thought it was just because we lived in a small village."

"I had a feeling you'd be a target, and so I paid him to follow you. When he called me to say you were alone with Bowman, I told Walter Campbell. I had a bad feeling about him."

"Why? He was always so charming."

"Call it lesbian intuition," Agnes said. "I didn't buy his line."

Maggie laughed. "You saved my life then, Agnes Jorgenson. Thank you."

She harrumphed and turned her attention back to her sorting, but Maggie knew she was pleased. She could feel vibrations of good feeling coming off of her. Salvation came in many different forms, Maggie thought. You never knew where the most unlikely angels would be hiding. She supposed you just had to keep your eyes open. But who would have expected salvation to come in the form of Agnes Jorgenson?

"I have a proposition for you," Agnes said.

"Oh, I don't know," Maggie said, automatically.

Agnes looked at her in that way she had all her life, analyzing and probing and then she barked with laughter. "Oh get over yourself, Maggie Dove. Not that type of proposition."

"Sorry."

"The fact is," Agnes said, "we work well together and I thought we might want to continue our association a bit longer."

"How do you mean?"

"Well, I have all this money and I'm not doing anything with it, and I thought perhaps we could start up a sort of detective agency."

Maggie laughed. "You want to do this on a regular basis?"

"Come now. You can't tell me it hasn't been fun."

"Agnes, my neighbor died. My best friend was murdered. I was almost killed." But it was fun, Maggie thought. She had felt more alive in these last few weeks than she had for a long time.

"And I thought we could ask Helen to join as well."

"Helen?"

"You do know she's with the CIA?"

"Helen Blake? Mother of this treasure?" Maggie said, as Edgar came barreling into her. He'd put on a construction helmet and was a super-hero.

'One of their top Russian analysts," Agnes said, "though she's taken a few years off to take care of Edgar. To be perfectly honest I think she might do better hiring someone to take care of Edgar and go back to work."

"How on earth do you know these things, Agnes?"

"I listen. You'd be amazed what you can find out if you listen."

"Still," Maggie said, looking out the window, at the pretty little village that lay in front of her, the beautiful old houses, the trees, the Hudson River rolling by, "I can't imagine there'd be that much to do in a sleepy village like this."

"No?" Agnes said. "I suspect you'd be surprised."

Chapter Forty-Two

Some nights later, Maggie went down to the park again. She breathed in its sweet air and listened to the soft lullaby of the waves lapping up against the rocks and the distant thrum of cars on the Mario Cuomo Bridge. Order, routine, safety. How lucky she was to be able to sit here again. How close she had come to losing everything, to throwing it all away. That would have been a sin, she thought. She had been blessed. She'd been saved.

She sat on her favorite bench, next to her little spruce, and took out a sandwich and a thermos full of tea. She'd brought a book with her. Agatha Christie's *Murder at the Vicarage*. She figured if she was going to work as a detective she might as well learn from the best. She started to read, and got so far as the introduction of Miss Marple, when she heard a familiar sound. There was Billy Kim, on his dirt bike.

How he'd progressed. Only a few weeks ago he'd been crashing into a tree and now he was tearing around the park. Of course, he shouldn't be tearing around the park. He would get into trouble. She expected that at any moment Walter Campbell would come lumbering by, but for now he was here. Jumping. Flying, really. He'd found a bit of hill and he was jumping off it and soaring into the air. It was so dangerous. He could fall on his head. He could tumble into the river, and yet he seemed to be in control. Life was dangerous, life was uncertain, and yet, as he soared in front of her, Maggie felt swept up in the beauty of the movement.

Reckless angel.

Again and again, he flew into the air, each time creeping closer to the Hudson, each time going higher, until he flew as high as he could, and at the highest moment, he flung out his legs so he was actually hovering in midair. She couldn't help herself. She stood up and applauded. Who could not be touched by his youth and bravery and general insanity?

Then he got back to earth, landed safely, must have figured he'd pressed his luck as far as he could, because he turned in the direction of the exit. But first he rode past her, tipping backwards on his bike as he went by, as though on a rearing stallion, and smiled, a huge grin, a pumpkin-faced grin, and he tipped his hand in a salute and roared off.

"Be safe," she called after his roaring back.

"Thank you," she said. Thank you for saving me. Thank you to Winifred, for being such a dear friend. Thank you to Peter, who was willing to give up his life for her, and to Walter Campbell, for protecting her. *My dear.* Thank you to Edgar, for making her young, and to his mother, for making her laugh, and to Agnes, for protecting her, and to her church, for nurturing her, and to her community, for cushioning her. To her husband, for loving her, and to her daughter. To Juliet. Who brought so much happiness into her life, so much joy. It would never go away, she realized. That love she would never lose.

Maggie felt something warm in her heart. Something crack and melt, that had been cold for so many years. She felt free. She felt content; she even felt excited about the future. With a heart full of hope, she headed home.

THE END

Acknowledgements

Turns out it takes a couple of villages to write and publish a novel, and I'm very grateful to the people who populate mine.

Especially:

Keri Barnum of New Shelves Books, for her creativity and hard-work.

Paula Munier, Amy Collins, Gina Panettieri and the rest of the fabulous team at Talcott Notch Literary. I could not ask for better advocates.

Dana Isaacson, for believing in Maggie Dove.

Alex Steele and Gotham Writers and all my friends/students. There's no better resource (or joy) for a writer than spending hours talking with other writers.

The mystery-writing world, which has been so much cozier than you would think. Special shout out to the kind souls at Mystery Writers of America, Malice Domestic and Miss Demeanors (missdemeanors.com) Also to Linda Landrigan and Jackie Sherbow, who've given Maggie Dove a chance to tell her stories at *Alfred Hitchcock's Mystery Magazine.*

My beautiful little village of Irvington-on-Hudson, which is not exactly Darby, but shares certain trees.

The Irvington Presbyterian Church, which has been a place of grace and hope for me. Special shout out to the IPC book club, which has shown me what readers look for when reading a book. Also hugs to Chris and Rhett Omark, who have been Maggie Dove superfans from the start. Enthusiasm matters!

Chris Canning and Patricia van Essche designed a magnificent website for me. www.susanjbreen.com

My circle of friends, most especially Melinda Feinstein, Terry Gillen, Leslie Mack & Robin Freedman, and Kay O'Keefe.

My family of Breens, Bucks, Lujans, Murcotts, Turchettes and Zelonys (especially my brother, Robert Zelony). Special hugs for Rosey Singh and my friends at the Good Shepherd Agricultural Mission.

My treasures: Tom Breen and Lucy Gellman, Kathy and Alex Brennan, and Chris Breen.

My dear husband, Brad. Who is everything.

And for Will, always.

About the Author

Susan Breen is the author of the Maggie Dove mystery series, originally published by the Alibi digital imprint of Penguin Random House and now rereleased by Under the Oak Press. Her first novel, *The Fiction Class,* also published by Penguin Random House, won a Westchester Library Association Washington Irving Award for "readability, literary quality, and wide general appeal." Her short stories have been published in *Best American Nonrequired Reading*, as well as an assortment of magazines ranging from *American Literary Review* and *The Chattahoochee Review* to *Alfred Hitchcock Mystery Magazine and Ellery Queen's Mystery Magazine*. She has a story forthcoming in the anthology *Murder Most Diabolical,* introduced by Walter Mosley. Susan teaches novel-writing and does editing work with Gotham Writers in Manhattan. She lives in the Hudson Valley with her husband, two sweet dogs (cockapoos) and two slightly hostile cats. Her three children are flourishing elsewhere. You can find more information about her at www.susanjbreen.com.

Made in United States
Orlando, FL
30 September 2024

52169443R00186